CW01659035

THE BREAKUP BOOKSHOP

Breea Keenan was born and raised in Glasgow's southside. She worked as a journalist before moving into communications. Breea Keenan's debut novel, *Plot Twist*, won the Debut Novel of the Year Award at the Romantic Novelists' Association Awards 2025. She lives near Glasgow with her husband and three children.

Also by Breea Keenan

Plot Twist

THE BREAKUP BOOKSHOP

BREEA KEENAN

CORVUS

Published in paperback in Great Britain in 2026 by Corvus, an imprint of Atlantic Books Ltd.

Copyright © Breea Keenan, 2026

The moral right of Breea Keenan to be identified as the author of this work has been asserted by her in accordance with the Copyright, Designs and Patents Act of 1988.

All rights reserved. No part of this publication may be reproduced, stored in a retrieval system, or transmitted in any form or by any means, electronic, mechanical, photocopying, recording, or otherwise, without the prior permission of both the copyright owner and the above publisher of this book.

No part of this book may be used in any manner in the learning, training or development of generative artificial intelligence technologies (including but not limited to machine learning models and large language models (LLMs)), whether by data scraping, data mining or use in any way to create or form a part of data sets or in any other way.

This novel is entirely a work of fiction. The names, characters and incidents portrayed in it are the work of the author's imagination. Any resemblance to actual persons, living or dead, events or localities, is entirely coincidental.

1 2 3 4 5 6 7 8 9

A CIP catalogue record for this book is available from the British Library.

Paperback ISBN: 9781805465959
E-book ISBN: 9781805465966

Printed and bound by CPI Group (UK) Ltd, Croydon CR0 4YY
Corvus
An imprint of Atlantic Books Ltd
Ormond House
26–27 Boswell Street
London
WC1N 3JZ

www.atlantic-books.co.uk

Product safety EU representative: Authorised Rep Compliance Ltd., Ground Floor, 71 Lower Baggot Street, Dublin, D02 P593, Ireland. www.arccompliance.com

FSC
www.fsc.org
MIX
Paper | Supporting responsible forestry
FSC® C013604

PROLOGUE

They say bad things come in threes. But after the first two gut-wrenching, heart-crushing bombshells landed on me with full force, I thought that *surely* I would be spared the third. I mean, come on. There was no way that my job – the one thing I was clinging on to for dear life, while everything else went to shit – could be taken away too.

Spoiler alert: I was wrong.

I slump back on the sofa and kick my legs up, my shoes still on. High heels and everything.

Fuck you, Seb.

I look around my flat. Except this isn't even my bloody home any more. Not really. A one-bedroom flat that I'm allowed to squat in temporarily while I sort my life out.

I pour myself a large glass of the lukewarm white wine that someone handed me in the office lobby earlier. Her name is Claire Something – it doesn't matter now. Said she'd swiped three bottles from the company's communal kitchen on the way out. I'd lobbed it into the cardboard box they'd given each of us as a parting gift, when we were given thirty minutes to gather our belongings and get the hell out of there.

In the years since I left uni, I'd gradually worked my way from intern all the way up to team leader at Seed Creative, an innovative digital marketing agency that promised to break the rules. Turns out they barely broke even and now Seed Creative is no more.

I put blood, sweat and tears into that place. All three, in that exact order, since the downward spiral started two weeks earlier. How had my life fallen apart so quickly? It's almost comical now, thinking back on it.

First was the blood. I'd been in a client meeting, presenting our creative campaign ideas and social media strategy for the launch of a new sports-clothing brand, when I'd bent down to pick up my pen and whacked my head on the corner of the table. There was blood everywhere within seconds and, of course, I was wearing a white blouse. Our client stepped in triumphantly, offering up an oversized Hello Kitty plaster straight from her designer handbag, because she had, and I quote, 'such a clumsy two-year-old' at home.

Then, sweat. Huffing and panting, I took my clumsy twenty-nine-year-old self straight to the Tube after the meeting. No one gave my blood-splattered white blouse or the cartoon on my head a second glance; they'd all seen far more interesting oddities on the London Underground. As I hurried out of the station and around the corner towards our second-floor flat, I'd breathed a sigh of relief. Seb was working from home that day, and I'd been desperate to get back home and tell him everything.

I resist the urge to scrape my dirty heels across Seb's pristine sofa as I remember the sight – or, more accurately, the sounds – that greeted me when I unlocked the door that day. I'd stood in the doorway, confused by the strange moaning. Guttural. Barely human.

It was like my brain didn't *want* to make sense of it. All I could think of were the birds that had been congregating outside our bedroom window lately, cooing and tapping in the early hours of the morning. Seb had pointed out that one of the birds was pregnant and, for a fleeting moment, I imagined flinging the door open to reveal Seb coaching a bird through its birthing experience.

Instead, it was like some clichéd movie scene that I'd accidentally flicked on while channel-surfing.

As he hastened to pull on his boxer shorts, I had to stop myself from being sick in my mouth. The woman threw herself underneath our grey duvet cover, but not before I caught a glimpse of her face. That was the biggest shock of all.

Lastly came the tears.

It's too much to think about right now. I flick my shoes off my feet onto the floor and rub my eyes. Seb had offered to move out for a while and, like a gallant martyr, said I could take all the time I needed to find a new place.

Fuck you, Seb.

Just like Seed Creative agency, my whole life has gone into liquidation.

I scroll through my phone with one hand and take a large gulp of wine with the other, before thunking my glass down in the middle of the coffee table without a coaster. I feel a sudden pang of guilt. Not for Seb but for Anya, the cleaner he insists on having once a week. When I first moved in, I was gobsmacked to hear that he paid someone to clean the space. It's barely bigger than a shoebox. Plus, Seb isn't 'clatty', as my granny would have said. He's neat. He doesn't leave the toilet seat up. He has a small selection of almost identical navy-blue and grey items of clothing in his closet, which take up minimal space and are never left scattered on the floor (except when he is otherwise engaged). Everything he owns, be it his clothes or his furniture, matches because it's all black, grey or dark blue. And he is savvy when it comes to recycling, which I always rated.

At one point, I really thought I'd won the boyfriend lottery with Seb.

Now here I am, scrolling through SpareRoom, marvelling at the creative descriptions of each prison-cell boxroom on offer, each accompanied by eye-watering price tags.

Exhibit A: Woolwich. Flatmate required to share with four law students who enjoy quiet nights in and occasional parties. Own single bedroom (mattress available), access to communal bathroom, kitchen and living room. No central heating, BYOEH (bring your own electric heater. Lol). Must like snakes.

Exhibit B: Clapham Junction. £450 p/w. Clean female flatmate required who can share responsibility for walking large but friendly dog at least twice a day (since dog dad has left me high and dry!). Bedroom with garden views and living room with small office space. Non-smoker preferred, but vaping is okay.

Exhibit C: Acton. Quiet female flatmate. No access to bedrooms, living room or bathroom 6–10 p.m. due to filming taking place in flat. Small balcony available for use during these times. Offers over £1,100 pcm.

With an indignant snort, I take a screenshot and click the 'share' button. As my most frequent contact, Macy Miller's name pops up first. My closest friend since school. Even my phone knows that she's who I share everything with, but we aren't exactly on talking terms any more. Not since I caught her in bed with my boyfriend.

My heart hurts.

I put my phone down and sigh, looking around Seb's small living room. I'd thought I had it all figured out. Get the job, move to London with my best friend in the world, meet the guy. Tick, tick, tick. I'd been working towards the next points on my checklist: modest but beautiful ring, intimate wedding, two kids and a dog. I'd thought I was on track.

Now, I have to choose between becoming a dog parent, living on a questionable 'film set' or partying with four snake-loving students.

Closing my eyes, I will myself to rewind to a happier time when it wasn't all about achieving *results*. A level results to land a place at a good university, exhausting myself at uni to get the grades needed to secure the starry London job, perfect biannual appraisals to get promoted fast and buy a house in Zone 2 before I'm thirty. All the things my parents wanted. The moment Seb mentioned his six-point plan for early retirement, they were like putty in his hands. Dad almost asked Seb's permission to march me down the aisle there and then.

I'd been so close. It's like I've been playing a game of snakes and ladders, triumphantly climbing to the highest point, just a few spaces from the finish line, before a roll of the dice brought me crashing all the way back down to square one. To a box full of my things and a bottle of lukewarm wine, which, oops, is almost finished.

I pick up my phone, my mind whirring, as I gulp down the last of it. Everyone always talks about the ridiculous London prices, don't they? How much better off you could be elsewhere? You'd think that my parents, as accountants and self-proclaimed money gurus, would suggest widening my search area to achieve better value for money outside the city. But they've been tied to their high-flying careers in Leeds for years now, while I was encouraged to go for gold in London. They thought I'd be raking it in in no time. It was true for a while, maybe, but like all good things, it didn't last.

Closing the Indeed 'Jobs in London' tab, I minimise the SpareRoom results and open another window on my phone.

Instinct takes over. A whim. Let's just see. In Rightmove, I type 'Ullapool'.

The first time my parents shipped me to the Scottish Highlands was when I was nine years old. I'd thought it was a punishment. Six whole weeks at my granny's house in the middle of nowhere just so they could continue working endless hours without me as a distraction during the school summer break; I thought I'd done something wrong. I was hardly old enough to appreciate the idyllic scenery: the perfect pastel village nestled in the mountains, the small pier where boats bobbed on the loch, the quiet streets where other kids raced on their bikes. I huffed as Granny tried to cheer me up, luring me to the kitchen with the smell of her freshly baked scones and bramble jam. She leapt on my love of books, creating a reading nook for me in the garden, and she let me stay up way past my bedtime as we huddled underneath a blanket on the bench at the front of her tiny cottage, counting the stars in the sky.

By the end of that first summer, I didn't want to leave. I begged her to let me stay. Instead, she promised I could come back the following summer. And the summer after that. My parents were delighted to be rid of me, although they didn't understand what I saw in the place. Dad couldn't hide his disdain for his Highlands hometown, where Granny worked in the local primary school as a dinner lady. She said it was the perfect job when you were raising a young child as a single parent. He'd grown up mortified by her lack of ambition. Leaving home as soon as he could, he'd adopted an English twang to his accent over the years. When I would call him and accidentally end up speaking like Granny – saying 'aye' and 'naw' – he would sigh and ask me to speak *properly*.

My parents were both glad to get me out of their hair for the summer breaks that they always said were too bloody long.

Granny said the summer holidays weren't long enough.

I vowed that I'd move there and live with her permanently one day, but she would shake her head and say I should spread my wings, stay in the city with my friends and live the exciting life that a *smart-cookie-like-me* was destined for.

Well, the cookie has well and truly crumbled, and here I am dreaming about Ullapool all over again. Granny passed away very suddenly when I was sixteen. It was the deepest pain I'd ever experienced. Just when I thought it couldn't get any worse, Dad insisted that her final resting place would be some burial plot near our home in Leeds. I argued with him until I was blue in the face. He was an only child and Granny never married, so I was the only one left to speak up for her. She would have hated to be so far away from her much-loved hometown, from the mountains and the water, but Dad insisted.

I'd longed to return for years, but life always seemed to get in the way. Moving to London with Macy, meeting Seb and climbing the career ladder had taken time. I'd promised Seb and Macy I'd bring them to visit one day, but they always had somewhere else they wanted to see more: Marrakech, Vegas, Milan. Still, I wanted them to explore the village that I held so close to my heart. The heart they'd both broken.

Suddenly, the pull to go back feels stronger than ever.

I scroll through the results. The first property that appears is a real-life castle. A historical B-listed estate, situated in a wooded area next to a small river a few miles from the village. Featuring eight reception rooms, ten bedrooms, nine bathrooms, a basement bar and a cinema room, the property has breathtaking views towards Loch Broom over its own private nine-hole golf course.

Okay, so I can't afford *that*.

But I see promise in each of the properties on offer, from a detached bungalow bathed in sunlight, surrounded by acres of greenery, to a small semi-detached property on the seafront, with uninterrupted views of the water and the majestic mountains in the distance.

My heart pounds with longing. Now, *this* is the dream. The fresh air, the space, the slower pace – it's a million miles away from what I have now.

As I scroll to the second page, searching for the cheapest property on offer, I squint at my phone and sit up. The listing on display is a retail space with a one-bedroom apartment above it. The mortgage rate listed beside it is the exact same as the monthly rent for the five-person flat share in Woolwich, where I'd have to queue in the narrow kitchen to make a Pot Noodle, stroke the reptile they all love and bring my own electric heater. Lol.

My redundancy payout isn't much, but it will help towards a deposit for somewhere like this in Ullapool. If I stay in London, I'll need to sell a kidney to get on the property ladder by myself.

My heart beats faster. I could have a place to live on my own, with a retail space below it that I can use to… do something, sell something, create a space that somehow makes money. I'm not sure what, obviously, but I can decide that later. I've invested so much time mapping out marketing strategies to turn other people's business dreams into reality over the years; surely I can do it for myself?

Underneath the picture are four words: 'For sale by auction'.

I blink. Is it a sign? Have I had too much wine? Without thinking, I click 'enquire about this property'. It can't do any harm to ask. Not to brag, but I'm kind of a pro at bagging bargains on Vinted and I'm rarely outbid on eBay. Maybe auctions are my forte.

I turn up the 'independent women' playlist Spotify recommends and leap up to dance around the living room. Wiggling my hips with my eyes closed, I throw my head back, enjoying the beat of the music and this new sense of possibility that has opened up. Maybe this series of very unfortunate events isn't *only* taking me downwards. It could lead to the fresh start I didn't even know I needed. Perhaps I don't need everything mapped out, like I always have. Screw the six-point plan!

Or yes, maybe I've had too much wine, but whatever. My newly hatched, five-minute-ago plan feels much more promising than my prospects here.

Maybe it is time for me to take the Highland coo by the horns and break up with London.

1

Three months later

Please don't let me die before I've had the chance to prove everyone wrong.

The knot tightens in my stomach as I grip the steering wheel, the windscreen wipers working in overdrive to clear the rain that bounces off my small car, as I finally approach Ullapool's main street.

I dreamt of the rolling hills and stunning greenery, but all I've seen on the almost eight-hour drive from my parents' house is biblical rain battering my front window. The ominous grey clouds warn that it isn't about to get better any time soon.

Welcome to summer in the Scottish Highlands.

Like any logical human being, I planned to view the property in real life before buying it. Who would invest their life savings in a property they'd never actually *seen*? You'd have to be totally out of your mind.

Well, maybe I am, because everything happened so

quickly. One minute, I was looking at the street view of the property to check how close it was to the beach. The next, I'd inserted my maximum bid online, trying to outbid an anonymous and very persistent potential buyer whose offers kept creeping up behind mine. My heart thumping wildly in my chest, I awaited the outcome with bated breath until, finally, my bid was confirmed as the highest. A done deal. Ready to sign on the dotted line.

I still can't believe it. My parents were horrified when I explained that every penny of my redundancy package had been swallowed up by a flat I'd never seen right bang in the centre of what Dad called the 'arse end of nowhere'.

But I didn't care. As I packed up every item I owned into a series of brown boxes, I felt surprisingly calm and relieved, like everything was happening exactly the way it was supposed to. I only wish that feeling had followed me for the past six hundred miles.

As I turn the engine off, the tension drains from my body and I let out a huge sigh of relief. Wiping the window to get a clearer view doesn't make much difference. I check the weather app on my phone to see when the rain might pass, but, of course, there's no reception. I'm not sure whether it's the fault of the village or the ancient phone I intended to upgrade before I was made redundant. Closing my eyes, I remind myself to breathe. This is what I wanted, after all. I knew what I was signing up for.

The rain continues to batter the windows. I can't just sit here all day. I fling the car door open and step outside, pulling my hood over my head. Cold rain dances around my toes and I sigh, looking down at my wholly unsuitable canvas trainers. I'll need to invest in some wellies, by the look of this weather. Surely it's not like this *every day*? My childhood memories of Ullapool feature hazy sunshine, the scent of coconut sun cream, and ice lollies on demand. Not this crazy summer downpour that has managed to soak my hair, even with my hood up. This rain defies the laws of physics.

From the boot, I grab my precious box of second-hand books and my backpack full of my favourite novels. I fish out the envelope inside my bag, which contains the key (literally) to all my dreams. Squelching with every step, I run to the door and balance the box on my knee while I wrestle with the lock. This is it. The moment I've been waiting for. I try to take it all in, savour the moment, but I am well and truly soaked. I shake my jeans and a raindrop somehow runs down the *inside* of my leg.

Today is beyond 'dreich', as my granny would have said, which translates to 'damp and miserable' weather. And I am definitely 'drookit'. Completely drenched. Some of the village would remark that it is 'fair pishing it doon', but Granny would tut and roll her eyes at that kind of language.

I can't believe I'm finally back here, that this special place that always *felt* like home is now my *official* home. It's different, but good-different. No, I won't miss having an abundant choice of restaurants and shops on my doorstep.

I won't miss the 'buzz' of the city. Definitely not. I can't wait to escape the noise. I won't miss £5 coffees and trendy cafes. Not even the baklava from the Turkish bakery down the road from Seb's and my place. Just Seb's place now...

This has to work out.

As the door to the shop finally flies open, my heart thuds in my chest. I step inside, soaking the floor, and set the box of precious books down on a dry patch further inside. I touch the exposed brickwork of the entrance way, my heart beating wildly in my chest. I'm here. I'm finally here.

I feel like I know the shop already, after endless hours spent poring over the images online, sizing up the space and dreaming up potential business ideas. I'd researched every inch of Ullapool, from the gift and coffee shops to the bed and breakfasts, the local walks, festivals and celebrations.

After weeks of careful consideration while I waited for everything to be finalized, I'd settled on the idea of a second-hand bookshop to replace the small cafe, known as The Old Tea Shop, which had been there since my granny was young. I can't remember ever visiting, but it seems familiar to me. Once I'd decided on a bookshop, I couldn't visualize the space as anything else. Books made Ullapool feel like my home when I was nine years old and now, twenty years later, they would do it all over again.

I put one hand on my hip, gazing around. It's going to be perfect. Shelves will line the walls. My desk will be in that corner, available for people to approach but tucked away so they don't feel as though I'm watching them. I'd resolved to find a local artist to paint a mural on the largest wall in the shop. The concept I'd drawn on the back of an envelope features stick-figure Highland cows and birds with no wings or eyes, but I know the right person can bring my vision to life.

I glance along the width of the whitewashed walls. I'd refused to take a single thing belonging to Seb from our flat, even though his tape measure would come in handy right about now.

As I clutch my backpack close to my chest, there is a tap on my shoulder. I screech at the top of my lungs and, without thinking, swing my heavy bag, which is full to the brim with heavy books.

'Arrrgh!' I shout.

'Arrrgh!' he shouts back, as my bag clashes with the side of his knee.

He comes into sharp focus, grabbing his knee with one hand as he clutches several white envelopes, flyers and leaflets in the other. He wears a bright red waterproof jacket, droplets of rain sitting on his shoulders. The postman. I've just attacked the local postie, all five foot two of him. I note the receding hairline and wisps of white-grey hair from my viewpoint, a few inches above him. He looks to be only a few years away from retirement, hardly in a position to defend himself against me and a bag full of my best hardbacks.

'Oh, I'm so sorry,' I say, placing my bag down on the ground. I'm so glad I didn't lob it at his head; it could have really done some damage. 'I thought you were going to attack me. I've just moved here from London.'

I add the London part, hoping that will somehow explain my violent impulses. He nods, rubbing his knee. 'You have a package that needs to be signed for and you left the door open. You might want to lock that in future.'

'I will,' I promise, nodding solemnly, before scribbling my signature on the paperwork. 'Can't be too careful.'

'It would be for our safety more than yours,' he says with a wry smile. His gentle lilting Highland accent has a slight mischief to it. 'I'm Pete. The whole village is waiting with bated breath for your arrival, by the way. Look out there.'

I follow Pete over to the window, where the thundering rain has finally eased to a dismal drizzle. He points across the road to a shop with a bright pink sign that reads 'On Edge'. Like me, right now.

At least five women stare back, straight at us. Two have their hair covered entirely in foils and wear fuchsia cutting gowns, another has curlers in her hair and someone else, a younger girl, clutches a floor brush in her hand. Someone stands outside in the street, talking on the phone, while gazing straight at us. As we peer back over, they all dart away from the window, trying to appear inconspicuous.

'The hairdresser,' he explains with a smile.

Yes, Pete, thanks for that.

'The hub of the village. It's owned by my daughter, but she's on holiday the now. So, you're Agnes's granddaughter?'

I'm not sure how Pete knows about my link to Ullapool already, but I am pleased at the mention of Granny's name. People will be more welcoming, knowing my connection with the village. At least, I hope they will.

'Yes, did you know her?'

Pete nods. 'Of course! Your granny Agnes was the dinner lady when I was at school, would you believe? She loved each of the pupils there like they were her own. She had a penchant for caramel squares, if my memory serves me correctly. She was a great cook herself but said she never mastered the caramel squares, so she came to my wife's bakery to buy them.'

'I'll have to try them.' I grin at Pete's recollection, but his eyes cloud over with sadness and he glances to the floor. I feel guilty, knowing I've made a misstep somehow.

He coughs and recovers himself. 'Donna's away just now, but when she's back…'

'Wait,' I say, holding my breath for a moment. 'You don't happen to mean Donna Wilson, by any chance?'

He smiles widely and nods. 'The very same. She wondered if you'd remember her.'

'Of course I do! She was one of my best friends here! She used to spend hours plaiting and styling my hair when we were younger. Oh, I can't *wait* to catch up with her again. When will she be home?'

'A few days,' he says with a smile. 'She's sunning herself in Tenerife, the lucky so and so. But one thing's for sure about our Donna, she'll do you a great deal on your roots.'

He offers up a mini salute, like he's doing me a huge favour, as I clutch the top of my completely natural auburn locks. I can almost hear Granny reminding me to be gentle with him. Men don't know much about that sort of thing, she'd have said.

He gives me a cheery wave goodbye on his way out, so I keep my mouth shut. I've hardly made the best first impression myself. The women across the road all witnessed me attacking poor Pete the postman. I note a tiny spring in Pete's step as he makes his way to his daughter's salon to deliver the juicy goss on me, the lass from London who's armed with a bag of books and isn't afraid to use it. Beware of any stray kneecaps.

As I climb up the creaking stairway at the back of the shop, my stomach fizzes with excitement. Donna is here. I already have an actual *friend* in Ullapool, who is also my work neighbour. This is the small-town living I've always craved. Everyone knows everyone. Not like in London, where you rarely see the same server twice at the local coffee shop. At work, you'd never admit to knowing someone's name outside your own department, for fear of being tied into a conversation. There were deals to be done and targets to hit.

My own targets had been enough to contend with. At Seed Creative, I'd juggled weekly goals, monthly managerial overviews and continued professional development, while organizing partnership and mentoring opportunities for local college students. Oh, and doing my day job: creating and executing social media campaigns, meeting existing clients and pitching for new ones. All achieved while maintaining a wide, I-can-handle-it-all smile and pretending everything was okay.

When I'd taken on responsibility for a social media team in their early twenties over the last year, my eyes had been well and truly opened. While many were just a few years younger than me, collectively they were my work antithesis. This group clocked in and clocked out for their exact work hours, took a *full hour* for lunch, went for daily 'mental health walks' in Hyde Park, and prioritized family and friends, even when the work was piling up. A part of me had been impressed. Meanwhile, every day I stuffed a Pret baguette into my gob, sometimes as late as 4 p.m., because I hadn't quite got around to eating that day; only achieved 3,800 steps on my walk to and from the Tube and going to the office loo; and missed countless social occasions. The longer I worked at Seed Creative, the fewer events I seemed to miss. Until I realized that somewhere along the line, I'd been dropped from the invitation list.

In fact, when I decided to move here, I realized that, after my parents, I had no one to tell. My 'friends' had been whittled to Seb and Macy.

This move is going to change everything, though. I'm determined to find that elusive work-life balance everyone talks about. I've firmly left behind my London self, and all associated stress. I'm going to be my own boss, set my own schedule and take breaks for nature walks, friends and fun in my new world. After a shedload of hard work to get me where I need to be, of course. Bookshops don't grow on trees, after all.

The top of the staircase takes me straight into my lounge area. Fully furnished, as promised. A small wooden coffee table and chocolate-brown sofa complete the space. Basic but liveable. I follow the beige carpet through to the bedroom, which contains a small double bed, a desk and a wardrobe. It needs a lick of paint and a lot of love, but for now, it is… fine. Passable. The small galley kitchen is exactly as the online pictures showed: dated, with brown and cream wall tiles, but it has everything I need to cook. I can barely swing a cat in the space, as Granny would have pointed out, but thankfully I don't plan on doing that any time soon.

I hesitate at the door of the bathroom, peering tentatively inside. It is the one room I instantly disliked when I saw the pictures. Sure enough, the garish green, diamond-shaped tiles overwhelm the long, narrow room. Not only is it an assault on the eyes, but everything is covered in a thick layer of dust. I'm tempted to rip the tiles straight off, but one step at a time. Plus, I'll need a serious YouTube DIY education before I can retile the place. I close the door and decide to start with a really good deep clean instead. I'll have it all spruced up in no time.

This place is all mine and, best of all, it is a blank canvas. I can't wait to get started on it. The buzz of excitement settles back in my stomach, with just a hint of nerves.

The neighbours' eyes follow me as soon as I step out onto the main street again. It's bizarre, like I'm some kind of celebrity – or someone who's just been released from jail – that they have to keep a very close eye on. Do they also think I'm mad for moving to Ullapool?

I shift from foot to foot, wishing I didn't have an audience. Lifting the boot of my car again, I reach in to retrieve the planks of wood I took from my dad's shed that I plan to turn into shelves. It's lashing it down again and I need to get this stuff inside as quickly as possible.

'Can I help you?'

I bang my head on the side of the boot and let out a loud curse that Granny would certainly not have been proud of. Clutching the plank of wood over my shoulder, I turn to see who is speaking to me, but the rain is making everything bleary from my viewpoint under my hood and...

'Ah, Christ!' the man groans, as the plank swings quicker than I can control, landing on the side of his forehead with an almighty crack.

For fuck's sake.

I've managed to assault not one but two people in the first thirty minutes of my arrival. But this guy doesn't look like someone I'd expect to bump into, not in Ullapool, anyway. A sweet, old man like Pete the postman, yes.

This guy, definitely not. He has thick, curly, dark brown hair and sharp, strong features. Much taller than me (and Pete, although that wouldn't be difficult), he has broad shoulders that tug at the seams of his navy jacket, which is lacking a hood. He is apparently too manly for practicality.

I can almost hear Granny's voice: *Put your hood up, son, you'll catch your death out here.*

His bright green eyes throw me an inquisitive look as I pull my hood closer to my ears. He rubs his forehead and checks his hand, presumably for bleeding. Dramatic. I didn't hit him *that* hard. This guy, with his stature, could probably lift the plank of wood and smash it over his knee in a swift wrestling move.

He arches an eyebrow. 'Do you often whack people before you've said hello?' He has a thick Scottish accent that dances through the rain. 'I was trying to give you a hand.'

'I wouldn't have whacked you if you hadn't crept up on me! Why does everyone seem to do that here?' I exclaim. 'No, I don't need help. I'm fine. I just want to unpack my car without injuring anyone!'

And then he does the most annoying thing. He flashes me a wide grin, his teeth white and perfectly straight.

'Mission not accomplished.'

Wait, is that a *dimple* in his left cheek? I fight my eyes not to roll. This guy is mocking me, with his chiselled jawline and dreamy eyes, standing in my way. I don't have time for nonsense like alarmingly attractive Highland men. I have work to do.

'You came too close!' I protest, pushing past him to get to my shop.

'To offer you help,' he points out, his tone moving into frustrated territory.

He obviously *loves* helping a damsel in distress. Well, not this damsel. I have ninety-nine problems and his exceptionally well-fitting jeans are not about to be one of them.

'I don't need help!'

He mutters something under his breath as I carry the plank of wood into my new shop, closing the door behind me.

For God's sake. A handsome stranger offers me some help – which I clearly need – and how do I respond? Not with, 'Oh, yes, that would be wonderful, thank you. Do you happen to know a good local joiner?' Instead, I assault him with a plank of wood, tell him to get away from me and screech that I don't need anything from anyone. Not exactly the best first impression.

I'm wired and shifty and I blame Seb. I used to be able to hold civilized conversations with men. Now, the sight of any man my age apparently sends me into a spiral. Especially that big burly Scotsman. The low, gruff accent paired with mischievous green eyes and dimples is too much. My mouth can't keep up with my brain and now I'm annoyed.

With any luck, I won't have to see him again. It's a small village, but it's a tourist hotspot too. He could be a tourist.

Some Glaswegian who's capping off a week of Munro-bagging by helping woefully unprepared small-business owners.

Hurrying back to the car to get the rest of the boxes from the back seat, I spot the sign of the shop next door.

The Toolbox, the DIY store. Now that's something that could help me. I need my own tape measure. And a drill. And nails. In fact, I probably need pretty much everything The Toolbox has in stock if I'm going to turn my new space into the amazing bookshop I've envisaged.

I let out a determined sigh, straighten my shoulders and puff out my chest. I've really messed up my first impressions so far in Ullapool, but I'm determined to do better with the owner of the DIY store. They will be my next-door neighbour and go-to person, especially over the coming weeks.

Getting off on the right foot is crucial.

2

A little bell dings above my head as I push open the front door of The Toolbox. How old school. Perhaps I should invest in a bell for *my* shop. It's cute. Although, it might be too distracting for readers. They could be right in the middle of a tense scene when DING! they're brought back to the real world. I wouldn't want that.

A customer stands behind the counter with her back to me. She looks to be an older lady, with short powder-white hair resting above her cream-coloured raincoat.

As she moves her head to one side, I see the shop attendant standing there, examining a bottle of whisky in his hand as he grins at the old lady with those familiar white dazzlers. Ah shit. It's the man I just bashed outside with the plank of wood. The one who sent me into a verbal spiral. Now he's inside, he's removed his jacket and his broad shoulders are held tightly by a black T-shirt displaying The Toolbox's logo.

So much for not seeing him again.

'You didn't need to do this, Margaret,' he says, admiring the whisky bottle. 'I'm always happy to help, you know that. Although I'll also be very happy to try this too.'

'Well, you wouldn't take money from me, as usual, and I do know you like a wee dram on a special occasion.'

'Aye, special occasions like Tuesdays.'

She bursts into high-pitched laughter. 'Oh! You have a wicked sense of humour. Right well, I'll be off now.'

'It's very kind of you, Margaret. Thank you.'

'No, thank *you*. I appreciate it, as always. Right, I'll leave you to it,' she says, swinging around.

Despite all her gushing towards him, Margaret seems to actively avoid even glancing in my direction on the way past. Head down, she shuffles past with the aid of her stick.

When he looks up, he doesn't exactly offer a smile of recognition. In fact, a scowl has emerged across his sculpted features, as he narrows his green eyes and scratches his brown hair, still damp, on the back of his head. I clock the small dent on his forehead, courtesy of me and my trusty plank of wood. Yikes. No wonder he isn't all smiles.

I place my hands on the countertop and glance over his shoulder at the display of tiny boxes behind him, featuring screws of all different shapes and sizes.

It's time to try to bury the hatchet. Judging by all the handy-looking things he has on display, he has everything

I could ever need stocked here, all within touching distance of my shop.

'Can we start again? My name's Ava. I'm your new neighbour and I'm screwed.' I hope he will be unable to resist my friendly charm, but his face remains deadpan. 'Let's just say that it's as well your shop is right next door to mine. The place needs a complete overhaul, from top to bottom.'

His frown deepens as he crosses his arms in front of his broad chest and shakes his head. 'It's fine.'

'Sorry?'

'The place next door,' he grumbles. 'It might not be to your *taste*, but there's nothing wrong with it. Archie kept it in really good nick, right till the end.'

The side of his mouth turns down. My cheeks redden. Great job, Ava. First, a whack to the head. Then, I refuse his offer of help. Now, I'm insulting his dead neighbour.

I lower my voice to a whisper. 'When you say *right till the end*... Is he... I mean, did Archie die... in *there*?'

To an avid reader like me, this conjures countless gory possibilities. I forget my small-town romcoms and remember my small-town thrillers and horror stories. My bookshop could be built on top of a plague graveyard, former home to a mass murderer or, yes, there could be a dead body under the floorboards. It's not exactly something they'd boast about on the listing. Maybe that was why I could afford the place.

'He did, aye,' he replies with a curt nod. 'I *think* they took the body out, but it could still be decomposing in the cupboard at the top of the stairs. You might want to check that.'

As my eyes widen, he throws me a withering look.

'Don't worry, you're safe for now. Archie is quite well and currently touring New Zealand in what we're calling "The Old Teashop Part Two: Campervan Edition".'

'Oh, thank God.' I let out a relieved sigh and wipe pretend sweat from my forehead.

He pulls out a notepad and starts to scribble on it, like he's declaring our conversation is over. Tough luck for him. I've only just begun.

'Archie, eh? I never had the teashop owner down as a man.'

'It was his wife Evelyn's. She passed away last year. In a hospice, so you can calm your jets there too.'

'Good. Well, not good that she died. I mean, you know.' I blush as my verbal inadequacy makes a comeback. 'Well, you're probably right. I just need to give it a good clean. The decor is mainly fine, aside from the awful green tiles in the bathroom, but I ordered some sample tiles online before I left, so it shouldn't be too long until I can change it up.'

He narrows his eyes. 'They're the exact same tiles we have in the bathroom here. And I picked them for Archie.'

Another foot-in-mouth situation. Bloody hell.

'You're joking?'

'They were sourced from a local supplier,' he explains. 'We do that around here, when we can. Our small businesses support one another. We don't just order everything for next-day delivery from big chain stores, like you city folk.'

'How do you know I'm city folk?'

It's my turn to frown, as I cock my head to one side and look up at him. Suddenly, he stops scribbling on his notepad. He seems to buffer for a moment before clearing his throat and shrugging, picking up some papers on the counter to leaf through.

'Ah, everyone knows. Plus, your accent is hardly local. Ava Campbell, isn't it? Word spreads like wildfire around here. We all know you're moving from London to open a *bookshop*.'

'Why did you say it like that?'

'Like what?'

'*Bookshop*,' I sneer. 'Like it's a dirty word.'

'We don't need a bookshop around here.'

'How do you know?'

He shrugs. 'I just do. We have everything we need. If we'd needed a bookshop, we'd have a bookshop.'

'Well, thanks for that enthralling piece of in-depth market research, I'll be sure to bear it in mind. Now, I need some nails, please – 16-gauge finish nails,' I ask with the most confident tone I can muster, hoping I've repeated the correct phrasing from my earlier Google search.

He slides a box across to me and shakes his head. 'It's just a bit cliché, isn't it? City girl moves to a village to open a bookshop. Probably been through a breakup and decided there's more to life than money and men, am I right?'

It catches me off guard. In fact, it stings. I'm trying to make amends, and now he's analysing me. Worst of all, he's right. As he moves his hand along the light dusting of stubble of his jawline, I note the twinkle in his green eyes. It feels like he's caught me wiggling my hips to my independent women playlist and is laughing his arse off.

Having him roll his eyes at what was a huge decision for me makes me feel small. To leave behind my whole life and restart here, it's not easy.

I've been trying to feel proud, but his diminishing stare is making that very difficult. What would this man, with his big beefy arms and general manly man-ness, know about heartache?

'Well,' I cough, trying to keep my voice steady, 'you're hardly living up to the village cliché, are you? You know, where everyone is *friendly* to newcomers and doesn't act like a complete *dickhead*. You haven't even introduced yourself.' I do my best Agnes Campbell impression, tutting loudly and folding my arms in front of me.

He carries on, as though speaking to himself, 'Wonder how long you'll last before you get bored around here. Pretty sure you'll lose interest. Most people do. I'd bet on three months. Maybe you could open an overpriced crepe shop in Edinburgh next?'

My mouth falls open. Who the hell does he think he is? I may have just moved here, but I *know* Ullapool. My granny's village and the hometown of my summers. It's not like I just closed my eyes, pointed at a random place on the map and decided to move here. Admittedly, buying at auction without seeing the place was out of character for me, but this isn't just some whim.

'How much?' I ask, raising an eyebrow.

He frowns. 'How much what?'

'You said you were willing to bet on whether or not I'll stay here,' I say. 'What are you offering up, if I make it past the three-month mark?'

'A bottle of whisky? I like Talisker Skye, if you're wanting to order it in.'

'I was thinking more about a DIY job, once I start working on my flat. If I'm still here, you can remove the green tiles from the bathroom, if I manage to stop myself ripping them off the wall.'

'And here's me thinking you said you didn't *need* any help.' He smirks as I roll my eyes.

'Do you accept the terms?'

'Fine. If you are still here with your green tiles in three months, I'll remove them. It'll be the equivalent of eating my hat.'

'Good.'

'Anything else?'

'Nope,' I reply. 'That's it. Unless you sell cleaning stuff?'

He reaches beneath the counter and pulls out a basket of disinfectant spray, a cloth and some bleach. He pushes it towards me.

'Here – you can use this. On the house. Bring it back when you're done,' he says, before adding, more quietly,

'And it's Rory, by the way. Rory MacGregor.'

He stares across the counter at me, a question in his eyes. What is it with the long, brooding gaze? Am I supposed to be happy that he's finally shared his name with me, like I'm being let in on some deep, dark village secret?

'Well, Rory MacGregor, thanks for the not-so-warm welcome,' I say, grabbing the basket. It's lighter than I'd anticipated and it almost flies out of my hands. 'I'll bring it back when I'm finished.'

He remains still, leaning over the counter, like there should be something else. What is he waiting for?

Finally, he shakes his head. 'You do that.'

I stop for a moment in the doorway before turning back around to face Rory.

'I am so glad to hear everyone around here supports local business,' I say with my sweetest smile. 'I can't wait to welcome you to my bookshop when it opens.'

He looks me dead in the eyes. 'That's another thing about you city folk.'

'What's that?'

'Always trying to get the last word.'

With great difficulty, I restrain myself from retaliating as I exhale sharply and turn on my heel to leave.

3

It turns out Rory MacGregor can hold a grudge.

In the days that follow our first encounter, he pops a series of leaflets, handyman posters and junk mail through the front door of the shop. I never see him doing it, but Pete says he never posts junk mail, so it must be Rory. Who else would want to clog up my front door with useless tat? Pete says that Rory is likely trying to be helpful, but I know better.

As I walk around in a dust-covered daze, I ignore his attempts to make me unwelcome.

My head buzzes with grand plans featuring bright and bold colours, luxury wallpaper and beautifully upholstered furniture. I post an appeal for a local artist on the bookshop's newly launched Facebook page, hoping to find someone to paint the mural that I can already picture vividly. Having all the vision but none of the skill is incredibly frustrating. I wish someone could just hand me a paint-by-numbers template for the wall, but I know this isn't some step-by-step craft project. It should look bespoke, specific to the community, not some stereotype of Highland coos and rolling hills. The Facebook post has had plenty of interaction, with some people recommending local painters and interior decorators, but there are no artists among them. In my wistful imagination, a beautiful place like Ullapool would be a retreat for reclusive creatives, where artists, writers and great minds hang around sipping whisky and discussing ideas, but apparently that's not the case.

While I want to do everything quickly, I keep reminding myself Rome wasn't built in a day. My tiny apartment and all associated Pinterest boards will have to wait. The shop space is my priority, especially if I ever want to see an increase in my stagnant bank balance. Even though the garish green tiles will be ever-present in my nightmares, they have to remain for now. At least in three months I can watch Rory remove them, one by one, from the wall, as I nurse a glass of celebratory fizz. That will be my moment of triumph.

The thick, padded wallpaper is easier than expected to scrape from the shop walls and, before I know it, I can barely move in the shop for the black bags that are filled to the brim. Pete calls in with a wave, makes a remark about protecting his kneecaps this time, and leaves yet another box of books I've ordered at the door, beside the three Amazon packages he left yesterday that I haven't had the chance to open yet.

I pick up some of the black bags and lug them outside to make some more room.

The auction website described the space at the back of my shop as an 'enclosed courtyard', but there were no pictures. I didn't have high hopes, and I assumed it would just be a small, concrete eyesore. I was surprised to find that the area was really quite big, enclosed by a brick wall with a gate leading out onto the back lane. There was a washing line, along with an old mop and bucket, and the trusty green, blue and brown recycling bins.

It's not like I'm planning a picnic out here any time soon, but, like everything else here, it has potential.

The ad also failed to mention that the courtyard is shared with the shop next door: The Toolbox. Luckily, Rory rarely seems to grace the courtyard with his presence. Pete told me that, thankfully, Rory doesn't live above his shop, like I do. Margaret, his favourite customer and whisky supplier, does. A single, narrow staircase outside the courtyard's black door leads to Margaret's flat above, so she's in spitting distance of the bookshop and The Toolbox.

As I catch glimpses of Rory arriving at work, I suspect that he's avoiding me. In the week since our scuffle, literal and metaphorical, he hasn't crossed my shop's threshold once to see how I'm getting on or to ask if I need any sugar, or whatever it is that nice neighbours are supposed to do.

He is clearly annoyed at me, the city girl who has come to gentrify the village with a bougie bookshop and the occasional threat of grievous bodily harm. However, two can play at this game of cat-and-mouse. I have more than enough things to occupy myself, thank you very much.

Since the move to Ullapool, I've been up at the crack of dawn and working till late every evening. So much for the work-life balance, but I'm hoping that will come once I'm more settled. The bonus is that the work is so physically demanding that I haven't had the energy to panic about all the things that kept me awake while I was in London. Instead of lying awake at 2 a.m. thinking about client presentations and regretting that dinner-time coffee, I retire to my bed above the shop and immediately slump into a dreamless sleep.

Rory clearly has the laidback Ullapool lifestyle down to a fine art.

The low hum of his car engine signals his arrival at 8:56 a.m. sharp every single morning and he leaves at 5 p.m. on the dot every single day. Not one minute before or one minute after. There's no casual eye-flick towards my shop, even when I'm hanging out of the window contemplating the great blinds versus curtains debate.

Instead, he keeps his eye trained on his phone as he walks by. I bet he's replying to a series of different girls from villages the Highlands and Islands over whose names he can barely remember but who hang on his every word, just because he looks all dreamy and brooding.

The prat.

His efforts not to meet my eye are becoming absurd. When I left the borrowed cleaning products on his doorstep, he was so intent on ignoring me that he tripped over them on his way into the shop. I was sanding some furniture outside and, even after he stumbled and I checked if he was okay, he still didn't acknowledge me. All I heard was a clatter and an expletive as he bundled his way into the shop. Ava 1, Rory 0.

While I agree wholeheartedly with his 'shop local' imperative, I can't bring myself to venture back into his store. That would lose me a point in the game he doesn't know, or care, we're playing. I'd tried to build a bridge between us on that first day, but it felt like every time I opened my mouth, I pissed him off even more. And vice versa.

Reflecting on it, there was something charged in that first meeting. I saw how he spoke to Margaret, how warm and friendly he was. But with me, it's like there was this instant, chemical dislike.

I also don't want to face any more insensitive comments. In that brief conversation, he slated me at every turn: about moving here, opening a bookshop that according to him no one wanted or needed, and accusing me of being flighty, ready to take off from Ullapool when I bored of it. In his dreams. Until he apologizes or at least acknowledges my existence, I will not venture back over the threshold of his shop, even if I really need something. No chance. So, Amazon it is, unfortunately.

And while Rory isn't interested in my bookshop, plenty of others are. I keep the door wide open for the steady stream of visitors who love a good nosy around.

Several tourists stop to ask for directions each day, while locals say they look forward to seeing the bookshop in all its glory when it's finished. I reply to all of them in my loudest voice, repeating their compliments, so Rory gets an earful of how much everyone *loves* the idea of my bookshop.

Once I remove all the bags, I make my way along the street, past The Toolbox without a glance inside, and round the corner. Fiona, the local cafe owner, greets me with a wave. She's become my coffee dealer (and therefore my friend for life) since I moved in. She's a good-looking woman in her fifties with full, rosy cheeks and a boisterous demeanour. Between steaming milk and pouring espressos, she keeps me updated on how much better she feels since the menopause, with better skin and 'no *bloody* periods'. She takes delight in her male patrons' blushes. I pop into Fiona's cafe every morning for my caffeine fix. See, I do shop locally, *Rory MacGregor*.

Now I've been in Ullapool a full week, if Fiona hasn't seen me before midday, she nips around to the bookshop with a latte, knowing that I am likely knee-deep in some DIY disaster. She keeps it on a tab, like she does for other locals. *A tab! One of the locals!* I love that for me.

With her easy humour and her warm nature, Fiona has been fast-tracked straight into best-friend territory, especially while I wait for Donna to return from her holiday.

Rory obviously isn't on that same trajectory.

My life here isn't all about the shop, though. Moving to Ullapool from London has been about so much more than that for me. Every evening after I down tools, I set off for a walk, usually drenched in sweat and covered from head to toe in paint and dust. Pounding the pavements of the local area before disappearing up the grassy hills while listening to upbeat music has become the best part of my day. Those Gen Zs in the office were onto something with their daily walks. But they didn't have these views. Whenever I take a pause, I see something new: how the evening light sparkles on the loch, the quaint rooftops with the villagers going about their days, the green hills that stretch to the horizon. Even though I'm working all the hours under the sun for now, the summer days are long in the Highlands, and I'm determined to make the most of the extra daylight hours.

Today, I stroll along the seafront and I skim stones down on the rocky shore like I'm ten years old again. Sitting with the tourists and their fish suppers, I gaze at the fishing boats that drift out towards the sea beyond. I have to pinch myself, particularly on days like today, where the sun peeks out from behind the clouds, illuminating what has to be the most glorious place on earth. I pat my younger self on the back for the vivid memories of this place that I'd carefully stored away, but always kept close to my heart, until I needed them again.

My morning commute, which used to involve cowering in a crowded Tube carriage trying to breathe through the stench of someone else's underarm sweat, has been replaced with a short hop, skip and jump down the small spiral staircase to my new shop. The constant city noise – cars beeping at one another in traffic, trains screeching along the tracks and people barking loudly at one another on every corner – has been replaced with the blissful sounds of the sea rolling in and out on the shore and birds tweeting. Children run up and down on the road, as though I've been transported to some magical time and place where traffic and pollution don't exist. Watching them, I remember my own carefree summers here.

Those are the memories I want to hold on to, not my London life. But still, I feel a heavy tug in my stomach any time I see a couple holding hands while strolling side by side or, even worse, two female friends. It serves up the gut-wrenching reminder of what I've left behind and *why*. Seb, my boyfriend, the man I thought I'd marry. Macy, my best friend, my confidante. Seb and Macy in bed, together.

My chats with Fiona across the counter, while she busily offers up soya milk and cappuccino sprinkles, are lovely, but they are nothing compared to what I had with Macy. My ghost of friendship past is a firm fixture in my mind.

Macy and I always said we were soul sisters. We met at secondary school. I defended her against a group of lads who were calling her Racy Macy in the canteen and we became thick as thieves.

We went to the same university, graduated with honours, landed jobs in London and moved into a tiny two-bedroom flat together. As a trainee recruitment consultant, she put everything into her career, just like I did. We joined a dating app at the same time. We used to gossip about everything: our careers, bad dates, our hopes for the future. We could make each other scream with laughter.

But while I struck gold with Seb (or so I thought), she struggled to meet anyone. When I moved in with Seb a couple of years ago, she had a work friend lined up and ready to take my room. Still, even when we weren't living together, we messaged most days. But maybe life got in the way, and we saw each other less and less. The week I caught them together, she had said she was too busy for coffee, but she had managed to squeeze in a session with my boyfriend.

Seb swore it had only happened a few times before I found out. But how can I believe a man who could sleep with my best friend during the day and wish me good night as we went to bed together?

I try not to think about Macy, but despite everything, it's hard not to miss her. I picture her wide smile, curly deep-black hair and collection of the brightest clothing I'd ever seen. Fluorescent pink and bold orange blouses that she matched with lime-green trousers or bold red dresses and pink tights. The mismatched combinations were her staple. Seb always joked that her clothes were so bright that they hurt his eyes. I kept my wardrobe plain and neutral to match him. In the end, I'd been blinded by them both.

I head back to my shop, hoping I haven't missed the new drill that I've been waiting for days for Pete to deliver. He arrives just as I do with a couple of envelopes, most likely bills I don't want to open, but no sign of any boxes.

'Don't shoot!' he says as he enters, already making himself laugh.

The bruise on his knee from my attack on the first day must have faded, but the joke is still very much alive.

'Any sign of my drill, Pete?'

'Sorry, love, sometimes these places have a wee bit of trouble finding us all the way up here.' Then, he has a light bulb moment. 'Rory will have a drill – you can get one right next door!'

He holds his finger in the air, like an exclamation mark.

I shake my head. There is no way I am going back next door to ask Rory for a drill. Not a chance.

'I've ordered one now, Pete. I don't want to double up, you know?'

'You could borrow one in the meantime then? Rory is the *nicest* bloke, I'm sure he'd love to help you out.'

I roll my eyes. Nicest bloke, my arse.

'Ah, I don't think that's fair, asking to borrow something he sells. You know?'

'I don't think he'd mind. He's not one to hold a grudge, not our Rory. It'll be water under the bridge soon.'

'You heard about a grudge?' I ask. 'What's he been saying?'

'Oh no, he hasn't mentioned anything. I just mean, with you pipping him to the post to buy this place.'

My eyes widen. 'Buy this place? My bookshop?'

He nods. 'Yes. He was in the running for it. Second highest bidder, so I heard. You swooped in and beat his offer, at the last moment. It was all very dramatic. We were all gathered around in The Toolbox cheering him on as he made his offer. Never mind, though, eh? You're here now and we're glad to have you.'

My heart sinks. So that's the reason Rory hates me so much; he was the mystery second bidder. I'd stolen all of his hopes and dreams with the click of a mouse. But this had been my dream too and, regardless of how he feels about me moving here, he'll need to accept that.

'What was he planning to do with the shop? Expand The Toolbox?'

Pete shrugs. 'Maybe. He didn't want it to be bought by a big chain or by someone who was just going to bugger off abroad and rent it out. That's become quite common around here, you see. Anyway, I'd better get on with the post. Busy day. See you later, Ava lass.'

After Pete leaves, I step into the courtyard and hop up on top of the green bin to make the call to Amazon customer service. Although hardly stable, it's the only way I've found I can get reliable service on my temperamental phone. Just as I'm getting as comfortable as I can be while balancing on a bin, Rory emerges from his door holding a large black rubbish bag. He raises his eyebrows at the sight of me.

A-ha. He can hardly avoid me now.

Game on.

Some jaunty hold music buzzes in my ear and I hum along.

I should wait for him to say something to me first. Play it cool. Let him hang for a moment.

But I can't stop myself.

'Dead body?' I ask, nodding at the bag in his hand.

'You're thinking of your upstairs cupboard,' he says. 'Aren't you on the phone?'

'On hold,' I explain, holding it towards him for proof, so he can hear the tune.

'Why are you on the bin?'

'Phone reception. It's best on top of the green bin.'

His facial expression remains neutral, although I detect a hint of amusement in his eyes. 'I won't ask how you found that out. But I would say the blue bin is better. In my experience, anyway.'

'You just want to see me clambering down to shuffle onto the other bin, don't you?'

I'm sure I see his lips twitch as he hides a smile. 'You won't know unless you try. Alternative is to climb into the bin and close the lid.'

'Oh, very funny,' I say, as a voice begins jabbering in my ear, and I realize my call has been connected. 'Hello, yes, I'm calling to enquire about a drill that I've ordered, please? It should have been here on Wednesday, but there's still no sign of it.'

Rory's eyebrows shoot up as he shakes his head. He opens the bin, places the bag inside and turns to leave. Before he enters his shop again, he thinks better of it and scrapes each bin along the ground, making a racket so loud that I can't hear the speaker on the end of the phone. Like changing the order of the bin line-up is necessary right now while I'm taking a call. Standing back from his wheelie-bin masterpiece, he appraises it and flashes me a grin before making his exit with a crashing slam of his door. A real Tool for The Toolbox.

The customer service team promises me that my drill will arrive any minute now.

Spoiler alert: it doesn't.

4

Sitting cross-legged on the floor contemplating paint samples, I spot Rory across the street. He's talking to a short, curvy woman with long hair and a blonde balayage wearing a black leather jacket and a wide smile. They chat animatedly as they cross the road together. The shop door is wide open, so their conversation filters into my shop as they approach. I appear nonchalant, gazing at the samples, while casually eavesdropping.

'Ah, come on, Rory, you haven't said anything yet? It'll all come out eventually, you know that,' the woman says, nudging him playfully in the ribs.

'Mind your own business.' He ruffles her hair and she pushes him away. He continues, his voice dropping to a whisper, 'But please, seriously, promise you won't tell.'

I hear her sigh. 'Your secrets are safe with me. However daft I think they are.'

'Thank you,' he says before he heads to The Toolbox.

Instead of following him, she skips straight towards me to my surprise.

'Ava Campbell?' she says in a mock-serious tone, peering through the door.

'Am I about to be sued or something?' I squint, before I recognize the familiar face in front of me. 'Oh my God! Donna?'

As I say her name tentatively, she throws her whole body into mine, while squealing at the top of her lungs. I find myself jumping up and down with her, joining in the squeal-fest.

'Oh my God, I can't believe you're here!' She pulls back from the hug but keeps a tight hold of my arms, and grins widely at me. A woman stands in front of me, but I can still see the girl I spent the summers playing with, her kind eyes and beautifully crooked smile. 'Fuck, Ava, you're just as gorgeous as you always were!'

I hug Donna closer. I've missed this: a real friend. A live one.

'Your hair is beautiful,' I say, gripping her hand tightly so she can never leave. 'And your tan! How long were you away for, six months?'

She grins as I pull her to sit beside me on the floor because I haven't managed to source any chairs yet. 'It felt like it! I couldn't believe it when I heard you were moving back. I wanted to be your welcoming party. I've been calling Dad every day for updates, though. He's been singing your praises – says you work like a Trojan.'

'Did he tell you about the—'

'The first time you saw him and whacked him with your bag? He hasn't stopped talking about it. Most interesting thing that's happened to him in months! We know you London lot are tough as nails.'

I smile and offer up a little bow. 'Glad to be of service.'

'It's nice for him to have anything to talk about, really. Between you and me, he's been struggling since my mum passed away at the end of last year.' Donna's voice becomes small and quiet, even though there is no one around. Her brown eyes flicker and I see the glisten of fresh tears under her false eyelashes.

'Oh, I'm so sorry, Donna,' I say, rubbing her arm. I realize then how silly I must have sounded to Pete when I asked to try one of his wife's caramel slices. 'That's awful. I didn't know your dad was grieving. He's always so cheery. And your mum was – well, I know I didn't know her that well, but I remember meeting her once or twice when we were younger. She was just lovely. I'm so sorry.'

'Thank you. I know, Dad is trying his best to put a brave face on it. I was so worried about leaving him alone, even for this holiday. Then we heard you were moving in, so I sent him on a mission to check you out and report back. Imagine his delight when you assaulted him on day one! And now he keeps telling me how he's walking about pretending you're going to attack him again at any moment. Sorry, he's always thought himself to be a bit of a joker.'

'Ah well, it's pretty funny,' I say through only slightly gritted teeth.

'I'm sorry about your granny, too, Ava. I know it was a long time ago now, but I never got to say it at the time. I thought you'd be back for the funeral but then we heard it was in England, and after that I kept thinking you'd be back the next summer, but...'

I let out a sigh. 'You have no idea how much I wanted to come back then. But my dad sold the house and there was nowhere for me to stay.'

Donna leans over and throws her arm around me, pulling me in for another hug. 'Well, you're here now. And you're opening a bookshop! Why am I not surprised? You always had your nose in a book when we were younger! I remember you even brought a book around the village with you in the basket of your bike. Elle and I used to call you Matilda, you know.'

'Elle! How is she? Is she still around?'

I can still picture Donna's and Elle's baby faces. Donna, with her long hair always styled to perfection, with an endless supply of sweets that she was more than happy to share with us. Her best friend, Elle, had shorter dark hair, dazzling blue eyes, and could never resist throwing herself into a cartwheel or handstand. We became a summertime trio every year.

'She moved to Edinburgh. She's a hot-shot corporate lawyer there now, would you believe?'

'Ah,' I say. 'Shame her gymnast dreams didn't come to

fruition, but I guess a lawyer is the next best thing. What about you, running your own salon? That's amazing!'

Donna flicks her hair back over her shoulder and grins. 'There was never really any doubt, was there? Eight years I've been open now. It was all I ever talked about! Remember I used to do your hair down at the beachfront, in between the cartwheels, dance moves and skimming stones?'

'Yeah, and you've done it! Your very own business. I just hope I can follow in your glossy-haired footsteps and make this place a success too.'

'You will. I can't wait to see your plans coming to life.' She gazes around the empty shop and smiles. 'Do you know what? I used to like reading. I read loads of romcoms until I went to high school and my teacher called them trashy. She said I should read the classics and then I might develop some *taste*. It put me off reading, to be honest. I've not read a book since.'

I do some quick maths and resist the urge to gasp. Donna hasn't read a book in over fifteen years. What a travesty.

'Good news for you then,' I say. 'Because you have years of *amazing* books to catch up on.'

I disappear to locate my best romances, which are covered by a dust sheet in the corner of the room, and tug at *One Day* by David Nicholls. I hand it to her.

'This will reignite the spark,' I promise, with a knowing nod. 'It's got a bit of darkness to it, but it's a gorgeous romance at the end of the day. You'll love it.'

Donna mentions something about the Netflix series, but

I don't quite catch it. Her response is completely drowned out by a loud, shrill noise.

I frown. What the...

The noise stops for a moment before resuming again.

There's no mistaking it. The Tool has a power tool; Rory is drilling next door. 'Bloody Rory MacGregor.'

'It must be good having Rory next door, right? He'll have everything you could possibly need to get this place whipped into shape.'

I frown.

He obviously overheard my phone conversation about the delayed drill delivery and is now showing off with his big, stupid, shrill drill, rubbing it in my face. Screw him. Pardon the pun.

'I'd like to get him whipped into shape,' I say.

Donna grins. 'Steady on!'

'I don't mean like that. He's been a complete pain since I moved in. He's been spouting all sorts of crap about me being a city girl who won't last five minutes in Ullapool and how the village doesn't need a bookstore.'

'He did not say that,' she says. 'I'll kill him.'

I continue to detail my run-ins with Rory – the assault with the plank of wood (my bad), the dumping of junk mail through my letterbox, the bincident – through the intermittent drill noises from next door.

'Ach, Ava,' she says after I've relayed Rory's and my failed first impression. And second and third and whatever number we are on now. 'I'm sure it's not as bad as that.

You've just got off on the wrong foot. Rory's a sweetheart. He wanted this place for himself and is a sore loser, but he doesn't hold a grudge, honestly.'

As though right on cue, the drill noise takes on a higher pitched tone and I raise my eyebrows at Donna.

'Everyone keeps telling me that he's *just so lovely* and that I have the wrong end of the stick.' I shake my head. 'But I am definitely holding the correct end, I assure you. He hates me. And the feeling is mutual.'

'He does not,' she says emphatically. 'And you don't. How could you hate him? He's a puppy dog! Just like Finlay, his best mate. Have you met him yet?'

'No. Why? Please tell me he was third in line for my shop throne? I can't afford to offend any more of the men of Ullapool.'

'No, no. Finlay's just… he's a good friend of mine too. He's our local dog walker; he takes my beautiful Bonnie out for walks when I'm working.' Donna laughs, although I'm not sure why, her face flushing. 'Anyway, Rory may be a bit put out, but he's very loyal. Once you have him as a friend, he's yours for life.'

'And once you have him as an enemy?' I arch my eyebrow. 'I take it that follows the same premise. He hasn't even come into *my* shop to say hello.'

'You left his cleaning stuff outside the shop instead of saying thank you,' Donna points out.

Damn Donna for being surprisingly good at recalling small details.

'Ah, c'mon, Donna! I need you on my side here,' I say. 'He has a whole army of people here in this village. Mr Loyalty or Popularity or whatever. I'm sad and lonely and *English* – you're my only real friend. Well, you and your dad. And Fiona, my coffee dealer.'

'Of course I'm on your side!' Donna promises. 'But I do think you need to try a little with Rory. Once you've cracked him—'

'Oh, I could crack him, alright…'

'Give it a try. Just think, you could be nipping next door if you need something, rather than waiting for deliveries that don't turn up.'

The noise of the drill pierces the silence as my head whips up. He's only gone and drilled a hole right the way through the wall into my shop and straight through my Dusty Blue paint sample. My mouth falls open. Donna attempts to hide a little smile behind her hand and coughs to cover it up.

'Excuse me!' I say, advancing towards the tiny hole. I put my eye to it, peering through. 'What do you think you're doing?'

'Ah, my mistake,' Rory calls back. 'Don't worry, I'll fix it up in no time.'

'What if I had been walking past and you just drilled through the wall and hit me?'

'What, as you slid casually along the wall?'

I ignore Donna's muffled laugh behind me.

'I should be able to do that if I want,' I retort. 'Without fear of being drilled to death.'

He doesn't respond. I peer through the hole, wondering where he's gone.

'Rory? Rory!' I call, but there is no response.

'I'm sure he didn't mean it,' Donna says.

I frown and spin around as Rory enters the shop, all big, burly and bloody annoying.

'Hey, again.' He grins at Donna. 'Did I mention you've got a great colour?'

Donna gives him a friendly slap on the arm. 'You flatterer. This Highland skin doesn't tan. This is courtesy of St Tropez.'

'Coulda fooled me.'

My mouth falls open. Who *is* this guy, full of friendly chat, who is so *nice*? I certainly haven't met him before.

'Well, don't mind me and the hole you just put in my wall.' I glare at him, folding my arms across my chest. 'I've got enough that needs fixing here. The last thing I need is new things to repair.'

'I'll sort it in no time,' Rory assures me. Already swinging out the doorway, he adds, 'Back in a minute.'

'He will, you know. *See*, he's a sweetheart,' Donna says. 'Anyway, I'll leave you both to it. Pop over soon for a cut or colour? Although I wouldn't want to do anything to that gorgeous auburn. We can have a good gossip. You can tell me all about making up with Rory.'

I want to say that she shouldn't hold her breath, but she is clearly a founding member of the large Rory fan club in the village, so I refrain.

'I do need a trim.'

'Come any time,' Donna calls over her shoulder as she crosses the road to her salon. 'We can have a right good blether.'

Before any more holes are drilled into my wall, or anything else can distract me from my long list of tasks, I set to work tidying the shop. I pull at the stepladders that I was using earlier to daub paint samples on the wall. Folding them up, I place them on the floor, then turn around to pick up the paint tray. Within seconds, a loud scraping noise, a short '*waaaaahh*' and a loud thump vibrates around the room.

I spin around and there he is. Rory's lying on the ground, clutching his ankle, his face scrunched into a tight grimace.

'Where the hell did the ladders come from? Was that my punishment for drilling a hole in the wall?'

'No. Although you were only drilling the hole to rub it in.'

'Excuse me?'

'You heard me saying outside that my drill hadn't arrived. You were making the petty point that if I'd bought it from you, I would have one.'

It sounds ridiculous now I'm saying it out loud, but I'm not about to back down.

He frowns at me, then his ankle. As he tries to move, he grimaces. 'I didn't hear you say anything about a drill. And I was using *my* drill to fix some shelves. It had nothing to do with you.'

Moving towards him, I extend a hand to help him up from the ground. He glares up at me, and we lock eyes.

'No thanks. We're a disaster waiting to happen. First the wood, then the hole in the wall, now the ladders…'

He manages to pull himself upright on a nearby chair, without my help. Shit, what if he has broken it?

'You'll need to get it looked at,' I say, with a pang of worry. 'I'll take you to the hospital.'

He shakes his head. 'I'll hop along to Dr Peters at the surgery and see what he says. It's just at the end of the road.' He stops and his lips curl. 'But I've got a huge stock delivery coming that I need to be in for…'

'I can wait in the shop for it?' I offer, glad of the opportunity to make up for his terrible luck in my presence. 'It's no problem.'

'No, don't worry, I'll just—'

'Rory.' I adopt a serious tone. 'It's not up for discussion. I'll look after the shop and take in the delivery; you go and see the doctor. It's my fault, with the ladders and all anyway. Let me help.'

'Fine. Take my number, in case you need anything.'

'I won't. I can handle it.'

He ignores me, reeling off his phone number, which I tap into my phone.

'You're welcome,' I mutter, as he hobbles out of the shop.

5

Rory's shop has more customers than I anticipate.

I thought I'd be able to sit with my feet up, playing on my phone, especially when I discovered that Rory has phone reception *in his shop*. I'd been balancing outside on a bin while he could just tap away in here, in the warm and dry, without a care in the world.

Unbelievable. Rory 5, Ava 3.

Yes, I'm still keeping score.

How many people ordinarily come into a DIY store anyway? It feels like he's lined all these people up to ask for a host of random stuff: shower seals, thermostats, hand tools, sockets, cables – you name it, the people of Ullapool want it. A village of DIY fiends, apparently. I'm up and down Rory's little ladder like a jack-in-the-box searching for whatever they want, determined not to call him. I want to prove that I can run his shop myself, even if I have no idea what an armoured cable is and why you would ever need one.

Luckily, it appears that Rory is meticulously organized. Every single thing in the store is labelled within an inch of its life, all present and correct. His workstation is also perfectly primed, with a desk organizer containing all the usual suspects – rulers, rubber bands, a calculator – but also, strangely, some fancy art equipment, like a tin of pencils and a couple of brush pens. A notebook featuring his to-do list lies open. The majority of items have been diligently ticked off. I wonder if he gets the same dopamine boost from marking items as complete that I do. Sometimes, just to give myself a little thrill, I'll even write a task down after I've completed it, so I get to cross it out immediately.

As I put an adjustable spanner away, I spot a sketchbook lying open on a desk. The shop is quiet for once and I can't resist checking it out. Rory's name is written in black ink in the top right-hand corner of the front page, like a child's school jotter. I can't help but smile – it's cute.

I'm not sure what I expected to find as I flick through the pages, but it's not this.

The landscape drawings feature the mountains I spent hours staring at during my Ullapool visits, alongside beautifully drawn fishing boats and mesmerizing sunsets. There are vivid sketches of the surrounding area, from a field of sheep and a telephone box in a grassy field to a red squirrel and an eagle, soaring in the sky. I bend my head to admire an intricately rendered butterfly wing. There are some portraits of people in the village that I recognize. The attention to detail in every picture is jaw-dropping. There's

Pete's warm half grin and Donna's sweet blush; he's even managed to capture some warmth from steely Margaret upstairs. The whole collection is breathtaking.

This is not the Rory I've met so far. Seeing this, it's like I'm getting a glimpse of the real him, like I've had a sneak peek into his soul.

I snap the book shut as the bell rings to signal another customer's arrival. Fleeing back behind the counter, I feel all jittery, guilty somehow.

I recognize her instantly: Margaret, my neighbour and Rory's biggest fan.

Her face drains of colour as she catches my eye.

'Where's Rory?' she spits as she leans on her walking stick.

'Oh, hi, it's Margaret, isn't it? I'm your neighbour, Ava. I've moved in next door.'

With all the politeness and charm I can muster, I smile at her. I'm not going to give her any excuse *not* to like me.

She narrows her eyes at me. 'Yes, so I've heard. So, where *is* Rory?'

Hearing her reply in the stern, no-nonsense accent of my granny, I'm suddenly conscious of my own rounded, so terribly *English* syllables. I try to tone it down as much as possible, but I can't change it altogether. It's not like I can dive into a full Scottish brogue or start conversing with her in Gaelic.

'I'm sorry, Rory's at an appointment just now. Can I help you?'

She frowns, as if a bad smell has overtaken the shop. I'm certainly not going to tell Margaret that her precious Rory was injured by the ladders I'd left lying out. She's likely to whack me with her stick.

'I'm here to help you with whatever you need,' I say, with a tight smile. 'And I'm looking forward to welcoming you to my bookshop next door, once it's opened. Are you a reader?'

'I'll pop back in tomorrow,' Margaret says, ignoring my question. 'See if Rory's back then.'

With a harrumph, she turns to leave.

What was it Granny always used to say? Kill them with kindness.

As I gallop ahead to open the door for her, she glares at me.

'Goodbye, Margaret. It was lovely to meet you!' I call, determined to go high when Margaret goes low.

No response. She does mutter under her breath, though. I think I hear something about a bookshop being a pale replacement for The Old Tea Shop.

After she leaves, her words swirl around my brain. Tears spring into my eyes and, feeling silly, I blink them back, but I can't help it. What if Rory and Margaret aren't the only ones who think a bookshop isn't needed here? Maybe the whole community feels the same. They may all miss The Old Tea Shop, the gorgeous coronation chicken sandwiches I'd read TripAdvisor reviews of and the delicate teacups that I'd found forgotten in a box under the till.

I've been so focused on what I love about Ullapool and what *I* want that I haven't properly considered what they might want from me in return. Certainly, Margaret wants to keep The Toolbox and Rory, patron saint of Ullapool; he's *needed*. Maybe Margaret wanted Rory to place the highest bid and secure my shop too. Maybe I am just a flighty girl with a pipe dream.

Just because I want Ullapool, it doesn't mean Ullapool wants me.

I sigh as I peer through the hole in the wall to see the disaster area that is my own work in progress. I see my uneven shelves and my shoddy carpentry. The to-do list on my phone is growing by the minute. Fixing the hole also needs to go on the list now too, thanks to the Tool himself.

I wonder how Rory is getting on at the doctor. In an attempt to combat the guilty feeling hanging around my stomach after Laddergate, I sweep the floor of The Toolbox and clean all the surfaces until they're spotless. I hold off on sending him a text to ask for an update. I don't want him to think I can't handle things here. He needs to know I can run a shop. I need to know it too. Instead, I pass the quieter time flicking through his drawings again.

While I'm hardly a member of the Rory fan club, I can't help but be impressed by his sketches. Then comes my light bulb moment. Rory is an *artist*. I need an artist. I appealed for someone on social media, shared the post to local artist forums as far as Inverness and even wrote a press release for local media to find someone to create the mural, but I've had no luck so far. Perhaps the right person has been sitting under my nose all along. One who strongly dislikes me, and who I've inadvertently attacked on more than one occasion, but this is business. While Rory might not share my vision for the bookshop, maybe I can still get him to create the mural. It might even bridge the gap between us.

It seems like I've found my artist. Now, I just have to convince him to help me.

*

I serve customers with a big smile and a can-do attitude, figuring out along the way where to locate what they need. My eager, over-pleasing mode is met with nods and tight-lipped thank yous, but I slip in mentions of the bookshop where I can.

Gosh, doesn't retiling feel like a hard bit of Crime and Punishment? *Do you know who else liked doing a bit of joinery? George Orwell.* I don't know if that's strictly true, but I'm sure old George wouldn't mind.

When one customer confirms they will visit when it's opened, I do a little victory lap around the counter after they leave.

Rory returns from the doctor with a small bandage around his ankle.

'Just a sprain. I'll survive.'

'That's a relief. I was worried you were going to sue me.'

'That's not a bad idea, you know,' he muses. 'I'll get my lawyers to call your lawyers.'

'You do that. You'll need to rest your ankle, though. I can work in the shop until it's better?'

I pull over a chair and gesture for Rory to sit behind the counter. Although I feel bad about Rory's injury, I hope he won't take me up on my offer. I have so much work left to do in my own shop, I can't afford to look after the Tool *and* The Toolbox. Time is money, and I am quickly running out of both. Thankfully, he shakes his head.

'I'll be able to take it from here,' he says, ignoring the chair. 'Did the delivery come?'

'Yes, sir, all present and correct.' I gesture to a large box on the floor. 'I also had your biggest fan here while you were away.'

'Michael Roberts?'

'No.'

'Jamie Brennan? He's got a bit of a wire fetish.'

'That sounds like something you should report to the police, but no, not Jamie. How big *is* your fan base, exactly?'

'There's a waiting list for membership,' he says, a smile playing at the corners of his mouth. 'Who was it, then?'

'Margaret. She was *not* pleased that I had the audacity to stand behind your counter.'

'Ah, of course. Go easy on her, I think she's a bit lonely. Lots of people that way up here. Margaret's husband, Bill, died recently. Not in your flat, in case you're worried.'

I roll my eyes at Rory's old joke, but inside I feel a pang of sadness for Margaret. Turns out there's a lot of lonely people in Ullapool, not to mention myself.

'Well, it's good that Margaret's got you to look out for her,' I say. 'The fan club may well double as an anti-book club. She wasn't much impressed, either, by the idea of a bookshop in the village.'

'As soon as you change a plug for Margaret, she'll be like putty in your hands.'

'That's not exactly in my business plan.' I clear my throat. 'Speaking of which, I have a business proposition for you.'

I stride purposefully to the desk and retrieve the sketchbook, bringing it over to the counter. I lay it open at a sketch of the mountains. 'You're an artist.'

The statement seems to take him by surprise. 'You looked in my book?'

'Yes, sorry,' I say. 'I saw it lying there and I couldn't resist. I need an artist for the bookshop. I've been imagining a mural of Ullapool for weeks now. It will be the focal point of the shop.' I consider my next words carefully. I don't want to stroke his ego too much, but I have to get him on board. It's a fine line. So I add: 'You're good. Very good. Seriously.'

'Thanks,' he says, unmoved. 'But no thanks.'

It's firm, but nevertheless I persist. 'I've got a fee set aside for it. Plus, I could manage your shop while you do it. I'm basically looking for your entire sketchbook in mural form on my wall. In fact, that's exactly what I'd like. It wouldn't have to be—'

'I said no thanks,' he repeats, somehow even more firmly. 'I'll fix the hole in our wall, though. It doesn't look good for a DIY store to be falling apart.'

He takes some Polyfilla from the shelf and busies around under the counter as I swallow my disappointment. It's not as though I asked him a favour. I offered him a fee. But he won't help me even if I pay him. Does he really dislike me that much?

'Well… I'd better get back next door – to get everything ready for the mural,' I say. Rory opens his mouth to speak, but I cut him off. 'Why don't you at least think about it? I don't need an answer right now.'

The bell gives a jaunty ding above my head as I pull the door open. At least I had the last word this time. Factoring in the hole in the wall and Laddergate, I reckon the score is starting to even up.

Let's say Rory 8, Ava 7. If I can get him to agree to the mural, I'll definitely give myself a few extra points.

6

Perhaps surprisingly, Donna's salon is the place to be on a Thursday evening.

As soon as I walk in, I'm hit with the scent of strongly scented shampoo, the wail of hairdryers and the most glorious sound of all: gossip.

Welcome home, Ava.

I've mostly been happy in my own company since arriving in Ullapool, but my limited interactions are starting to take their toll and I've started to yearn for some small talk. Most of my conversations are with Fiona from the coffee shop, but she's always so busy balancing coffees and taking orders that it doesn't go much further than a throwaway comment about the weather or a brief update on the bookshop. My exchanges with customers in Rory's shop were transactional, despite my overly eager, people-pleasing tendencies.

When I received a spam call earlier asking whether I'd

ever been in an accident at work, I contemplated playing along to see where the conversation might lead. I also had a full-blown discussion with myself this morning about whether to buy orange juice with or without pulp. Things got quite heated, let me tell you.

So, I've come to Donna's salon.

Her face lights up as soon as she sees me and she pulls me into a tight hug.

The chat with Donna is top tier from the start. Ten out of ten. In the space of a five-minute hair wash, Donna reveals to me that she's recently split from her boyfriend, Lewis from Glasgow, after trying to make a long-distance relationship work for a couple of years. I discover what he looks like, which football team he supports (apparently it's a loaded question in Glasgow), and that sometimes he likes to eat cold baked beans from the tin. They split because he refused to move to Ullapool and she couldn't possibly move to Glasgow to be with him because her pet poodle Bonnie suffers from terrible anxiety, which he'd *always* known.

'Can you imagine wee Bonnie in *Glasgow*?' she asks, incensed by the idea of it. 'Bad enough when I take her to the vet here, never mind venturing to Glasgow. She'd have a complete meltdown. I think she might die of shock, to be honest. And what about Guy Fawkes Night? Had he ever thought of *that*?'

I stretch back in the faux-leather seat and shake my head.

'I guess he hadn't,' I shrug, ignoring the fact that the water is getting hotter by the second as she rubs a coconut-scented conditioner into my scalp.

'He did not. He always said he'd like to make the move somewhere quieter, but that's what they all say, isn't it? All I want is to settle down in Ullapool with the love of my life. Is that too much to ask? But every guy I meet around here is either a tourist or a pensioner.'

'Erm, the water is getting pretty hot.'

It's burning now. I have to flip my head to the left to escape the scalding flow.

'Oh, shit, sorry,' she says, switching the water off. 'Don't worry, you're done now anyway. So, Lewis is in the bin. Next! I updated my Tinder profile, but around here you have to have your radius set to about a thousand miles to find someone you're not related to. I just want to meet someone, you know?'

'There must be some decent men around here. You like Rory?' I say, ignoring the strange, unpleasant feeling in my stomach as I suggest it.

Donna scoffs. 'Rory's like a brother to me. Absolutely not.'

'What about that other guy you mentioned the other day? The dog walker?'

'Oh!' she exclaims, rubbing my hair with a bright pink towel. 'I didn't even realize I mentioned Finlay to you. No, gosh no, not *Finlay*.' It may be the hot water, but I swear I see Donna's cheeks flush. She straightens and moves the conversation on. 'Anyway, what was it that made you move from London, then? Was it man trouble too?'

'Something like that,' I mumble. 'Everything trouble, really.'

Donna nods as though she understands, wraps my hair up in the towel and gestures for me to sit down in front of the mirror as she searches for her scissors.

'You didn't fancy a complete makeover then? New do, new you? That's what we always say,' Donna asks, throwing in some jazz hands for good measure.

'Just a trim, please.'

'Are you sure? Any time we have a breakup or tragic life event, or any minor inconvenience really, we whip out the dye, order extensions or jump on the latest hair trend. How bad was your breakup, on a scale of straighten-only to pink highlights?'

'Oh, it was a complete and utter shitstorm. A spiky, purple mohawk of a breakup,' I confirm. 'But I'd still just like a little bit off the ends, maybe add in an extra layer or two for volume?'

Donna nods knowingly, glancing at me in the mirror with a sympathetic smile. 'You're not over it.'

'I am!' I protest. 'I just don't really dye my hair.'

'It is a lovely colour,' she says, twirling my wet auburn locks around a finger, before setting to work with her scissors. 'It always was. Elle and I thought you were so cool when we were younger, you know.'

I burst out laughing. 'Me? Cool! Donna, I stayed here with my granny and you had to drag me away from my books to get me outside. How could you think I was cool?'

'You were mature. The big city girl who swanned in and out every summer and didn't care about being away from your parents. We were in awe of you.'

I throw my head back, a loud laugh escaping my lips, as Donna steadies my head back into position.

'I was in awe of you and Elle! You both knew everything that was going on in the village and you were so close. I was lucky you let me be the third wheel.'

Donna snorts. 'The third super cool wheel who arrived with highlights in her hair when she was fifteen! I begged my mum for highlights after you left that summer, but she said I had to wait until I was at least sixteen. I genuinely think your hair made me realize I wanted to be a hairdresser. I remember thinking you looked amazing. The boys all drooled over you too.'

'I doubt that. I was always terrified of the boys. There seemed to be so many of them swarming around like bees on their bikes. I've always been much more of a girls' girl.'

Unlike my London bestie.

I keep the thought to myself.

'Girl, same,' she says, her eyes serious as she snips at my hair. 'I'm much happier without Lewis. Really, I am. I love working here and being my own boss. It's a vibe, you know? Plus, we hear it all in here – breakups, affairs, tragic love stories. It's usually people gossiping about other people's misfortunes, rather than coming straight from the horse's mouth. They wait till after the storm has passed, then come in for their new look.'

'No way,' I say. 'Affairs and tragedies in Ullapool? I thought this place would be peace and harmony after the city.'

Donna shakes her head. Her expression softens and her voice shakes as she says, 'You wouldn't believe half the stuff that goes on around here. It's a very supportive community, though. When Mum died last year, you couldn't move in this shop for condolence flowers. It turned into a florist's overnight.'

'That's lovely,' I say. 'That's exactly why I'm back here, for the community part. London just feels so… soulless in comparison.'

'We have plenty of soul here. And yes, it was Mum rather than Lewis that brought on the balayage, by the way. Lewis was barely worth a fringe,' she explains, flicking her glossy locks. 'On the day of her funeral, everyone lined the streets as the coffin drove past. The bakery that she worked in for more than twenty-five years closed for a whole week as a mark of respect. Then, as the week progressed, everyone worried that the bakery might lose out on too much money. So, as soon as it reopened, people flocked from around the village to help them out. They were completely sold out of stock by midday.'

'Your mum must have been very loved by the village. To have had such an impact.'

Donna's eyes shine again as she nods, lost in thought for a moment, before adding, 'It's funny how quickly life moves on, though, and everything is supposed to go back to normal. I want to talk about her now more than ever, but no one ever asks about her and it's hard when you don't have the space to do it. I just don't want to forget her, you know?'

I nod. 'Of course.'

She purses her lips and lets out a long sigh. 'Anyway, silly me going on and on about it when you just want to have a nice chat and get your layers in. Sorry, Ava.'

'Donna, seriously, I'd love to chat more about your mum. Now, or any time.'

I mean it. I remember feeling the same when Granny died, wondering why my parents stopped talking about her. I wanted to scream from the rooftops how much I missed her advice, her warm hugs in the summer and our frequent phone calls throughout the year. The silence was too much. I wished I had someone to talk to about it; somewhere I could *go* to meet people who felt the same as me. When I started university, I heard about a 'death cafe' where you could talk about your lost loved ones, but I never had the guts to go. It sounded morbid, for a start, and I was paranoid everyone would think my grief ship should have sailed by then.

Judging by Donna's pensive expression and sad brown eyes, I see that she feels the same.

She coughs and nods. 'Thank you. I might take you up on that.'

'Please do.'

'Anyway, did you make up with Rory?'

'Not likely. I last saw him through the hole in the wall he still has to fix.'

'Maybe he was trying to make that hole surreptitiously,' she suggests. 'So he could spy on you.'

'That would be a) creepy and b) illegal.'

'He's not that kind of guy, don't worry.'

'Well, if I *am* murdered in my sleep, he'll be suspect number one. I don't think anyone's ever taken such an instant disliking to me. Did you know he wanted to buy the bookshop? Do you think that's it? Because it's just business, it's not personal. I had no idea he existed.'

Donna shakes her head. 'Yes, I did, but he won't be holding a grudge because of that, don't worry. Rory comes from a big family – he's the youngest of eight children – so he's used to fighting it out for what he wants. They've all buggered off to live in other places – at least one of them lives in Australia and I'm sure some of the others are abroad too. His mum and dad are in Edinburgh, helping his sister who's just had a baby. He's the last man standing here to take care of the family business.'

'Lucky him, having a business handed to him on a plate,' I sniff. 'While I'm killing myself to try to fix mine up. You don't happen to know a good accountant, do you? I've been trying to work things out on my own, but I need help.'

'Oh, you need Eilidh. She does all my accounting.'

‘Brilliant. My parents both work in finance and they keep passive aggressively offering to help. The last thing I want is to have Mum peering at my figures while Dad shakes his head, wondering where they went wrong with me.’

‘I’ll give you her number. And mine,’ Donna promises, peering across the road towards the bookshop. ‘Are you nearly finished with the renovations? It’s really taking shape now.’

‘Yes, I’ll be having a launch night as soon as it’s ready. Will you come?’

‘Try and stop me,’ Donna smiles, as she starts blasting my freshly cut hair with the hairdryer. ‘Maybe that’ll be the night to officially launch the purple mohawk?’

*

I feel every one of my twenty-nine years, and more, a few hours later.

I step out to place myself on top of the green bin to call Eilidh, the local accountant Donna recommended, when I discover I’m not alone.

Two teens, a boy and a girl, are locked in a steamy make-out session in the small courtyard beside the bins. Yes, the bins. Gross. The things we do for young love.

I clock them as their hands lace around each other (the boy has one hand on the girl’s bum, as the girl places hers on his waist). Their heads move back and forth quickly, like birds pecking against a tree, without coming up for breath. I find myself completely frozen to the spot, unsure of my next move. Should I call over and insist my courtyard isn't a suitable snogging location and they should find somewhere else? Throw a bucket of water over them both? Leave them to it?

Deciding on the latter, I creep backwards.

'Jesus!' Rory shouts, as I bump into him on the way.

I spin around as the bag he was holding falls to the ground, the contents spilling everywhere.

'Sorry!' I apologize in a whisper, bending down to pick up the rubbish. Unfortunately, he does the same, and our heads collide.

'Fuck's sake,' Rory mutters, rubbing his head. 'We shouldn't be allowed near each other. It always ends in injury.'

He isn't wrong. Some people, like this teen couple, are drawn to each other like magnets. Rory and I seem to have the opposite problem. He rubs his head, close to the spot where I hit him.

'Another whack to the nugget,' he mutters.

'You've got quite the sharp skull yourself.'

The couple peer at us with startled expressions. Their baby faces are clouded with concern; they think they're in huge trouble. The young girl's make-up is over exaggerated and completely unnecessary for her perfect, clear skin, and her lipstick is smudged all around her mouth.

Rory exhales and the pair practically tremble at the sound. 'Jen. Evan.'

'Please don't say anything, Mr MacGregor,' Jen pleads. 'We promise we won't come here again. We thought The Old Tea Shop was still empty.'

'Mr MacGregor,' I mutter to him under my breath. 'Makes you sound like an OAP.'

Rory ignores me, but I feel him stiffen at my side. 'Don't worry, you two, your secret's safe with me. But Miss Campbell here, who's just taken over The Old Tea Shop, is a bit of a blabbermouth.'

'Oi,' I say. 'That's *Ms* Campbell to you. And don't worry, my lips are sealed. I was young and in love once too. I won't say a word.'

Jen and Evan stare back, their wide eyes blinking, as though they aren't sure whether to believe us or not.

'Off you go,' Rory urges, flapping them away with his hand. 'Go exert yourselves in someone else's garden.'

They scamper out of the courtyard, along the back lane, with mutters of 'Thanks, Mr MacGregor. Thanks, Ms Campbell.'

'"*I was young and in love once too*",' Rory repeats with a chuckle. 'Call me an OAP. What are you, a hundred years old?'

'Don't you know I run a bookshop in the middle of nowhere? I'm in my geriatric era, Mr MacGregor. How old are they anyway?'

He shrugs. 'Thirteen, fourteen maybe. Jen works on a Saturday helping Donna in the salon and Evan's parents own the fish and chip shop on the main street.'

I lean against the brick wall in the courtyard with a nostalgic smile. 'First love. Do you remember being that age? Snogging in bike sheds for hours?'

Rory's face clouds over. 'Some of us were late bloomers.'

'Ah, I see. No one wanted to kiss teenage Rory?' I tease. 'Did you walk around telling all the girls how bad their business plans were and lecture them on shopping locally too?'

From the look on Rory's face, I realize I've hit a nerve. I've never seen his face flush like this. He avoids looking in my direction, searching for some distraction in the empty courtyard.

I look him up and down. I may not get on with him, but I have eyes. He's about my age. He is every inch the picture-perfect guy, from his tanned skin – how do you even *get* a tan in the north of Scotland? – to those gorgeous green eyes. If he was in London, rather than Ullapool, he'd likely have a model on his arm. I doubt there are many models our age in Ullapool, but there are certainly plenty of girls out there who would kill for a bit of Rory action.

Maybe he was a late bloomer, as he said. But if he had gone through an ugly phase as a teenager, he'd clearly grown well out of it now, *and* he obviously knew it. It would be hard to miss. He couldn't think he was Mr Popularity just because of his excellent customer service. Donna is prepared to defend him to the death, Margaret worships the ground he walks on. Even Pete sings his praises. So, what exactly is his problem? I must have stirred up bad memories of being dumped at a school disco, or something equally traumatic.

Despite what Donna and Elle believed, I hadn't exactly had an easy time of it at school either. Aside from my Ullapool summers, I found it difficult to make friends. Until I met Macy, I was a bit of a loner. And while Macy was my best friend, she always had plenty of other options. She played sports and her parents took her to endless clubs and activities, while I buried my nose in books and waited for my Scottish summers to roll around. And when we got older, she easily made friends with her colleagues and people she met in passing, too, while I spent what little free time I had with Seb.

Until she decided to see what it was I liked so much about Seb.

'I didn't lecture you,' Rory protests, bringing me back to the here and now. 'I was just pointing out that, as a new shop owner looking for support—'

'Yes, I know, I get it,' I cut him off. 'And just so you're aware, I am shopping locally. I do it all the time. I ordered a pizza from the new takeaway place, I buy coffee every morning from Fiona's down the road, I'm researching local accountants that I can use *and* I've just had my hair done at Donna's. Put that in your *shop local* pipe and smoke it.'

'Just not the DIY store next door.'

'Sorry, did you mean to say "Oh, yes, your hair, I was just thinking how lovely it looks"?'

He blinks, without taking the bait. 'No, I didn't mean to say that at all.'

'I bought nails from you on the first day,' I point out. 'Then I asked you to paint the mural for me and you said no. There was no discussion about it, either. I want to shop locally; I want to pay you for the mural, but you're the one that's blocking *me*.'

He shrugs, placing his rubbish in the bin. 'I'm not an artist.'

I roll my eyes. 'Stop fishing for compliments! You're good and you know it. I will keep asking until I break you.'

'Like you've been trying to do the whole time you've been here?' He gestures at his ankle.

'Mishaps,' I say, with a wave of the hand. 'Anyway, stop avoiding the subject. Will you paint the mural for me?'

'Nope.'

I exhale, walking back towards my shop. If he is hoping that I'll beg for his help, he'll be waiting for a very long time.

What would Granny have called someone stubborn? *Thrawn*.

I call it being an arsehole.

7

Slapping on the factor thirty suncream before an early evening walk makes me realize that high summer in Ullapool has crept in while I've been working behind closed doors.

The mornings usually start off dry but overcast, and as the day progresses, the sun starts to break through the fluffy white clouds. By the time evening lands, the whole village basks in sunshine along the shoreline where the ferries go out to the Outer Hebrides. Children cycle along the streets, just as I did when I was younger. I'd barely been able to ride when I first arrived here as a child, but Granny borrowed a bike for me. I was a pro by the end of my first summer, whizzing around the grassy fields and streets near her house, and growing in confidence with every turn of the pedals.

I can still picture the faces of the other kids. The endless stream of boys who'd jeer at us from their bikes. I think of how few young people there are in the village now. Those kids must have all grown up and left. Just like Rory's siblings. More than likely he and some of his brothers were part of that faceless gaggle of boys I was afraid of.

There was one boy, though, I remember more clearly: Mackie. A self-proclaimed geek who vowed to travel the globe once he'd had his braces taken off and had laser eye surgery to correct his vision. I'd loved chatting to Mackie, who was less intimidating than the rest of the lads. He'd been so *interesting*, and interested. In our shy childish way, we spoke of the places we wanted to go. Me, I wanted to come here, to Ullapool. He wanted nothing more than to leave.

I told Macy about him when I returned home after the second summer, after we'd developed a secret handshake. She teased me that I'd landed my first boyfriend, which instantly shut me up. Mackie was *not* my boyfriend. My cheeks flushed at the accusation. I had seen him the following year, and all those after until Granny passed away. We'd slip back into light conversation about our studies and his travel plans. He wanted to backpack as soon as he finished school, which I'd never even considered, though it sounded amazing. I told him my plans to study marketing and move to London, like my parents wanted, before I made my millions and could see more of the world. Looking back, I can admit that I had a bit of a crush on him, as nerdy and lanky as he was. I looked forward to seeing him every year, but nothing ever came of it. He was far too awkward for anything like that. And then, I didn't return. He's probably long gone by now, off travelling the world like he always wanted.

As I walk along the pebbled beach, I scan the ground for a good skimmer. It's just like when I was a teenager. I can picture us lined up along the seafront, lukewarm cans of cider clasped in our hands. We'd spend hours trying to get the stone to jump out two, three or even four times. I do it now, too, alongside families who are soaking up some sun before eating their picnics. I breathe in Ullapool's magic before progressing with my exploration of the surrounding area, captivated by the beauty of the rugged landscape.

Just when I'm most at peace, a thought enters unbidden into my mind. I remember that the only person I'd been sad to leave for my Ullapool summers is the reason I am here now.

Macy.

It's inevitable that I'm thinking about her today, when she's celebrating her thirtieth birthday. It's such a milestone that I can't quite believe I'm not at her side. We'd talked at length about our thirtieth birthday plans. I'd even put in some calls earlier in the year to start arranging a party for her. We'd discussed a trip abroad in September, when the sun was likely to be kinder on my pale complexion. Macy didn't need to worry about that, with her gorgeous, bronzed skin, but she was willing to go when it suited me.

I can't help but wonder who she's celebrating with today. Is she having her party? Have her brothers come to visit? Will her mum and dad ask where I am? What's she told them about me?

Once we became friends, Macy was the only pull away from Ullapool that I had. I couldn't have given two hoots about leaving Mum and Dad, but I always missed Macy. I hate to admit it, but part of me still does, in spite of everything.

We spent every summer texting back and forth. I'd call on this day each year to wish her happy birthday. She was usually in Spain, Greece or somewhere equally beautiful with her family. They'd all take turns saying hello to me on our calls, while playing volleyball on the beach or chilling by the pool. Her older brothers would tease us about missing each other, that we were soulmates, but we never denied that. We solemnly confessed we missed each other like mad and couldn't wait to be reunited.

Oh God. Is *Seb* celebrating with her today instead of me? Are they toasting her over some champagne? Is he singing 'Happy Birthday' at the top of his lungs? The thought makes me queasy. Grabbing my phone, I check their social media pages for any evidence of family celebrations, boozy brunches or, my stomach drops at the thought of it, a romantic getaway. But Macy hasn't posted anything since completing the marathon she spent months training for last year. She beams at the camera, clutching her medal proudly with both hands. I check Seb's page, but he hasn't been active since his work trip to Dubai two years ago. He'd been so excited about flying business class for four days of back-to-back meetings and client dinners. I'd secretly thought the whole thing sounded exhausting.

I glance down at the pair of sturdy boots on my feet that Granny would have been proud of. My London look of tailored trousers, blazers and high heels are, thankfully, long gone. I'd never felt truly comfortable in the formal workwear. When I first moved to London, I lived in comfortable clothes, but my wardrobe evolved over the years. Now, I'm back to casual wear and wouldn't look out of place hopping on board with the fishermen at 5 a.m.

I did contemplate dressing up to visit the finance guru, Eilidh Stewart, to look as though I've got my shit in order, but I decided against it. An unexpected letter from the tax man sent me into a flap earlier, so I plan to turn up at Eilidh's listed address to see if I can catch her. It seems she isn't willing to answer her phone, no matter how many times I call. I am determined to shop local, so even if the local accountant is a recluse, she is going to be my accountant.

At the bottom of the pier, a group of tourists huddles together at the Summer Isles boat-trip stand. It's something I never got round to when I was younger, but always wanted to do. Once the bookshop opens, I vow to finally do the trip, as a mini celebration for myself.

I haven't managed to bring myself to venture up to Granny's old cottage just yet. Although she's constantly on my mind as I traipse through the streets, it's like there's a mysterious force repelling me from venturing in that direction. I'll need to own up to it and go eventually – in a village as small as Ullapool, you can't avoid a whole section of it – but I can't seem to do it just now. I don't want to see someone else standing at the window, washing dishes the way she used to, weeding the front garden on hands and knees or reading a book in the garden nook she created just for me. I'm pretty sure the sight would break my heart, and it's been through enough recently. I think I'll just stay on my own path.

I cross the road towards Eilidh's house on the edge of town. Following my phone's map I find myself on the outskirts of the village, surrounded by greenery. In the distance, I spot Finlay, the village dog walker that Donna mentioned, ambling down the hill, surrounded by his army of pups. He often comes to the courtyard at the back of our shops to chat with Rory, but I'm not going to hold that against him. Everyone loves chatting with Rory, after all. Everyone except me.

Looking ahead, I climb up the hill and follow a long and winding path. The views of Loch Broom and the village below are incredible. I can even see my own little piece of Ullapool, my flat and future bookshop, and my heart swells with pride. I've almost done it. I escaped, like I said I would. I've started taking the walks that I promised myself. The bookshop is almost ready to unveil and then I'll be able to start my apartment makeover. Take a boat trip. Keep on breathing. The future will be here soon.

I turn the corner to see the home of the elusive Eilidh Stewart. Gasping at the sight of the elevated house on the hillside, I realize that Eilidh must be quite well off, as most finance types are. I'd be a recluse, too, if I lived in a house like this. The sprawling stone-built house is set over two levels and boasts a balcony the whole length of the upper floor. Behind the house, I spot a long, flat grass area with a football goal at each end. Lucky kids growing up in a house like this. Walking up the long drive, I picture the superwoman who lives in this house, a pen in one hand, kids' football boots in another, phone crooked between her neck and shoulder.

But as I approach the front door, I hear a quiet whimpering noise. A woman, who looks to be in her late thirties, sits on the bench outside the door with her head in her hands. She's clearly having a moment, interrupted by my stomping up the grassy path. I think about turning around, but she clocks me before I can back away.

'Can I help you?' she calls, wiping her eyes.

'I'm, erm, sorry to intrude. I'm looking for Eilidh Stewart? I've been trying to call, but…'

'Ah,' she says, raising an eyebrow above her bright, blue eyes that are red from the tears. 'You're 658.'

'Sorry?'

'Your phone number ends in 658. I've been wondering who it is that keeps pestering me,' she said. 'I thought it was a scam caller.'

'Oh, yes, that's me. I'm not a scammer, though. I've just

moved here to open a new business – a bookshop in the village. Donna recommended you as the one-stop shop for all my accountancy needs. But I can see you're in the middle of something, so shall I come back?'

She thinks for a second, before shaking her head. 'No, come on in for a cup of tea and you can tell me what I can help with, 658.'

As she pulls open the heavy wooden front door, I'm eager to get a glimpse of this beautiful house's interior. I follow her straight up the stairs, past the array of family pictures featuring Eilidh, her partner and two young sons, to the expansive open-plan living area, which includes a kitchen with a huge marble island and a dining space that overlooks the balcony, with an uninterrupted panorama of the loch and the sea beyond.

'Wow, your house is amazing,' I breathe. 'Look at that view!'

'Yep, it is beautiful.'

She doesn't seem too happy about it. In fact, as she pulls her cardigan around her sunken shoulders and lifts a coffee cup to put it in the sink, all she radiates is sadness.

'Well, it *was* beautiful,' she continues, as she starts scrubbing at the coffee cup. 'It was pretty perfect, in fact, until Mark decided it wasn't.'

She lets out a long sigh, places the cup on the worktop, and promptly bursts into tears. Oh shit. I've obviously picked the worst possible time to drop in unannounced on Eilidh. Advancing towards her, I think of Donna and her love of big hugs, but somehow Eilidh doesn't seem like the type. I place a hand on her shoulder instead.

'Sit down,' I say. 'I'll make the tea.'

She lets me. I busy around her kitchen, opening random drawers to look for spoons and mugs. Eilidh doesn't move. She sits at the breakfast bar, staring out at the view with a melancholy expression.

'Do you want to talk about it?'

'I'm sorry you've found me this way. It's the first time I've had to send the boys away with my husband. My *ex*-husband,' she sighs. 'My sons, Harry and Caden. They're only five and seven. They didn't want to leave. They kept asking why I wasn't coming too.'

Her eyes fill with tears again as I place the cup of tea in front of her. She grips the cup with her hands but doesn't bring it to her lips.

'You've separated?' I ask.

She nods her head. 'He had an affair. He's been coming here to see the kids, but now he's "settled" in Inverness. Settled with her. He was meant to be settled with his own family, but instead he buggered off to start a new one.'

My eyes widen. 'A new family?'

'Baby on the way,' she says, her voice flat. 'Due in December. A girl, obviously. I wanted our third to be a girl. Shit, sorry, I'm oversharing. I just… I haven't really told many people about it.'

I suck in my breath. Poor Eilidh. I think my predicament with Seb is bad, but what she is going through is proper grown-up shit. Kids. Divorce. Heartbreak on another level. Looking around the perfect family home, you'd think she had it all.

It doesn't seem right that Eilidh should be dealing with this all on her own. The death cafe at uni pops back into my mind – what she's experiencing is another kind of grief. There should be somewhere she could go to share her story with people who are on hand to listen and help, rather than opening up to someone who just popped by for advice on their tax return.

'I'm so sorry,' I say. 'I can't imagine how hard that must be for you. You can talk to me about it. I'd like to help if I can.'

'Thanks,' she sniffs. 'It just doesn't seem fair, what he did. It should be illegal. You sign a legal document when you get married, don't you? Shouldn't you be locked up if you break it?'

I nod. 'I can see your logic.'

'Anyway, you're not here for my sob story. Sorry, what did you say your name was?'

'It's Ava. Ava Campbell. But we can stick with 658 if it's easier,' I say, with a small smile. 'I wanted to talk about business plans and finances, but we can do that another time. What are your plans for when the boys are away?'

'To wallow in self-pity,' she admits with a self-deprecating look.

'You're not planning on moping around in this big house by yourself all day, are you? When are the kids back?'

'Tomorrow evening,' she says. 'But I wasn't planning to—'

'Grab your coat. Let's go out.'

*

Eilidh puts up less of a fight than I expect. She grabs her trainers and jacket from a large walk-in closet filled with children's wellies, shoes and backpacks. As she ties her laces, I study the family pictures on display all over the house. Mark is attractive, but Eilidh is much more striking, with her long deep-red hair flowing loosely around her shoulders in each picture, and her piercing blue eyes that her sons have inherited. The boys beam widely at the camera in various baby and toddler poses, their chubby cheeks replaced with boyish grins as they grow up.

'Happy families,' she groans, as she catches me staring at them. 'I paid a fortune for those professional photos. It's taken all my strength not to take a permanent marker to erase Mark's stupid face.'

'You look so happy,' I say. 'I can't believe that he could turn his back on all this. What more did he want?'

Eilidh shrugs as she holds the front door open and gestures for me to walk in front. 'Everything's always been handed to him on a silver platter, so he thought he'd go for gold. Her family is eye-wateringly rich.'

'And you're not?' I snort, before I can stop myself, gesturing to our beautiful surroundings.

Eilidh allows herself a small smile. 'Some people are never content. Anyway, what brings you to Ullapool? Have you come here with a partner or on your own?'

'I'm very much flying solo.'

I share my Seb story with Eilidh during our walk to the village. It's only fair, a heartbreak for a heartbreak. I don't mention the best friend element, though. I can't seem to put Macy's name in my mouth. Somehow, it's the worst part of it all.

'What an idiot,' Eilidh says, shaking her head.

'At least we're in it together,' I say in a cheery voice. 'Both screwed over. Now, I'm not looking for your professional advice or anything. But I thought you might like to see my bookshop on the way and then we can head to the pub?'

Eilidh nods. 'Sure. It's better than anything I'd planned for the evening.'

We walk along side by side on the pavement until we reach the front of the bookshop. I gaze up at the building in front of me, filled with a sense of pride at my next chapter.

'So, wait, you just bid in an auction for a shop and turned up here to get started?'

'It was a little more complicated than that,' I say, not wanting her to think I'm a complete flight risk. 'I had to speak to some lawyers and my granny used to live here, so I know the village. But yeah, I suppose that's it. In a nutshell.'

'That's… I could never do something like that.'

In a way, I'm lucky that I can just up sticks and move here. I've got no ties to Seb; I can move on with nothing holding me back. With their sons, Mark will always have to be in Eilidh's life.

'I never thought I could do anything like it either. But when Seb and I broke up, it suddenly seemed like the only thing that made sense.'

I push open the door to the bookshop and follow Eilidh inside.

It looks like a completely different shop from the one I bid on a few weeks ago. I'd settled on a vibrant, bold blue shade for the walls and fixed various sizes and shapes of bookshelves to the walls, thanks to the drill that finally arrived and several hours spent studying DIY videos on YouTube. It could have looked totally shoddy, but somehow the eclectic aesthetic works. I'd started categorizing and shelving the books, from the Scottish section that was bound to be popular with tourists, to the fiction, non-fiction and children's books. I'd kept one wall blank for the mural and I've been using stencils to paint famous book quotes in gold paint on the wall behind my desk.

I take videos of the transformation work for my social media pages each day, omitting my swearing and despairing moments, and post them online. It's part of my strategy for the business, and it seems to be working. I've already amassed a healthy following, plus the interactions keep me busy in the evenings, when I have no one else to talk to.

There is still work to do before it's completely finished, but as I try to see it for the first time through Eilidh's eyes, I feel pretty bloody proud of myself.

'This is amazing, Ava,' she says. 'I can't believe you've done all this by yourself.'

'Neither can I,' I admit with a low laugh.

Eilidh takes her time observing the space, remarking how much she loves the bright armchairs I've selected. I'd sourced bits of furniture online, mostly for free, driving to neighbouring villages and squeezing the bits and pieces into my tiny car. Initially, I'd planned to reupholster them, but they are all in good condition, so I'm keeping them as they are for now. The burnt-orange stripy love seat is my firm favourite, and it faces a teal armchair with a matching footstool. It shouldn't work, but it does.

I spend hours curled up on the chairs in the evenings, blinds down, reading the books that I've bought for the shop. I've been devouring all genres of books for years and can't believe that I've turned my passion into work that I love. Reading is now market research, so I can recommend books to my customers when my shop opens. It's becoming more real every day. I am building a life, a future here. I shiver at the realization.

'Can you show me what it looked like before? I hadn't been in The Old Tea Shop for years.'

'You should follow me on TikTok,' I suggest, holding my phone out to show her my transformation videos. 'Is there anything more satisfying than watching these? They're like home renovation shows in thirty-second bursts.'

'I'm not "down with the kids" enough for TikTok,' Eilidh shakes her head, transfixed by my first DIY bookshop video. 'But I'll join if it means I get to watch these. How did you get so many followers?'

'Consistent, relevant and fun content,' I say. 'I was the campaigns manager at a marketing and social media agency in London before I moved here. I worked every hour under the sun for other people's businesses. Now I'm putting my money where my mouth is.'

'Well, it's definitely working. Although I'm not exactly sure how many people in Ullapool are on TikTok.'

'Not many, from my analytics. But it should work well for the tourists who come here. My engagement goes through the roof when I post videos of the Scottish scenery, the wildlife and Scottishisms I pick up along the way. I post some of my granny's favourite words and sayings. Everyone loves that. Who knew that a short video about my granny calling me "peely wally" would resonate with so many people?'

'I call my boys peely wally sometimes too,' Eilidh says with a smile. 'What are you going to call the bookshop?'

'I'm not sure. Nothing has really clicked yet. I'll need to decide soon, for the grand opening. I just need to get a few more things set up and I'll be good to go. I can't wait to get started. Are you a reader?'

Eilidh blushes. 'I hate to say this, but I've not managed to finish a book since I had the boys. I used to be such an avid reader too.'

I shake my head. 'No need to be embarrassed. What's your favourite genre?'

Eilidh thinks for a moment. 'I've always liked thrillers.'

I smile, setting off for the downstairs loo, where I've stored three boxes of my favourite thrillers. 'I've got just the thing.'

I locate a Frieda McFadden book and hand it to Eilidh on our way out of the shop.

'Try this one and report back,' I urge her. 'I'm not a mum, but my granny said reading was how she made room for herself when she was raising my dad. Try and make a bit of time for yourself, especially when the boys are away. This will be a good distraction. No pressure, but I bet you'll love it.' Eilidh accepts the book gladly before I continue, 'Anyway, I promised you a drink.'

8

As we pass the Tool's Toolbox and find the bar down the road, I feel quite smug. First, I have a new friend to come to the pub with. Second, Eilidh looks much brighter than she did earlier. Win-win. I text Donna to see if she'd like to join us. Donna invited me to form a trio with Elle every summer, and now it's up to me to return the favour. She replies to say she'll be here as soon as she finishes at the salon.

'Not seen you in here in years, Eilidh Stewart,' the barman says, as he fills our glasses with ice.

'Haven't been thirsty, Tom,' she jokes, but I hear the air of sadness in her tone.

We take our drinks over to a table in the corner.

'I take it you haven't been out much recently? Since everything happened with your husband?' I whisper, aware that Eilidh probably doesn't want her business becoming everyone else's business. I know word travels fast around here.

'Way before all that,' Eilidh explains. 'Mark wasn't a big fan of the local pubs. He wasn't a big fan of Ullapool in general, if I'm honest. He's a property developer, all about business, making money, doing deals. There wasn't enough of a buzz around here for that kind of thing.'

She sighs.

'I chased the big deals, the promotions and the money in London for a while,' I confess. 'It didn't bring me any more happiness. As soon as it was all gone, it was like the fog lifted and I could actually see that. I bet he'll regret it one day.'

'I don't think his enlightenment is coming any time soon. He regrets the time he *did* spend here,' she says, shaking her head. 'He kept pushing me to move to a city, but I wanted the boys to grow up surrounded by nature and greenery, like I did, rather than smack bang in the middle of a concrete city, you know?'

'More fool him. He's missing out on more than just a lovely place to live, that's for sure,' I say, as I tap my glass against hers. 'Anyway, cheers. To new beginnings.'

'To new beginnings,' she repeats, with a half-hearted attempt at a smile. 'Oh my God, is that Rory MacGregor I see over there?'

Ah, shit. It's bad enough that Rory and I have to share a wall every day, never mind sharing the pub in our free time. At least I can say that Rory's true to his word: earlier today he did come round to fix the hole, though he barely uttered a word while he did. I consider hiding under the table, but Eilidh looks so excited to see him. Of course she does. He is Mr Bloody Popularity, isn't he? Now I've got to explain to her why he hates my guts. Not that I'm 100 per cent clear on that.

I glance over and, sure enough, Rory is sitting there beside the roaring fire, sipping a pint across from Finlay the dog walker. One of the pups has taken up residency on the carpet under the table at their feet. I hope Eilidh isn't about to—

'Rory!' She stands up and starts waving her hand in the air as I slide down in my seat.

Double shit.

Rory turns around to face us, smiling as he sees Eilidh. His expression quickly clouds in confusion when he spots me sitting across from her.

'Eilidh,' he calls, moving towards us. 'Where have you been hiding?'

Rory envelops Eilidh in a friendly hug. I frown. Who is this cheery village creature that everyone seems to love and why does he disappear around me?

'Ah, you know, the kids, the husband, all that stuff,' Eilidh says, her eyes still sparkling at him. 'Why don't you come and join us?'

Rory glances down at me, as I sip my gin and tonic. It tastes exceptionally bitter. Fitting. 'Ava,' he nods towards me, acknowledging my presence like a state official.

'Rory,' I nod, tight-lipped, in return.

Curt. Polite. We can be civil towards each other, just for one evening. Can't we? Maybe it is time to have a day off hating each other.

'Ah, you two know each other already!' Eilidh beams. 'I was just about to say that you must be work neighbours. Rory's my cousin, Ava. Well, not really. Our mums were best friends growing up, so we called each other cousins. You know how it is.'

I nod although I don't know how it is. I had no cousins growing up, never mind pretend ones.

Eilidh beams at us both like we are one big happy family. Does everyone love Rory MacGregor, apart from me? And does he love everyone *except* me? Every time I make a friend, he seems to be waiting in the wings to swoop in and claim them. He is always there first. It is getting beyond annoying. Now, Eilidh's inviting him to sit with us, and he looks to be considering it. Bloody hell.

'Where's Mark?' Rory asks, looking around the pub.

'He's… we've… He won't be coming tonight,' Eilidh stutters, before finding her words. 'Anyway, sit down! Join us. Ava doesn't mind, do you, Ava?'

I bloody well do mind.

'Of course not.' I smile sweetly, aware that I want to keep the new friend I have made. And what is it they say? Keep your friends close and your enemies closer. 'You'll need to invite Finlay over too, though. We can't leave him all on his ownsome.'

As a dog lover, I already rate Finlay. I decide then and there to make it my mission to get him on my side. That way, I can get in first before Rory infects him with his tales about me, the big-city girl who'll be gone before everyone knows it. Despite Eilidh's lifelong friendship with Rory, to the point that they consider themselves practically related, Eilidh and I also definitely have strong friendship potential. I still have time to salvage this situation and show everyone that I am a nice, civil person.

Finlay, with his pale skin, cheeky expression and short red hair, has a look of Prince Harry on country vacation. He's almost as tall as Rory and about the same age. As we wave him over, he brings a German Shepherd to sit beneath our table.

'Nice to meet you, Finlay,' I say. 'Donna, my friend from the hairdresser's, mentioned you.'

He splutters his pint. 'God, sorry,' he says, wiping his mouth. 'That went down the wrong way. You know Donna? She was in the same year at school as me and Rory.'

'Ah, Donna and I go way back,' I say with a smile. 'We've been friends since I was a kid and, before you say anything about my accent, I'm at least half Scottish. I used to come here every summer to visit my granny.'

'Well, isn't that something?' Finlay smiles widely at Rory, who shoots Finlay a withering look.

I catch a glimpse of Donna over Finlay's shoulder.

'Ah, here she is.' I grin, standing up to hug her. 'Speak of the devil.'

'Donna… hi.' Finlay stands up behind us, as though waiting in line for a hug, and then realizes it's not a queuing situation. He clasps his hands together like a jilted groom before taking a seat again. 'Didn't know you were coming.'

'Neither did I. Ava invited me. Hi everyone.'

As Donna attempts to drag a heavy chair over to join the group, Finlay leaps up to help her. Their hands meet on the back of the chair and Donna jumps back like she's been electrocuted. Finlay clears his throat and stands tall, squaring his shoulders.

'The usual?' he asks, gesturing to the bar.

'Yes, please,' she nods, not meeting his eye.

'What a gentleman.' I smile widely at Finlay before directing my gaze over to Rory, who hasn't moved a muscle to help. So much for being a helping hand to everyone. He sips his pint.

Finlay's dog edges his way towards me and places his paw on my shoe. I let out a loud 'aww' and lavish all my love on the dog, exclaiming how utterly gorgeous he is while stroking his fur. The dog yawns in return, bored with being adored.

'What's your name?' I say in a sing-song voice.

'Piper,' Rory responds, looking me dead in the eye. 'She's mine.'

'She's *your* dog?' I ask. 'I thought she belonged to Finlay.'

'Nope, she's mine.'

'I didn't have you down as a dog owner,' I say, pursing my lips.

'Why's that?' He cocks his head to the side.

'I thought you'd be more the goldfish type,' I shrug. 'Maybe a cat, at a push.'

He frowns. 'A *goldfish*? What does a goldfish owner look like?'

His face flushes with annoyance. Why is he so touchy about everything with me?

'Just, you know, they're very low maintenance. Don't require too much *affection*,' I say as Finlay returns with Donna's 'usual' drink. 'Anyway, I see Finlay out walking with the pups all the time, so I assumed he'd have a dog of his own.'

'I walk Piper,' Rory interjects, before Finlay can respond. 'We're out all the time.'

Now Rory is getting defensive because he thinks I am insinuating he never walks his own dog.

'Erm... congratulations?'

Eilidh and Donna look at Rory, then back at me, with puzzled expressions. Donna quietly thanks Finlay for the drink, and he nods as he rests his welly boot over his knee.

Rory takes a long sip of his pint and plonks it back down on the table, the last of the frothy foam dancing at the bottom of his glass. 'I'm going for another round. What's everyone else having? I take it you're okay, Donna. Eilidh? Finlay? Ava?'

There is an edge to the way he says my name. A stumble. A hesitancy. The last thing he wants is to buy me a drink, but it would look strange if he didn't offer. Around his friends, he is being forced to conform to social norms, and I like it.

'Yes, please, that would be lovely,' I say.

As Rory makes his way to the bar, Finlay makes conversation with me. He's energetic, easy to talk to. I can see why Donna likes him so much – not that she would admit it. But I notice her looking at him proudly as he leads the chat. When he hears about my daily walks, he takes his phone out to show me the best local walking routes. As Rory returns to the table with the promised drinks, we are in full discussion about local landmarks, gorges and waterfalls.

'You should definitely go further afield,' Finlay advises. 'There are a few routes and climbing paths that are a short drive away but well worth it. Corrieshalloch Gorge has some great scenery. You're not afraid of heights, are you?'

'How high up are we talking?'

'Just don't look down when you're on the viewing platform and you'll be fine,' Donna says with a knowing grin.

'The Summer Isles tour is the best,' Rory proclaims. 'I've not been on it for years. I'd love to do it again sometime.'

'Oh, I want to do that too!' I say eagerly, before sitting back in my seat to tone down my excitement. I don't want anyone to suggest a group trip. Rory will probably make plans to throw me overboard.

'Knockan Crag National Park is great too,' Finlay adds. 'If you like climbing for an amazing view.'

'And rocks,' Rory chimes in. 'Are you much of a geologist, Ava?'

'I can't say I'm a fan of rocks, per se,' I reply, lifting my gin. 'I do like my whisky on the rocks, though, if that counts?'

I smile around the table but am met with a cold, hard stare from Rory. Finlay frowns too. Eilidh gives me a small shake of the head, her smile turned into a grimace. Even Piper seems disappointed, slumping her head onto her paws.

'Typical,' Rory mutters.

'Ach, it's not her fault. She's not from around here,' Finlay says in my defence, shaking his head all the same, as though he disagrees with himself.

What am I missing here?

'I thought your family was Scottish,' Rory says, accusingly. 'Didn't your granny teach you about Scottish whisky?'

'Well, no, funnily enough, single malts weren't at the top of the list for our conversations when I was *a child*.'

Donna snorts.

'Did you just say single malt?' Rory splutters.

Eilidh taps her glass and clears her throat. 'I think it was just an example.'

'You can't have a single malt with ice,' Rory shakes his head.

'Why not?' I ask, tipping my head to the side with a smile. 'It's delicious. I wouldn't have it any other way.'

I have no idea whether the whisky I'd had before was a single malt, a double melt or a triple Malteser. I can't even remember if I had it with ice or not. Whatever. It seems to really be winding Rory up, though.

'The ice dilutes the flavour and numbs the palate. It's pointless drinking whisky with ice,' Rory says, all fired up, ready to go full Braveheart in defence of his national drink.

I contemplate starting on Irn-Bru next, but I worry that would start a bloodbath the Highlands haven't seen since Culloden.

'What's pointless about drinking something the way you like it?' I frown, sipping my gin calmly. 'Surely that's the whole point?'

'Yes, of course it is, Ava,' Eilidh chimes in, throwing me a smile. It is a bit of a pity smile, as though she secretly agrees with Rory, but it's a show of solidarity and I take it.

Rory sits back in his creaky wooden chair, his arms folded across his chest. 'There's nothing else for it. We know what we've got to do.'

'Absolutely,' Donna agrees.

'Oh, please no,' Eilidh says. 'I have things to do tomorrow.'

'What?' I say, perplexed.

'A whisky tasting session,' Finlay says. 'That's the only way to settle this.'

'Now, Finlay, I'm not sure that's strictly true,' I protest. 'Anyway, they all taste pretty much the same, don't they?'

There is silence for a moment, before Donna throws her head back and begins to cackle, while Eilidh giggles.

Rory nods at Finlay. Without any further discussion, they stalk to the bar.

'I hope they're not about to spend a fortune trying to prove me wrong,' I whisper. 'Why are they being all weird and neanderthal-y about whisky? They're practically thumping their chests.'

'Oh, Ava, they're on a mission now,' Eilidh laughs, bending down to stroke Piper.

'They're about to go full master blender on you, talking about nosing your whisky and the *hints of oak* and *how you can taste the barrel*.' Donna rolls her eyes.

'Do you think I should go and get an ice bucket and start popping little ice cubes in just as we start?'

'Next you'll be saying whisky is spelt with an "e",' Eilidh says with a grin. She looks around the table at Donna and me. 'Before I get blootered on whisky and can't form a sentence, I want to say thank you for dragging me out of the house.'

'Blootered! That's another good word. My granny used to say "steamin". That's next on my TikTok: all the different Scottish words for "drunk".'

'I don't think TikTok would let you make a video long enough,' Donna laughs.

'Right, well, I need you two to help me with my Scottish vocabulary and stop me from making cultural faux pas. We can get blootered along the way.'

'This is exactly what I needed tonight. Some pals and no pressure,' Eilidh says. 'And I'm so glad you came, Donna. It's funny that we've grown up in the same place, but it takes Ava for us to get together, isn't it?'

Donna nods. 'Definitely. I'm so glad to see you here, too, Eilidh. It's been ages!'

'I think small communities can be like companies,' I muse, my gin and tonic reaching my head. 'After a while, you stop communicating outside your own circle. We used to accuse people of "working in silos". Maybe villages have that too.'

'Yes!' Eilidh exclaims. 'Then as time passes, it's past the point where you can socialize. It shouldn't be like that.'

'You pair of corporate shills,' Donna says, as she raises her glass in the air. 'Cheers to turning that on its head. We'll break down the silo, one dram at a time.'

9

Finlay swirls the last drop of amber liquid in his glass and downs it, before sitting back in his seat. 'I'd best stop now, or the dogs will be walking me tomorrow.'

The whisky is flowing, the chat is good and a traditional Scottish band is playing at the opposite end of the bar. I bounce my foot to the tunes, grateful that I can barely hear Rory at the other end of the table over the noise. We've all been nursing our drinks for a couple of hours now, and there's a pleasant, warm feeling throughout the pub.

'This band plays at the local ceilidhs,' Eilidh says. 'You should come sometime, Ava.'

'Wait, did the elusive Eilidh Stewart just ask me on a *date*?' I joke. 'Yes please, I'd love to come! I've never been to a ceilidh before, though, I don't know any of the moves.'

The ceilidh band's catchy melody pauses before the accordion rings out a final flourish. After a couple of seconds, a new energetic rhythm starts up. Finlay taps his foot while Eilidh nods along.

'Stand up. I'll teach you,' Rory says suddenly, his green eyes boring into mine.

'What, now?' I ask, glancing around for someone to laugh and say he is joking.

Eilidh, Donna and Finlay don't seem too concerned. They don't know Rory the nightmare neighbour that I do. They're used to Rory the nice guy. All they see is a well-meaning Scotsman offering to teach me a dance.

But I know better. Rory doesn't *like* me. He's made that perfectly clear. I'm always tripping him up with ladders, putting my foot in it and pissing him off with pretty much everything that comes out of my mouth – when I don't mean to and when I do. And yet, this dance offer doesn't seem to be a question. Perhaps my lack of ceilidh dancing and whisky knowledge, despite my Scottish roots, is pushing him over the edge. But his broad shoulders, in his deep-green T-shirt, rather than his usual black Toolbox work top, seem relaxed. He is with his friends, out of work mode and drinking whisky. There is a look in his eyes that I can't quite put my finger on. Amusement, maybe. Or perhaps this is his attempt to be friendly at last. I'm not sure.

'Yes, now,' he nods, his gaze intensifying by the second. 'No time like the present.'

'We'll butt heads,' I remind him subtly of our previous conversation.

We can't be trusted in close proximity. He and the fading dent in his forehead know that all too well.

But the warning doesn't stop him. He reaches down and pulls me to my feet in one swift movement. My mouth falls open as he whips his arm around my shoulder and takes my hand in his.

I am a head smaller than him and fit snugly under his arm. I can smell the sweet musk of his aftershave, or perhaps it's the whisky. All I can think of is how weird it feels to be so close to someone, to feel another person's body against mine. I haven't shared a close space like this with a guy, not since Seb. The thought makes me dizzy.

'The Gay Gordons,' he says, before propelling us forward, then, with a slight turn, flipping us in the opposite direction. In perfect step with the music, we dance.

My face flushes, even though no one is giving us a second look in the busy bar. Rory lifts my hand above my head and begins twirling me around. I catch the warm and smoked scent of whisky on his breath, or maybe it is mine, I'm not sure. My fingers tingle at their edges at the feel of his hand taking charge of mine. His strong arms lead me through the moves and, despite some clumsy footwork here and there, I manage to keep up.

He guides me through the dance with a practised strength, holding me close by the waist before flinging me into spins and twirls, and then pulling me back again. We alternatively jump, shuffle and dance, finding what space we can in the crowded pub. A few neighbouring punters hoot and clap along to the music. I can feel the heat of his body on mine. When I glance up at him, there's a playfulness in his eye. He's having fun.

His jaw is strong and set. He wants me to learn. This is serious business, this Scottish dancing. Not to be messed with. But I'm sure I see a small hint of a smile on his lips as I turn underneath his arm in an expert motion. I'm conscious of my heart thumping in my chest. I don't want him to know how he is making me feel.

How *is* he making me feel?

Uncertain. Breathless. Hot. God, it is *hot*.

The song comes to an abrupt end. Or it feels abrupt as he lets go of my hand, and I land back on my chair quicker than I anticipate, my heart beating wildly. I gaze up at him; his eyes meet mine as he takes a sip from his glass.

'And that's the Gay Gordons,' he proclaims with a nonchalant shrug.

'Well,' I say, regaining my breath. 'That was an experience.'

'Ah, you're not a ceilidh virgin any more, Ava,' Donna grins. 'No excuse not to come along now.'

I feel my cheeks burn even more. I want to turn the attention away from me, but I struggle to form a sentence.

'Where did you learn to ceilidh dance?' I ask.

'School,' they say, in unison.

'You learn that dancing in *school*? Like, as part of the curriculum?' I ask, my mouth falling open.

'As part of our PE lessons,' Finlay affirms.

'We did sports too, obviously. It wasn't like we did the Gay Gordons or Dashing White Sergeant instead of basketball or anything,' Rory says.

'Who is this Gordon? Is he the Sergeant too?'

The others laugh and explain that these are all dances. 'And the boys had to ask the girls to the end of term ceilidh,' Donna says, with a nostalgic smile. 'It was a huge deal. Mating season for Scottish teenagers.'

'Ah, the annual walk of shame back to your seat after asking someone to the ceilidh followed by the "*Aw, cheers but no thanks*",' Finlay says wistfully. 'Those were the days.'

'You didn't have to ask in our final year,' Donna reminds Finlay with a swift nudge from her elbow. 'It was the girls' turn to approach boys.'

Finlay smirks, glancing sideways at Donna, like they share a secret.

'Yep, those annual moments of ritualized torture we look back on so fondly,' Rory says. 'The real nightmare before Christmas.'

'Don't give us that, Rory MacGregor.' Eilidh rolls her eyes. 'You refused to ask anyone. Ever. You were always waiting for that girl—'

'Anyway,' he cuts Eilidh off, looking flustered as he shakes his head into the last of his whisky. She frowns into her own whisky and shrugs, while Donna grins at Rory. 'This has been a fun trip down memory lane, but I've really got to head off.'

It's strange being in this group who have so much shared history between them. Sometimes, you can see it in the looks they exchange, other times they say something that seems to have a deeper meaning. As an outsider, I'm grateful to be in the mix, but often it's confusing. The conversation feels full of pitfalls. The time will come when I might know an inside joke or two myself, if I'm lucky.

'You need to be at work at 8.56 a.m. sharp tomorrow,' I say to Rory, giving a small salute.

'8.56 a.m.?' he repeats.

As his eyes narrow, I wish I hadn't reminded Rory of our daily interactions, rather than whatever that had been during the impromptu dance. I'd hoped to launch my own inside joke, but it falls flat as he shoots me his usual disdainful look.

'That's the time you arrive. On the dot. Every morning,' I say. I can't exactly stop now. 'Never a minute later or earlier.'

'How do you know it's the same time every day?'

'Well, I was taught to tell the time at school, while you were all dancing around in your kilts. And I am your next-door neighbour, remember.'

He nods, pulling his jacket on. 'Well, some of us have a schedule to stick to. We can't just swan around with a latte doing whatever we feel like.'

'Swan around? I've been working my arse off to get my shop in shape for opening,' I say. 'All that's left now is an empty space for the mural that you've been refusing to paint.'

'Mural?' Finlay repeats, glancing at us both over the table.

Rory rolls his eyes. 'Ava wants me to paint a mural in the bookshop.'

'Did you guys know he's an artist?' I ask with a flick of the wrist, as though I am painting in the air. I've clearly had too much whisky. 'Trapped behind the front desk of a DIY store, *which* I said I'd look after for him, by the way, while he paints, *which* I also want to pay him for.'

'I didn't know you painted, Rory,' Eilidh says.

'I don't,' Rory replies, his expression now hard.

'Ah, you should do it, mate,' Finlay urges. 'I reckon you'd enjoy it. Wasn't that what you wanted that shop for? A space to work in and display local artists and some of your work?'

Rory stands up and shakes his head. He looks livid, as if Finlay has just outed him as the customer with a wire fetish. So *that's* what Rory planned to do with my bookshop. He was going to take it over as his artist's studio and shop, right next to his family's store, until I swooped in and snapped it up.

No wonder Rory hates me.

I swallow and look away, hoping to avoid further conflict. It's not like it's my fault. I had a dream too. I just happened to get the last bid in to secure the shop, that's all.

The barman nods goodbye before calling for last orders. We file out of the door into the dark of the night. It's still pleasantly warm, so I shrug my jacket off and hold it close to my chest.

Across the road from the pub's entrance, a couple are in the middle of a full-blown argument. A 'stooshy' as Granny would have said. Eilidh links arms with me as Rory fixes Piper's lead.

'Susie and Cormac McFall,' Finlay whispers. 'They've been back together for five minutes and already fighting again.'

'You always know everyone's business!' Donna exclaims. 'You'd think he worked in the hairdresser's.'

'They got back together? I thought Cormac was leaving Susie for her cousin?' Eilidh whispers back.

'Second cousin,' Finlay nods, knowingly. 'That didn't last.'

'Ullapool has a lot of drama, for a small place. And it feels like people really want to talk about it,' I muse. 'All I've heard so far is people splitting up and falling in love. Either that or they're hooking up by the bins.'

'Who's hooking up by the bins?' Donna asks.

'Oops,' I say, covering my mouth. 'That was supposed to be a secret.'

Rory rolls his eyes at me. 'A couple of frisky teens. No big news flash.'

'They were outside the shop, just before I practically begged Rory to paint my mural and he refused.'

'Ah, come on, you hardly begged,' Rory says.

'Is that what you want?' I stop to look at him directly. 'You want me to tell you that you're the most amazing artist I've ever met and that I'd be lucky if you would grace the walls of my bookshop with the sheer genius that is your paintbrush? Do you want me to—'

Eilidh, Donna and Finlay exchange a glance as Rory raises an eyebrow at me.

'Fine, I'll do it,' he mutters, as I continue my rant.

'—announce on my social media page that I've hunted high and low for someone to paint my mural and even though there is a guy that could do it *right next door*, he refuses and I...' I stop for a second, absorbing his quiet words. 'Wait, did you just say you'd do it?'

He nods. 'It won't be at 8.56 a.m. tomorrow because I've got to see a man about a dog, but aye. I'll do it. Come on, Piper. Night, everyone.'

Rory throws a wave in the air as he walks away.

'See, Ava, he is lovely,' Eilidh says with a smile.

'I knew he'd say yes,' Donna nods.

'Great guy,' Finlay adds.

Bloody Rory.

When it's just me and him he's belligerent, stubborn and downright unfriendly, but as soon as there's an audience, he becomes so amenable.

Can no one else see why Rory MacGregor is driving me mad?

'My taxi's here! Ava, I know you're just up the road, but Donna, do you want a lift home?'

'Erm...' Donna says, considering it. She sneaks a look at Finlay.

'I'll walk you home,' Finlay offers, looking at the ground rather than at Donna. 'Then I'll head home.'

'Great,' Donna gives a businesslike nod. 'Let's do that.'

As I make my way home in a whisky-fuelled daze, I wonder what exactly is going on between the pair of them.

10

I am barely alive by 8.56 a.m. the next day.

This hangover is like nothing I've ever experienced. As soon as I wake up from a sleep that feels like I actually died, albeit temporarily, it kicks in. This is my punishment for the ice comment and for winding Rory and Finlay up about whisky drinking. The Scottish gods have teamed up and struck me down with the hangover from hell.

I pull the covers back over my head, cursing Rory, the smug whisky dealer, for the sheer volume I consumed the night before. I hadn't even felt that drunk, although I can recall standing up in the middle of the bar attempting the Gay Gordons with him.

Did I initiate that? Oh, *God*. I shouldn't be allowed out.

Rory. My skin prickles across my neck as I think back to the moment he pulled me to my feet in the pub last night. Had he whispered ceilidh instructions in my ear, or was I embellishing now? It's all a little hazy. Dizzying. I now know that he'd hoped to buy my shop to use as his own art space, which makes me feel pretty bad. But he finally agreed to paint the mural, following a dramatic rant from me outside. Christ. Would he even remember agreeing to it? I should have whipped up a contract on the spot and urged him to sign it there and then so he couldn't back out on me.

Urgh. The headache is getting progressively worse.

I have so much to do today. I can't just lie around feeling sorry for myself. But as I fling back the covers, my body recoils, and forces me to climb back into bed. I have to take some paracetamol. If I can ever move again.

I look at my phone. A record of my drunken interactions. Last night, I'd demanded that Eilidh text me to let me know she'd arrived home safely, which she had. I'd replied with an SOS emoji sign by accident. She'd called immediately to check what was wrong. I'd apologized for giving her a heart attack and hung up.

And then I remember.

I check my messages with a shaky hand, my stomach churning. This is not happening. But the cold, hard evidence is there in black and white: a message to Seb, with a taunting blue double-tick to indicate that it has been successfully delivered and read.

Two words.

Why Macy?

I had done so well in the weeks since their betrayal. I never drunk dialled either of them or asked for an explanation or even an apology (though surely they owed me that?!). I went quietly about my business, making plans to exit London, and then duly left the keys in his flat. I didn't trash the place or cut up the blue and black designer suits he left behind (although I was sorely tempted). I maintained a dignified silence, which, apparently, could only be broken by whisky.

Damn the whisky. Damn all the bloody whisky.

A loud buzzing noise from downstairs makes my head feel like someone is drilling a hole right through to the core of my brain. I groan. This is *not* the time. If Rory is out with his bloody drill again... Another loud buzzing noise infiltrates the apartment. I can't get up yet. Please. I am in recovery.

Then I remember the delivery that's due this morning. Pete asked one of his postman pals to help him with the heavy antique book cabinet that I'd fallen in love with online. It is destined to be in my bookshop. The only problem was that it had to be shipped from a furniture store in the Cotswolds. Pete assured me they would be able to handle it, but now it's here, I have to let them in. Get up, be a grown-up and get moving. Forget about the text. I sigh.

As I put on my slippers, a thought taunts me at the back of my throbbing head. Seb hasn't even replied. I'd secretly imagined that if I ever reached out to him, he'd take the floor and offer me some long-winded apology. But he hasn't. He's said nothing. Nada. Zilch.

Why had I texted him? One night out in Ullapool and my whole brain drains itself of common sense. I'd managed to forget everything I'd built to protect myself. The six hundred miles between me and all that hurt. I blame Rory. Bloody Rory. He is infuriating, blowing hot and cold with me. Mainly cold, but then last night he held me far too close during that stupid dance. That was the problem. I hadn't been touched by any guy since Seb. It scrambled my head.

Damn Rory. Damn Seb and the stupid text.

The shrill noise rings out and I realize it must be the doorbell. I take the stairs down as quickly as my wobbly, hungover legs can carry me and fling the door open, not caring if Pete sees me in my polka-dot pyjamas with my hair sticking up and a line of last night's mascara smudged along my cheek. I squint in the sudden brightness, narrowing my eyes as Pete comes into focus. But he isn't alone. I groan at the sight of his grinning accomplice.

'Pete! You got *Rory* to help you?' I ask, hiding behind the door as much as I can. 'I thought you said you'd asked a postie pal.'

'Rude,' Rory grins, putting his arm around Pete. 'I am a postie pal. I'm everyone's pal.'

Everyone except me.

I arch my eyebrow at Rory, sure that he can read my thoughts. His grins widens. 'How's the head?'

I shoot him a look, determined not to reveal that it might take a week to shift this pounding in my brain, and shuffle back in my slippers to give them space to enter. 'Perfectly fine, thanks.'

'Good,' he says.

'I needed Rory's brute strength,' Pete says. 'Strongest lad in the village, or so was proven at the last village fete. Do you have any idea how heavy that thing is?'

Rory smirks at the compliment, while I contemplate throwing up.

'So where is it?' I ask, peering over their shoulders.

'In the van,' Pete explains. He seems out of breath at even the thought of lifting it, which doesn't bode well for my new piece of furniture. 'We just wanted to check you were in. Can't leave it outside.'

I move behind the counter and pretend to look as busy and professional as possible in my tired pyjamas and slippers. As much as I want to run upstairs, change my clothes, wash my face and brush my hair, I don't want Rory to know that I feel self-conscious in front of him. So, instead, I leaf through my book inventory, pretending to be terribly busy, important, and not in the least bit hungover and regretful of my recent life choices.

Rory's face strains with concentration as he positions himself at the bottom of the tipped antique cabinet, while Pete puts all his energy into the top end.

'Where's it to go?' Rory calls.

'Right there,' I point. 'Beside that blank wall where your mural's going. Unless you'd forgotten?'

'Of course not,' Rory replies.

They let out some muffled huffs and puffs as they set it down. The sight of the beautiful cabinet, looking just right in the spot where I'd pictured it, suddenly feels like a warm hug, like everything is going to be okay.

'Oh, I am in love,' I exclaim, clutching my hands together. 'Thank you for bringing it in. I can't wait to get started on it.'

'Started?' Pete frowns.

'Yes, I'm going to upcycle it,' I explain, running my hand along the edge of the dark brown wood. 'Bright canary yellow, I think.'

'You have great vision, Ava lass,' Pete smiles, shaking his head. 'Doesn't she, Rory?'

Rory gazes around the shop. 'I have to admit, it's looking alright in here.'

'Just alright?' Pete elbows him in the chest. 'This girl's been working like a dog. Every time I come in, she's sanding, painting or building something.'

'Or hanging out around the bins trying to learn how to do it all,' I say. 'But it's getting there. I'm glad you think it's "alright". The green tiles will be coming off in no time at this rate.'

'Okay, it looks good,' Rory concedes with a shrug. 'But I'm still holding off on the tiles.'

'It'll be better with the mural. That's the finishing touch.'

'You don't need to remind me of it every three seconds. I said I'd do it, and I will. Tomorrow.'

'Oh aye, Rory's a man of his word, don't worry about that,' Pete nods. 'Anyway, I've got to head off, these packages won't deliver themselves. Donna said to tell you she'll pop over on her lunch break to see you, Ava. Just giving you the heads up in case… Well, you know.'

Pete gives a mock whack to his knees on his way out of the door, and I groan inwardly. We'd managed to have a whole interaction without him mentioning the kneecapping incident – or so I thought.

*

I'm lying in a very strange position on the ground taking videos of my new cabinet for a DIY transformation TikTok when Donna's voice fills the space.

'Ava, why are you lying on the floor like a murder victim?'

'I'm filming.'

'Oh, shit, sorry,' she replies, before gasping and whispering, '*Oh shit*, quieter sorry.'

'It's fine, I'll play music over it anyway,' I say, as I scramble to my feet. 'May I introduce you to my new cabinet? Isn't she a beauty?'

Donna runs her fingers along the gilded edges. 'Ah, yes, she's gorgeous. God bless her, and all who sail in her. I take it you'll be painting her?'

'Bright yellow.'

'Course you are,' she says. 'You are to interiors what I am to hair: always desperate to get a makeover on the go. Speaking of which, we could get you booked in for your own transformation before the bookshop opening. Have you decided on a date?'

'Next Saturday.'

'And is Rory going to paint your mural on time? Or was that a drunken promise?'

'Yes, he's starting it tomorrow. Very reluctantly, but he's doing it. I think I had a bit too much on the old whisky front… Suppose I got a bit swept up in the moment – not by Rory!' I say, feeling the need to explain myself, although Donna doesn't seem concerned. 'It was everyone else's company. What about you and Finlay, though? What's the deal between you two?'

'No idea what you mean.' She shrugs, although her cheeks flush again. 'How did you manage to get Eilidh on a night out, anyway? I didn't want to say while she was sitting there, but she's not been seen inside a bar in the village for about a decade!'

I note Donna's fly attempt to change the subject from Finlay and make a mental note to revisit it at a later date.

'I asked her when I went to speak to her about financial planning.'

'Did you meet her husband?'

I shake my head, vowing to keep Eilidh's secret. I know the last thing she needs right now is to be the centre of the village's gossip mill.

'He's a tosser,' Donna whispers, even though there is no one around. 'Total waste of space.'

'What makes you say that?'

'Just passing on an opinion, based on fact,' she says, tapping the side of her nose to indicate she has a secret.

I wonder if the whole village knows about Mark's indiscretions. 'He's always been up his own arse, thinking he was too good for this place. When he first moved here, he made such a big deal of the fact that he sacrificed everything to come to live in Ullapool because that's what Eilidh wanted. And then she stopped coming to all the usual events she used to love: the fete, the bake sales, the ceilidhs, everything. We've barely seen her since she married him even though she's just up the road. No one would be sorry to see the back of him.'

I look over Donna's shoulder to see Eilidh at the shop's front door.

'Eilidh!' I exclaim. 'Come in!'

Donna almost jumps out of her skin.

'Oh, Ava, hi, sorry to interrupt,' Eilidh says. 'And hi, Donna! How are you?'

Donna shifts awkwardly from one foot to the other, wondering if she's been caught in the middle of her gossip session. 'I'm great, thanks. You?'

'I was just popping by to thank Ava for this book,' Eilidh smiles, handing the paperback to me. 'I couldn't put it down. When I got back from the pub, I had to stay up all night and finish it. It sounds silly, but it feels so good to finish a book again! It's like I'm me again, you know?'

I'm so pleased to hear it that I don't even question how Eilidh managed to keep her eyes open, never mind read a *book*, after our whisky-fuelled session. Scottish people must be born with some sort of magical whisky-repelling powers. My head gives another timely thump, like it's agreeing with me.

'Oh my God, Eilidh, I know exactly what you mean!' Donna says. 'I've started a book that Ava gave me, too, and I'm loving it. It feels so good to be reading again.'

'We should start a book club,' I suggest. 'We could get together, drink some wine and chat about our latest reads?'

'Not whisky?' Eilidh asks, her eyes sparkling with mischief.

'Definitely not,' I shudder. 'I've banned myself.'

Donna laughs. 'I'm keen. I'd love a girly night of words and wine.'

'Yes, definitely! Although, I mean, I love the books. Don't get me wrong, Ava,' Eilidh says, 'but it would just be nice to have somewhere to go and talk. That's what last night taught me.'

I nod along as Eilidh and Donna discuss the bookshop opening and how excited they are to have a new place to go, somewhere to read, but also somewhere to feel closer to other people in the village. It's exactly what I'd secretly hoped but was too scared to voice. And finally, it's all starting to come together.

11

Seb still hasn't texted me back. Not a peep. It's not that I want to hear from him, but it feels like I've given him the upper hand. I hate that. Plus, it hurts. I hate that it hurts.

I try to forget about Seb and Macy, but reminders sneak up on me when I least expect it. The morning sun creeps through the windows as I busy myself around the bookshop, slotting titles into the correct shelves. Then, the radio blasts out a song that takes me straight back to my twenty-first birthday: 'Chandelier', by Sia. Macy and I went to some horrible, sticky nightclub and danced into the small hours with our friends. On the way home, we'd all taken turns singing the song in high-pitched warbles while walking hand in hand through the streets of London. Hearing the song now, I can't believe how carefree I was then. Before Seb, before our 'grown-up' jobs, before real life kicked in and got in the way.

The nostalgia almost takes my breath away. I blink back tears. God, it is so stupid to feel this way over a pop song. We'd sounded like a cat's choir. Someone had shouted at us to 'shut the fuck up' from across the road and we almost doubled over with laughter.

I miss that feeling. I miss Macy.

Shaking my head, I remind myself what's happened since then. Things have moved on for a reason. There is no time to wallow, I have to move on, make the most of the new life I am creating for myself. I watch Rory's car pull up outside. I must put a brave face on and be nice to Rory all day, until he's completed the mural. It is the finishing touch to my bookshop, the focal point, so it has to be perfect.

I fling the door open, fixing the cheeriest smile I can muster on my face. I check my watch: 8.56 a.m. Even if I am practically having to drag him into the shop and force him to paint, at least he is reliable.

'Good morning!'

'I'll just get my stuff. Be with you in a minute.'

'Excited to get started?'

He stops and shifts from foot to foot, looking down at the ground. 'Look, I'm not usually… I don't normally get paid for this kind of thing. The art thing has always been a bit of a pipe dream for me. Maybe you should hire someone who knows what they're doing.'

I've never seen Rory like this before. Grumpy, yes, often. But nervous? Not so much. I can't help but like this more vulnerable side to him.

'I wouldn't have asked if I didn't think you could do it,' I say softly.

He picks up his paintbrushes and sketches from the back seat of his car, still not meeting my eye. 'I'll do my best.'

'There's no pressure. Best thing about painting is that it can always be painted over.'

'Or you could order a print from Amazon instead?'

'If it's shit, I'll just shove a chair and a huge plant in front of it,' I say. 'Hope no one notices.'

'Good.' He nods and offers me a small smile. 'As long as we have a back-up plan, I'm good to go.'

'We won't need it. I'm pretty confident about that.'

'Glad someone is,' he mutters.

*

I want to give Rory the time and space he needs to work on the mural. So, I hold myself back from bouncing into the shop every five minutes to check on his progress and, instead, I concentrate on serving customers in The Toolbox.

I finally unleash myself near the end of the day, popping my head through the door of my bookshop. Rory stands in front of the mural, peering at his sketches and then back at the wall. I clear my throat to signal my presence and gasp at the sight of what he's created. He has sketched a map of Ullapool, from the mountains to the sea, with characterful drawings of the local wildlife and quirky features of the village too. I spot the bookshop next to his DIY store, with Piper lapping some water outside. He's in the middle of painting the sky.

'Wow,' I breathe. 'It looks amazing, Rory.'

'It's getting there. I still need to build up the layers and add some details, but it's a good start.'

'An excellent start. Can I get a video of you working on the mural for my social media?'

'Social media,' he repeats with a roll of his eyes. 'That wasn't in the contract.'

'Do you know the impact social media could have on your business? We don't all have your dedicated fanbase in the village so I need all the help I can get.'

'Ah, come on.' He puts his paintbrush down on the counter. 'It's all bullshit. Influencers parading around, sponsored ads and Big Brother spying on your every click.'

'I worked for a creative agency in London specializing in social media. It can increase business revenue massively. My business strategy is based on it.'

'It's not about social media and all that nonsense around here.' He leans back on the counter. 'It's about supporting people in real life. Helping people with the things they need, like finding the right size of cable, ordering something in when you don't have it in stock or changing a plug for them when they can't do it for themselves. It's about—'

'I think you're right,' I interrupt.

'You do?' He raises his eyebrows.

'Yes, you can tone down your righteous speech, I've got it covered. Social media is a big part of my business strategy, but it's not the whole thing. I've been working on this other idea that could be great. In fact, I think it's going to be amazing, for the whole community. Even your fangirl Margaret. She might end up liking me more than you.'

'That's a bold statement. Go on then. I'm all ears.'

'A support group. In the bookshop,' I announce, proudly. 'The Ullapool bookshop breakup and grief support group.'

'Well, that's a bit of a mouthful, for a start. What do you mean, a breakup and grief support group?'

'I want the bookshop to be a space that the community really needs, as well as somewhere they can discover their next read. It would be somewhere people can go to talk about whatever they're going through. From my short time in Ullapool, I feel something like that is really missing from here.'

'You've completely lost me.'

'This village has so much heart, but also a lot of heartache: breakups, affairs, grief. People like Donna and Pete, even Margaret, they're all missing someone and want to talk about it. Every person I've spoken to has a story of something they're working through. Well, except you. You have a heart of stone.'

'A *breakup bookshop*. You really have lost it.'

'Rory, I'm telling you,' I say, putting my hands on my hips. 'People need a space to gather and share their stories.'

'They already do. It's called the pub.'

'It's not healthy, though, to go to the pub and drown your sorrows, is it? People around here are crying out for a space to open up and a shoulder to cry on.'

'Alright, Oprah Winfrey. You've got these big ideas with your woo-woo city therapy speak, but we don't need that kind of thing here. This is the Highlands. We don't need social media and support groups and breakup bookshops. We just get on with things.'

'You said yourself that people appreciate help,' I point out. 'It's not fixing their washing lines or whatever you do, but this is a different way of helping them. Plus, it brings the community together. Surely that's not a bad thing?'

'Next, you'll be suggesting we replace Fiona's caff with artisan coffee shops and bougie restaurants with minuscule small-plates you need to remortgage your house to afford. Fish and chips served in wee metal trays, just to be posh.'

'You're just scared that I'm going to take your halo,' I say. 'I'll be the new favourite.'

'There's no way that's going to happen because of a support group.'

'Just because you're dead inside doesn't mean everyone else is.'

'I don't want to see you crash and burn, Ava. I'm trying to help *you* here.'

'You want to help me? Come along to the first breakup support group and open up about what turned you into such a negative Nigel,' I snap. 'And get the mural finished. I'm paying you for that.'

I can't quite bring myself to leave it at that. I bite my lip to try to stop, but find myself adding, 'Please.'

12

Following my several requests for Rory to move his head to the left while I film, look like he is concentrating more, smile a little but not too much, and make sure there are some books in the background of the shot, he finally loses the plot and asks me to leave. I have enough content for the video, which I manage to edit in between customer chats at The Toolbox. I invite everyone to the opening of the bookshop. Rory relieves me of my duties at 5 p.m. on the dot.

Hanging outside around by the bins to get reception, I post the video, then go back inside to unpack more boxes of books. The website seller described them as a 'pick and mix of popular books' and my inner nerd can't wait to see what they've sent. I thought the novelty of book deliveries would have quickly worn off, but I still get that rush every single time. I read the blurbs of the books, one by one, and pick one I haven't read before. Scanning the first page, I find myself hooked and abandon the box to curl up on the lumpy couch in my flat, reading as the late afternoon turns into evening.

I'd never have been able to do this in London, just abandon the rest of my day to read. A pang of pleasure fills my stomach as I realize how lucky I am to have entered this new phase of my life.

It's dark now and I'd completely forgotten about my phone. When I finally check it, I see it's flooded with notifications. I scroll through the messages. The first is from Wren, an old colleague from Seed Creative.

Wren: *Girrrl, you need to start a new page. Hotties in the Highlands. Are you kidding me? *books a flight immediately**

Typical Wren. She is a renowned party queen, never without a man on her arm. There is no way I am showing that message to Rory; his head won't fit inside the bookshop door. But the likes and comments continue on my public feed.

booksamillion404: *Next video request: painting a mural IN A KILT. That'll be all, thank you xx*

user486027x7: *And suddenly the move from London to the middle of nowhere makes complete and utter sense!*

edi4lyfe: *Paint me like one of your Highland girls, Rory* 😍

The views and likes are through the roof. I've inadvertently turned my social page into a digital version of the Rory fan club. Brilliant. This is all I need. His antisocial media, anti-support group, anti-bookshop and, to be perfectly frank, anti-anything-I-have-to-say attitude is really grating on me.

Rory seems to have time for everyone in the whole village – everyone apart from me. I can't help but take it personally. Eilidh, Donna, Pete, Margaret, Finlay all love him. What stings the most, which I will never admit, is that he seems to love them too. He is friendly with every single person I've seen him meet. I've tried to subtly move things on between us, on to more friendly terms, but he always snaps back with a snarky or negative comment that results in me liking him even less.

As I take a sip of tea, an all-too-familiar name pops up on my screen. I nearly spit out the tea. My heart thuds in my chest. I put my phone down immediately, tucking it underneath a cushion, as if that will make the whole thing go away. Macy. I do not want to hear from Macy. Why is she messaging me, after weeks of no contact?

Oh God, what if *she* is replying to my message from Seb? Telling me to back off from their new relationship?

I swallow the hard lump in my throat. I am not going to cry.

I should have blocked her. I'd considered it when I was packing up my old life and came across a photograph of the two of us together, beaming at the camera. But I'd thought there was no way she would contact me, not after what she'd done. I assumed she'd wait for me to reach out.

Macy hates being in the wrong. She gets defensive at the mere suggestion of it. She was once accused of stealing someone's sandwich from the fridge at work and was affronted by the allegation. She talked about setting up a camera to catch the fridge thief. It turned out to be a coincidence, and someone happened to have a similar sandwich in the other fridge and had forgotten where they'd put it, but Macy still harped on about the accusation months later, like she would never trust her colleagues again.

This time, there is no denying she is in the wrong. No fridge camera, no mistaken identity. If I hadn't seen them together with my own eyes, I'd never have believed it. The stinging reminder that she never even apologized is the most bitter pill to swallow.

But I've moved on. Or I'm trying to. Why is she messaging me *now*?

I read the first line while my finger hovers over the delete button: *Hey, I know things are really weird between us—*

I quickly delete the message without reading the rest. I can't go there. Not now. There is nothing she can say that will change what she did or make it better.

My heart thuds. Weird between us. Things aren't 'weird'. It's not like we've fallen out because she forgot to return a top she'd borrowed. She borrowed my boyfriend. There is no coming back from that.

I turn on a home renovation programme on the TV, determined to forget about her, but my mind keeps wandering to the message. Perhaps she'd said: *Sorry, I know things are really weird between us, but I had to message after seeing that video. I'd really like to hook up with that hot guy. DM me! Lol.* Or worse: *Back off, bitch. Stop messaging Seb. He's mine now!*

Anyway, I'm doing fine now, much better. Everything is going well. The bookshop is almost ready to launch, I'm settling into Ullapool life, I'm not missing London at all. Even with the pressure of the business and its finances firmly on my shoulders, I feel freer than I have in a long, long time. The pressure to check and respond to emails immediately has gone. I'm no longer having to juggle clients and pretend I care for each of them like they're my favourite child. I don't have to review colleagues' work; all I have to do is concentrate on my work. On myself.

I curl up on my hard sofa, placing the cushion which needs extra stuffing under my head, and sigh.

This is the reason we need the support group at the bookshop. Just when you think you are over the heartbreak and are moving on with your life, it all comes straight back to bite you on the arse.

*

Rory's negativity around the breakup support group doesn't put me off. I am ready to go full steam ahead with the idea, and Donna agrees wholeheartedly.

'I can't tell you the number of times I've been doing someone's highlights and they've been in tears by the end of the appointment. But then, boom, our time is over, I have other clients to see and I need to charge them for it,' Donna says, with a firm nod. 'So, I'll be first in the queue for your support group, Ava, and I'll be recommending it to all my customers.'

I approach Eilidh with a bit more caution. While she has been welcomed back with open arms into the village fold, she's still only dipping her toe back into being part of the wider community again. I know that our book club, which we've hosted regularly since it was suggested, has been a big step for her, but that's just been the three of us. The support group could be a step too far for her.

'A support group?' Eilidh repeats. She looks down at her lap, serious for a moment, before lifting her eyes to meet mine. 'I think that's a brilliant idea, Ava.'

'Will you come?'

'Of course I'll come!' she says. 'I need to get back in the swing of things within the community, but I haven't been sure how to go about it. This gives me the excuse. The support group is such a good idea.'

It *is* such a good idea. No matter what Rory thinks.

'Oh, Ava, I've just had a thought,' she continues. 'Have you heard of Richard J. Walker?'

'The author who writes really gory bestselling crime fiction that people can't get enough of? Of course. I'm a huge fan!'

'He's… well, he's an old friend of mine. He has a new book coming out soon. Maybe I could ask him to come to the bookshop opening. He could give you a quote to send with the media releases you talked about as part of your communications strategy?'

This. This is exactly why you need supportive friends who champion you, not ones who sleep with your boyfriend behind your back, break your heart and then send you messages out of the blue.

Embarrassingly, I feel tears springing into my eyes.

'I can't believe you'd do that for me,' I whisper, blinking back my over-the-top emotions.

'I can't promise anything,' Eilidh says. 'All I can do is ask. I'm sure he'd be happy with the cross-promotion for his book, if you agreed to stock it.'

'Of course I'd stock it. I'll have a whole wall dedicated to him if he comes here. He's such a big name! How do you even know him?'

Eilidh pauses. Do I detect her blushing? She never blushes.

'He's an ex, actually,' she admits. 'We recently got back in contact online. We were at university together. He was a little older than me, a mature student, and, well... it just didn't work out. I've not seen him in over a decade, not since before Mark and I got together.'

'No way! Are you hoping something happens between you again?'

She shakes her head. 'No, it's too soon for that. It's just nice to have someone to chat to. It helps at night, when the boys are in bed and I'm feeling lonely, you know?'

'Well, I'm very pleased to hear it. Especially if he's able to attend the bookshop launch, then you'd both get to see each other in person again. Sparks fly, one thing leads to another and before you know it...'

'You've been reading too many of your romance novels,' she laughs. 'I'm definitely not ready for *that* again. Okay, I'll send him a message and see if he's free. It would be so good if he could come along. He's so popular just now. He used to say he wanted to visit Ullapool, so this would be a good excuse.'

As I wait for Eilidh to hear back from Richard, I forge ahead with my plans, handing out the launch leaflets on the street, posting on social media, telling everyone who'll listen about the bookshop.

It isn't long before we have a reply. Apparently, Richard is keen to see Eilidh again in real life too.

'Oh my God, Ava, he's booked a flight! He's coming to the bookshop launch.'

We jump up and down on the spot, spinning in circles, holding on to each other. Just as we are mid-jump, Rory opens the door to the bookshop.

'What are you two looking so excited about?' he asks.

'Richard J. Walker,' I breathe, 'is coming to the launch of my bookshop. I can't believe it!'

Rory stands still for a moment in the doorway and stares at us both. He backs away, turns around and leaves again.

Too much excitement on display for one grumpy git.

13

The bookshop opens tomorrow. After sweeping the floor for the millionth time, I gaze around. I am pretty damn pleased with myself. Everything is just as it should be, from the kids and teenage section, complete with a Highland coo footstool that I found online and couldn't resist, to the local interest/Scottish section, packed full of books about Ullapool, fishing, wildlife and walking trails. My thrillers section now features a large display of Richard J. Walker's books that his publisher kindly sent for the bookshop launch.

The cookbooks are arranged in my canary-yellow cabinet. I pasted blue and yellow floral wallpaper in the back panels of the cabinet, so there's a nice surprise if I manage to sell out of books. I've displayed some of the beautiful crockery I found in the shop when I arrived, as a tribute to The Old Tea Shop. My before and after videos on social media are full of praise for my upcycling abilities.

However, they still haven't attracted more views than Rory, the 'hunky Highlander', painting the mural. That's by far my most popular video.

Granny's handwritten recipe cards, including the 'Campbell family scone recipe', are displayed in a variety of colourful frames around the cabinet. I haven't been able to find her cookbook, which I was sure I'd brought with me to Ullapool, but I'm hoping it will turn up. I can almost hear her voice telling me how proud she is of me. It feels like she is here in the bookshop with me.

The walls feature golden quotes from my favourite books. Everywhere I look, I see something that I love: the small gift section full of products from local craftspeople, my colourful furniture, the brightly painted panels behind the till. The space is full of light and vibrancy. I used to beg Seb to let me re-cover his two grey armchairs in our living room, but he refused. He always called my taste 'a bit much'. I wish he could see it realized now. It works. The bold colours don't fight with one another but create a gorgeous, welcoming space. This is my shop, and I'm finally creating the home I always wanted.

The local interest section sits proudly beside Rory's mural of Ullapool, which is now finished. I have to give it to Rory – the painting is a complete showstopper. The beachfront, the fishing boats, the rows of shops and houses, the mountains, the sunset, he's recorded it all. The vibrant colours will catch the eye of everyone who walks in the front door. Not only that, but he's managed to capture something of the village's essence that only someone who knows and loves Ullapool could. Within the painting, you have the sense that these little houses are filled with people who know one another deeply, who care and look after one another. I love it, from the Ullapool title at the top, to the artist's signature at the bottom. Even if it is Rory's signature.

I can hardly believe that I've done this. Before arriving in Ullapool, I'd barely changed a light bulb. Now, I've completed a full renovation almost entirely by myself. There was of course help along the way. Rory was right that people do lend a hand here. I drafted in a local joiner to help fix some of the bookshelves and signage. A plumber fixed the tiny downstairs toilet that had been completely blocked when I arrived, and transformed it into the prettiest loo that I've ever had the pleasure of peeing in. Donna helped me finish painting the quotes on the wall. And then there's the mural, the work of art that takes centre stage in the shop.

The shop is my work, but it takes a village.

Now the only thing left to do is the launch tomorrow, to introduce my bookshop to the world.

I walk outside to gaze at the shop's exterior. It has changed completely, from the off-white dull unit to a mint-green shop front proudly declaring the shop's name: The Next Chapter.

As I look up at the bookshop sign, Rory walks outside and leans against a lamp post.

'Admiring your work?'

I nod proudly. 'Yup. I can't believe it's all finished. I think I've aged at least ten years in the past two months, but it's done. You're coming tomorrow, aren't you? You'll talk to everyone about the mural and not utter a single word about how my bookshop isn't needed in Ullapool, correct?'

'Scout's honour.'

King Rory of Ullapool is my local VIP guest, alongside the actual VIP in Richard the author, who is going to stay at a local bed and breakfast. The whole village has been on 'Richard watch' for days. No one has spotted him in the wild yet, but rumour has it he'll arrive very soon.

'What are your plans to celebrate?'

'I'm going to take my first ever soak in the bath upstairs,' I declare. 'I'm going to stare at the garish green tiles in the bathroom and picture you removing them. Only one month until I've won our bet.'

'Nothing wrong with the tiles.'

'There won't be, as soon as you change them. Anyway, I'm going. Don't work too hard.'

Climbing the stairs from the bookshop up to my apartment is like going from heaven into hell. I can't wait to start bringing in some cash so I can, first of all, break even, and second, start transforming my flat. The ideas are all lined up and ready to go, but my bank balance is sternly against me taking any action just yet.

As I start to run the bath, I glare at the green tiles that line the narrow bathroom. My nemesis. I can't wait for Rory to rip them off the wall. I plan to cheer triumphantly behind him as he does it. I run the water for a couple of minutes, the old pipes taking a while to warm up.

I take out some bubble bath and pour it under the water, hoping the scent overpowers the musty scent in the bathroom. Pressing play on my independent women playlist, I turn the volume right up as I start to undress while dancing around the small space.

I lower myself into the bath and stretch out, enjoying the perfect temperature. If I close my eyes, I don't even have to look at the tiles. I can dream of my Pinterest board instead. As the song comes to an end, I hear a weird screeching sound outside. I ignore it, hoping it will go away and stop disturbing my peace. But, as the next song starts, I hear it again, despite the beat of the music. I sit forward, turn the music off and listen intently.

'Ava!'

It sounds like a man straining his voice outside. Weird. I jump out of the bath, wrap a towel around myself, and listen for it again.

'Ava!'

There it is.

Even in the two syllables of my name, I detect the urgency.

I dash along the hallway wearing only my towel. I take the stairs as quickly as humanly possible down to the bookshop. Seb flashes into my mind. Is he *here*? I shake my head. Surely not. Just because the voice is male, it doesn't mean it belongs to Seb.

'Ava!' he roars again.

I fling open the door. Rory stands outside in the street, gazing up at my flat.

'I'm here,' I call over. 'What is it?'

He glances at my towel before rather too deliberately meeting my eye. Do I detect some hesitancy in his expression? Like he doesn't know where to look. He runs a hand over his hair and starts to knead the back of his neck. I pull the towel up higher and hold it tight to my body. Jesus. How embarrassing.

'I think your bath is leaking,' he says. 'I've got water seeping in through the ceiling.'

Oh.

Fuuuuuck.

My hand flies to my mouth. Rory averts his gaze just in case, but thankfully the towel remains in place.

'I can come and have a look?' Rory offers, before clearing his throat. 'At the bath, I mean.'

His face flushes. I wonder what he's getting all flustered about. I'm the one with water pouring into his shop space. I nod as he follows me inside. I pad along the bookshop floor towards the stairs. Rory stops and gazes up at the ceiling.

He points. 'You've got water coming in too.'

'Oh no, the mural!' I exclaim, running towards the wall.

Shit, shit, shit.

The mural's vibrant colours are blurring together as the water drips down the ceiling and splashes onto the floor.

Rory moves straight over to inspect the till area, grabs a cardboard box and places it underneath the mural.

'Not ideal, but it'll do for now. Let's go upstairs so I can have a look,' he says, moving towards the stairs. 'There's a lot of water coming down here, how many baths are you having?!'

I pad along after him, still very much in my towel. I suddenly feel guilty.

I'd let the water run for some time before I'd popped the plug in. I was supposed to be waiting for the water to heat up, but then I'd been distracted and forgotten about it. Meanwhile, I had been flooding Rory's shop, and my own, the night before my launch.

This is the last thing I need.

Rory takes the stairs two at a time. 'Have you got a bucket? That cardboard box is going to get pretty soggy.'

'Erm, I'll check in the cupboard upstairs.'

I grab my dressing robe and wrap it around my body, tying it tightly, then retrieve a small orange bucket from the airing cupboard and run downstairs to place it under the leak. Back at the scene of the crime, Rory has removed the bath panel and is inspecting underneath.

'I think it's just a faulty seal,' he says. 'I should be able to get something to fix it.'

I empty my toothbrush holder and and use it to scoop water out of the bath and tip it down the toilet.

'Less water means less strain on the bath seal,' I murmur.

Rory nods. 'Good idea.'

I continue to scoop the water out of the bathtub as he crouches down underneath.

'How bad is your shop? I'll get straight on to my insurance and pay for whatever it costs to fix it up... I'm so sorry.'

'It's not bad. I just saw some water coming down the wall. I ran upstairs to check on Margaret, but she hadn't been using any water, so I figured it must be coming from you. I think your shop is worse. The mural is the real victim here.' He smiles weakly, trying to make it a joke, but I can see he's disappointed.

I can't believe it. The mural that I pestered Rory to paint for me is ruined. He spent hours working on something that he hadn't even wanted to do. Now it looks like a rainbow has cried on the wall. I haven't even paid him for it yet. He keeps dodging my suggestion of a bank transfer, so my plan is to leave an envelope of cash in The Toolbox when he isn't looking.

'Brilliant,' I groan. 'The night before the grand opening. Although, it could have been worse. For a second, I thought you were my ex, hollering at me from the street.'

Why did I say it out loud? Any time something goes wrong, my thoughts seem to switch to Seb, but there's no need to voice it to Rory right now.

Rory frowns. 'Why would your ex be here? Is he coming?'

'Oh God, no. He's the last person I'd invite. I just, I don't know, my mind must have been playing tricks on me.'

The relaxing evening I'd planned has gone straight down the plughole.

Rory fixes the bath seal while I change quickly, before going downstairs and mopping up the water on the bookshop floor. I sigh, looking at the mural. It is supposed to be the focal point of the bookshop. How can I unveil the bookshop tomorrow when it looks like it has been shot by a paintball gun?

'I think I've fixed the bath, but you should get a plumber out to double-check it before you use it again,' Rory advises. 'I'm just going to close The Toolbox for the day. It's past closing time anyway. I'll be back.'

Now this is the helpful Rory the whole village praises at every turn. Apparently, all it takes is pouring water down his walls, ruining the mural he's spent hours painting and completely screwing up my grand opening plans for the bookshop. Who knew?

'Rory,' I say.

He turns around and looks at me, eyebrows raised.

'Thank you,' I say earnestly.

'Don't mention it,' he shrugs, before his face breaks out into a smirk. 'Because I will. Over and over again.'

Ah, there's the Rory I know.

'Bet you don't cast things up to Margaret,' I call, as he walks out of the door.

'Jealousy will get you nowhere.'

As he carries a dehumidifier into the bookshop, I realize I should just be grateful that he is willing to help me at all.

'So, we just stare and watch paint dry?' I ask, as he switches it on.

'Yup.'

'So, what should I do with the mural?' I say sadly. 'I wanted it to be a big reveal.'

Rory shrugs. 'As long as everything else is okay, you'll just have to explain what happened. We can fix up the mural at some point once everything's dry.'

'It's just – I was so excited about it. All the colours tied in so well with the rest of the shop. But I can't cancel the launch. I need to get opened and start making money or next time I'm in the bath, I'll have the bank manager breaking down the door instead of you.'

'You do love vibrant colour, don't you?' he asks, peering at the bright splashes around the room.

'My ex-boyfriend was very anti-colour,' I say. 'It was grey or nothing in our flat. I wanted to make this space as bright as possible.'

Rory stands stiffly, unsure how to respond. Why am I mentioning Seb again? It must be a psychological thing. The last time I felt this panicked and out of my depth was because of Seb, so my mind is rewinding to him over and over. I open my mouth to try to explain to Rory, but he is busy packing up.

'Right, well, I've got to head home for Piper.'

'Thanks again for all your help.'

He nods briskly and leaves.

*

Tossing and turning in bed, I replay the day in my mind. I'd been lucky. If it hadn't been for Rory, I could have completely flooded both shops and had to claim on the insurance, which had been in place for all of five minutes. The excess would have been huge. I'd be up to my eyes in debt, even more than I am right now…

Now the bookshop is one sleep away from opening, the reality of what I've done is closing in on me. My bank balance is pleading with me to stop the crazy nonsense and resume normality. Get a real job, get a salary. Maybe I should be listening.

My sleep is broken with half thoughts of no one turning up to the bookshop launch. Worse still, I have a nightmare in which *everyone* turns up – Seb, Macy, Rory, Piper the dog and, for some reason, my least favourite primary school teacher, Mr Johnstone. I welcome them all at the front door with a wide smile before I look down and realize I am stark bollock naked. I whisper to them in turn as they make their way past, begging them to lend me a towel. My primary teacher mutters that I should really have factored that into my planning and hands me my orange bucket.

Thanks, Mr Johnstone.

A sharp noise downstairs tears me from the dream. I sit bolt upright in bed, my ears on red alert. My heart feels like it's thudding in my throat. What the hell is that noise? Fuck, now someone is breaking into the shop and is about to murder me in my bed. Just what I need. Should I just lie here and hope they go away?

No. I can't just hope for the best. What would my independent women playlist think of me? I grab my phone, even though I know it won't work if I try to make a call, but I feel safer holding something. I try to make as much noise as possible, thudding around to alert the intruder to the fact I am coming. I hope they'll think better of it and scarper instead of killing me.

A foolproof plan.

Another noise downstairs reminds me that this is no joke. There is definitely someone in the bookshop below. I grab the heaviest thing I can find – which happens to be the ironing board – and creep down the stairs, clutching it tightly under my arm. I can swing it directly at them if needed, whacking them out of the way.

I tiptoe into the bookshop, ironing board at the ready. A man kneels at the foot of the mural. My heart thuds wildly in my chest until he turns his head.

'Rory?' I almost keel over in relief. 'What the fuck are you doing here? It's half three in the morning! How did you get in?'

He jumps slightly, holding a hand to his heart and then frowns. 'Why are you holding an ironing board?'

'I thought you were a burglar!'

'And you were planning to 'uncrease' me to death?'

'No, I was planning to… anyway, never mind, what are you *doing* here?'

'I'm fixing it,' he says. 'I practised the mural on a large canvas at home before I started, so I thought we could use that for the launch, until I can redo it. I've just fixed it to the space.'

I look up at the wall behind him. The blotchy mural is completely hidden behind the large canvas.

'It looks great. Better than great. Amazing. But, Rory, you came here in the middle of the night to do this?' I ask, my voice catching for a moment. 'For me?'

'For my reputation. I couldn't have Richard J. What's-his-face thinking I can't paint.'

I'm completely disorientated. I've had so little sleep, between all my embarrassing naked dreams and waking up suddenly to an intruder in my shop.

'So, wait a minute, you thought it would be a good idea to break into the bookshop and scare the shit out of me, just so Richard J. didn't think you'd gone too far with abstract art?'

'It's not abstract art. It looked like a rainbow had thrown up on your wall.'

'I thought you were breaking in to kill me!'

'That's a touch dramatic, no?'

He stands back to size up his work.

'I don't know whether to thank you or smack you over the head with the ironing board.'

'It looks better,' Rory says. 'Not as good as the original, but it'll do for now. Right, I'm heading home. I'll see you when you're better dressed.'

I look down at my pyjamas. 'I was actually going to wear these to the launch…'

'Lock the door behind me, just in case.'

I roll my eyes. 'I locked it earlier. How did you even get in?'

'Tricks of the trade.'

'The murderer trade?'

'I own a DIY shop. You don't think I know how to pick a lock? Good night, Ava.'

'Good night, Rory,' I say. 'And thank you.'

He raises a hand into the air and wanders off into the night.

14

'Bloody hell, Ava, I hardly recognized you there,' Fiona grins as she carries the first of the catering trays through the front door of the bookshop. 'You scrub up well, lass.'

I rush over to help her with the heavy trays of wraps, sandwiches and finger food. My make-up is done, hair curled, and I've finally settled on my outfit choice: a mid-length, floaty, pink and black number that I pulled from my London wardrobe. I plan to be barefoot until the event officially starts, but I have my heels ready to go.

'You're used to seeing me at my worst, Fiona: scraped-back hair, no make-up and, worst of all, before the caffeine that you supply me with to help me function like a human being. Wow, this food all looks amazing!'

'We can lay it all out and then I'll need to nip away and get my glad rags on! I can't be late for the most exciting thing to happen to this village in months! A brand-new bookshop *and* Richard J. Walker in Ullapool, who'd have thought it?'

'Are you a crime fiction fan, Fiona? Or just a Richard fan?'

Fiona's laughter echoes around the bookshop. 'God, no! I'm not… Well, let's say he's not my type. I know someone who loves his books, though. Devoured them, actually. A friend. A former friend.'

'Former?'

Maybe Fiona and I have more in common than I realized.

I don't want to think about Macy, though. Not today.

Fiona's cheeks flush. 'Erm, yes. Anyway, I've included some extra fruit skewers. We had some strawberries and mango going spare. Let's put them on the edge of the table here. Do you need some help pouring the Prosecco?'

'No, no. You go home and get ready! I need you back here with a smile on your face and a glass of fizz in your hand in approximately thirty-six minutes.'

'Oh, Ava, everything looks just wonderful,' she grins, gazing around. 'I'm so glad you moved here. It's so lovely to have fresh faces in the village and the bookshop is such a fantastic addition.'

'And I'm single-handedly keeping your business afloat with my coffee addiction?'

She winks and gives me a warm hug. 'Well, there is that. Okay, see you back here soon! Good luck!'

*

'He's even more gorgeous in real life, isn't he?' Donna whispers in my ear. 'Your pal, Richard. I know he's a wee bit older than us but *look* at him. Eilidh, what do you think?'

Eilidh blushes. 'Oh, I don't know. I mean—'

'Sorry, is it too soon for you to be eyeing up other men? After Mark?' Donna asks, rubbing her on the shoulder.

Eilidh eventually opened up to Donna about Mark at one of our book club meetings. Donna threatened to hunt him down and kill him, but Eilidh graciously refused, and we all lived happily ever after. Aside from the bookshop, being part of the three musketeers with Eilidh and Donna is my proudest achievement in Ullapool so far.

'It's not that,' Eilidh whispers. 'Richard is my ex. We were together for a few years before Mark and I met.'

'Oh my God!' Donna splutters. 'Eilidh, you sly dog.'

'Must have been an amicable breakup,' I say with a smile. 'Since you were willing to invite him along for me. Unless it was just an excuse to see him again?'

Eilidh's face flushes a deeper shade of pink. 'He's staying at a bed and breakfast. No funny business. Plus, I have the boys tonight.' Just as she says it, a pair of boys tear through the bookshop, squealing and chasing each other between the shelves. Eilidh tries to calm them, but I place a hand on hers and tell her it's fine. She continues, 'I'm not ready for anything like *that* just now.'

Donna nods. 'I get it. A quickie for old times' sake, then send him back to the bed and breakfast.'

'Donna!' Eilidh laughs, shaking her head.

The launch party of The Next Chapter is in full swing. The fizz flows, people chat, and the till is red hot. I paid Jen, Donna's Saturday girl and one of the courtyard snoggers, to take charge of purchases tonight so I can mingle, gather content for social media and try to soak it all up.

Margaret has backed Richard into a corner, interrogating him about one of his mysteries. As I make my way over to rescue him, I bump into Rory.

I've been hugging everyone on arrival since the event started. Without thinking, I lean in to do the same with Rory. My face brushes against his cheek as he jumps back, as though I've given him an electric shock. My arm, ready for the embrace, hangs in the air awkwardly. I let it drop as he steps back.

'Hi,' I say, clearing my throat. 'It's, erm, customary to return a hug from the host.'

He doesn't reply. He's made an effort for the occasion, or as much as Rory can. He's swapped his usual Toolbox T-shirt for a plain black tee paired with a pair of smart, grey trousers, and I can smell the deep, woody scent of his aftershave. As I look back up, he stares me straight in the eye.

'You have this habit of swooping in out of nowhere,' he says, tapping me awkwardly on the shoulder, presumably to avoid any further advances. 'I thought a plank of wood was about to come at me again.'

'Says the middle-of-the-night painting ninja.'

Donna sips a large glass of fizz as she makes her way over to me, bumping into Finlay, who has a smoked salmon canapé in hand.

I hear Finlay manage to cough out, 'I meant to ask… how was your holiday?'

'Just what the doctor ordered.' Donna flashes a wide smile. 'Sun, sea, sand, the works. Well, not the works as in sex. I didn't mean that… I didn't do that. Have sex, I mean. Not on holiday.'

Donna casts me a sidelong glance. She grimaces at me as she brushes her hand across her forehead.

I sneak a glance at Rory, who seems to be enjoying the awkward interaction, judging by the grin on his face.

'What is going on with these two?' I whisper to him.

'Keep watching, this is golden,' he says in a low voice.

'So, no more Lewis? Or, I mean, whatever his name was,' Finlay says, waving his hand around and almost knocking Donna's Prosecco out her hand. 'Sorry. I'm sure you said his name was Lewis. I remember because I thought of Lewis Hamilton, the racing driver. And the Isle of Lewis, of course. Which is stunning this time of year.'

'No more Lewis,' Donna confirms, flicking the edge of the false nail on her finger. 'What about Keira Stanley? Are you two still…'

Finlay shakes his head firmly. 'Oh, no. That wasn't anything to write home about. Finito. I don't mean that, it's just… we only went on a couple of dates. Dogging. Oh,

God, not *dogging*, in that way, I mean we went on a few doggy dates. She has a dalmatian. Gorgeous dog. But not any more. Well, the dog is still alive, I mean…'

Rory attempts to muffle his laughter. Finlay's face is crimson by the time he finally finishes spitting out what he's trying to say, but Donna just chimes in with her beautiful laugh.

'Good,' she says after she's recovered. 'That she has a nice dog, I mean. I love my Bonnie, so I'm glad that other people have that in their lives. Anyway, I'd best…'

'Yes, I'd better…'

'Okay then.'

They each try to move around the other, but keep choosing the same way, somehow managing to lightly headbutt each other. They cringe in unison. Finlay stands still so Donna can make her way towards us.

She downs her fizz, her cheeks aflame, and blows her hair out of her face. 'Ava, hello, you told me to let you know when it was seven o'clock for your speech. So, here I am, your walking alarm clock.'

'Erm, what was that?' I ask her.

'What?'

'You and Finlay. It's all so… strange. The tension – or whatever you'd call it – is off the scale.'

'There's no tension,' she protests. 'Why would there be tension?'

Rory smirks. 'Why, indeed?'

I check my watch. 'Okay, thank you, it's speech time. I'll

ask Richard to say something first. At least that'll release him from Margaret's grasp.'

I tap Richard on the shoulder as Margaret throws me a look of disdain. First Rory, now I'm stealing Richard. 'I'm so sorry to interrupt. Richard, would you mind saying a few words now? I'll introduce you.'

'Certainly. It was lovely to meet you.' Richard nods to Margaret before following me to the till area.

My palms are sweating as I call for everyone's attention. Butterflies parade around my stomach.

As I look around the room, there is a sea of familiar faces. But my heart pounds all the same as I catch sight of Eilidh, Pete, Donna, Finlay, Fiona and the rest of the villagers I've come to know these past two months. And Rory. Rory, holding a glass of Prosecco that he tastes before making a face. He lifts up his glass as he catches my eye. He nods with something that could be mistaken for encouragement.

I can do this.

'Thank you, everyone, for coming and supporting the launch of The Next Chapter bookshop,' I say, gazing around the room.

'Hooray!' Donna whoops.

The room erupts into a mixture of laughter and applause. Looking around the bookshop at the eager faces, I feel the waves of support. I wet my lips, which feel like they've turned to sandpaper.

'I'd like to thank the amazing Richard J. Walker for coming along to support the launch and am now going to invite him to say a few words. Richard, the stage is yours!'

I step back. Everyone applauds as Richard steps forward, looking slightly bemused at my abrupt introduction. He looks much more handsome than the author headshot from his novels. He is in his mid-forties, remarkably tall, with thick, wavy brown hair, warm, deep-brown eyes and a genuine smile that lights up the room.

Margaret swoons as his eyes sweep the room. In fact, everyone looks at Richard a little dreamily, even Pete. I wonder how many of them have read his latest novel, with several in-depth, gruesome descriptions of severed body parts. It's difficult to look someone in the eye when you know they could be considering you as their future fictional victim. But he could be anywhere right now, and he is here in Ullapool, standing in *my* bookshop. And while all eyes are on him, he only has eyes for one person. He talks about the importance of reading and bookshops for all people, especially small, rural communities like ours, and wishes The Next Chapter bookshop every success in the future. All the while, his gaze keeps drifting back to Eilidh. I wonder if his next book might be about the one that got away.

'So, I'll pass you back over to The Next Chapter's owner, Ava Campbell!'

I almost jump at the sound of my own name, as I smile and thank Richard, pulling my notes from the counter. What the hell am I supposed to say? My hands shake.

I meant to rehearse this speech last night, but it didn't happen, thanks to the flooding in the shop. I clear my throat and look around, muttering a thank you to everyone for coming.

My heart pounds. The Next Chapter is finally here, my next chapter is starting. A new beginning. My eyes land on the bright yellow dresser, with Granny's recipes displayed all around it. It feels like she is here, celebrating with me. I close my eyes, just for a moment, and offer up a moment of thanks to my wonderful granny, who welcomed me to Ullapool with open arms and made me feel like finally I had a home. The whole room is still as I open my eyes again.

Donna offers me the widest grin. Eilidh stands with Harry and Caden, who elbow each other as she reminds them to behave. I lock eyes with Rory for a moment as he offers me another nod. I clear my throat. I start by thanking everyone for coming, Fiona for the food, gesturing around the shop and saying vague breathless thanks for the help I received with the joinery, the plumbing. But I feel at a distance, as though I'm looking at myself from above. I try to centre myself.

'One of the things that has struck me since I've been in Ullapool is how much I've enjoyed connecting with every single person and hearing about your stories,' I say, pausing for a moment and taking a deep breath – in... and out. I continue: 'Whether it's how much Pete loves delivering the post because it *keeps him young*, or Fiona's daily update on the shenanigans of the sheep next door, or Finlay telling me about his latest, *very dangerous* climbing adventure, I love stories. Stories connect us all, and when we share our own, it brings us closer together.

'I've also been really moved that people have shared some special moments with me. Donna and Pete have given me permission to mention Elise, a much-loved parent and wife, who passed away recently, and have told me how much she would have loved this bookshop. My own granny, Agnes, who lived in Ullapool, would have been thrilled that I fulfilled my promise of returning to live here one day, especially to open a bookshop. It was Granny who fostered my love of books and reading.'

I take a deep breath as I feel tears in my eyes. I don't want to cry. Not here, not now, with everyone looking at me. The room is still as I clear my throat again.

'A couple of us have been meeting up to talk about books and share our own stories recently. We'd love to extend the invitation for others to join us, now that The Next Chapter bookshop is officially open for business. We'll be hosting book clubs and author events too, but this is a little bit different, more of a support group. If you'd like a shoulder to cry on, for any reason at all, be it a bereavement or that bastard of an ex, we'd like to welcome you to meet with us here on Monday evenings at seven o'clock for The Next Chapter support group. Anyone can come with their problems – they don't have to be romantic – or you can come just for a chat. The first one will be next week to let me get my feet under the till. For one night a week, we'll be the breakup bookshop!'

There's a ripple of knowing laughter and a few cheers at the announcement. I meet eyes with Rory across the crowd. He was right. The Ullapool bookshop breakup and grief support group was a bit of a mouthful. The breakup bookshop rolls off the tongue much more easily. He's among the throng, and I can't see his reaction to me using his words.

I exhale and finish my speech. 'Thank you everyone for coming along this evening. Please eat, drink and be very merry!'

Phew. It's over. The room erupts with applause as I step back and smile. My whole body is shaking, but I did it.

*

'Ava, we have another recruit for our group!' Donna calls over, gesturing with jazz hands to Fiona, who blushes and says she'd love to come if we're happy to hear the witterings of an 'auld bird' like her.

A series of 'not at alls' follow, as I grin at them.

The evening is full of chatter, exchanges of book recommendations and laughter. As it draws to a close, people congratulate me, many laden with books they've bought, and I wave them off with a grateful smile. Even Margaret manages to get into the spirit of the launch and approaches me on her way out.

'Thank you for coming,' I beam at her.

'Your downstairs toilet didn't flush,' she says, raising an eyebrow as she shuffles out of the shop.

Fabulous.

Okay, so not everyone is swept up in the excitement.

I spot Rory speaking to Finlay in the back corner. He is standing with his back to the room.

'Rory!' I call.

He doesn't hear me, so I make my way over to them.

I nipped out earlier to buy a little thank you present for Rory's help with the bookshop last night: tickets for the Summer Isles boat trip he'd mentioned he'd loved when he was younger. Gripping the tickets, I march towards them.

I raise my hand, preparing to tap on his shoulder for attention, when something stops me in my tracks. Rory is speaking in a more charged tone than normal, and I wait a few paces away from them.

'People don't come *here* to talk about their feelings,' I hear him say. 'This place is an escape from that. It's quiet. We help one another. We move on and we keep to ourselves. It's not like you want the whole village knowing your business, is it?'

Finlay's eyes widen as he tries to alert Rory to the fact that I am behind him, but Rory's on a rant, and he isn't about to pause any time soon.

I feel my face heat up. I am rooted to the spot, unsure of my next move.

'And then there's that fucking mural that she ruined in twenty minutes because she didn't check her bloody bath worked. I come along in the middle of the night to fix it for her, and she hasn't even mentioned it tonight. Not once. This is just like her. Forgetting everything – or not caring. God, I'm an idiot!'

My body slumps. I knew there was something I'd forgotten to say in my speech. I'd written a special thank you to Rory but then got sidetracked by the breakup bookshop idea and hadn't gone back to it. My nerves got the best of me. I wish I'd rehearsed, but the flood got in the way. Plus, I'd barely slept the night before. He knew all that. But, dammit, I know I should have said something.

I can't do anything about that now, though. I can't call everyone back and declare, 'And you'd probably all be standing in a foot of water if it weren't for Rory!'

Finlay, his pale face matching his red hair with vicarious embarrassment, gestures at me over Rory's shoulder.

Rory looks sheepish.

I thrust the tickets out towards him. 'Here.'

He stares back at me, his expression cold. 'What's this?'

'The "thank you" that you wanted.'

I want to storm off, but this is my shop. My launch night. Instead, I pick up a black plastic bin bag for the rubbish and hope he takes the hint.

And he does. Rory is gone.

15

The Next Chapter's first few days are so busy, I barely have time to sit down. Most evenings, I'm so exhausted that I can't even lift a book, never mind read one myself.

Locals and tourists alike are drawn in, thanks to my 'blind-date' stand that I roll out every morning. Each book is wrapped in brown paper with a few clues on the front – genre, tropes and comparison titles. I picked it up from a London bookshop, so it isn't an original idea, but everyone here seems to love it.

Margaret is the first to buy one, although she declares she might return it after she's read it depending on whether she likes it or not. I've come to expect nothing less from her. Eilidh picked up a couple when she popped in for a very important finance meeting with me about profit and growth projections, which we managed in between snorts of laughter, before she had to pick up Harry and Caden from school. Jen and Evan come in, hand in hand, and manage to restrain themselves from full-scale snogging in front of me, although I do observe a few pecks and hear an excessive amount of giggling. They leave with a Thai cookbook for Evan's mum's birthday.

A large group of American tourists who stop in the village for the day as part of their Highland bus tour practically empty the shelves of blind-date books one afternoon. Two women grab at the same time at a Scottish historical romance novel. Their raised voices float into the shop, but I am too busy at the till serving the rest of their tour group to intervene. Their tour guide begs me to wrap another book for them before they take each other's eyes out. I dash to my stock collection, seize the brown paper and write up the description as quickly as possible to prevent an American civil war on Scottish soil.

It's the first time I've seen Rory since our salty exchange at the end of the launch. He sticks his head into the shop once the drama is over and the two women are lined up in an orderly fashion to purchase their books. At the sight of him, they fix angelic looks on their faces, blushing and snickering like schoolgirls. When he leaves, they agree that he is the real blind date they pined for. One proclaims that his accent alone makes her feel a flutter *down there*, while the other asks if I have any pictures of him for sale that they could take home. A Highland Hunks calendar, perhaps?

Inwardly, I roll my eyes, but I show them my TikTok of Rory. All publicity is good publicity, after all.

Finlay pops his head in later that afternoon, asking if he can bring Piper and a small cocker spaniel called Lacey into the bookshop.

'Of course,' I smile, before stroking Lacey's tummy. Piper jumps up, jealous of my attention to Lacey. I rub them both between the ears, sharing the love.

'How's it going?' he asks, looking around. 'It looks brilliant in here.'

'It's great,' I say. 'Very different from London life, but that's exactly what I came here for.'

'By the way, I'm sorry you heard all that the other night. He was tired, but it's no excuse. Has he come in to apologize yet?'

'Who?' I ask, knowing full well who he is talking about.

'Your young Brad Pitt next door,' he grins.

'Brad Pitt? More like a Tad Shit. I know he's your mate, but he doesn't half blow hot and cold, doesn't he?'

'He's stubborn as a mule. But he has a heart of gold, really. He's a mate for life, once you get him on side.'

'Yes, so everyone says.' I roll my eyes. 'I don't have time to stroke his ego all the time. I didn't miss him off the thank you speech because I wasn't grateful. I was shaking in my boots at the launch. I hadn't been that nervous in a long time.'

'See, you *were* anxious. I told him you would be. He thinks you're some big shot without a nerve in your body.'

'Well, he's getting on my last nerve,' I sigh. 'He's labelled me as some sort of flighty gentrifier or something, but he doesn't know me and he doesn't seem to want to get to know me. I don't know what his problem is.'

'Rory's changed a lot,' Finlay says. 'He's got a lot of insecurities he never talks about. He was such a dork as a teenager. He was always moping around, pining for some girl he couldn't have. He started going out with Elle a few years ago and completely transformed after they broke up. Bulked up, got a haircut, and bam – everything changed. Think he feels a bit weird walking around feeling like a nerd but looking, y'know, the way he does.' Finlay's lips curl up in a smile.

'*Really?*' I ask, delighting in this insight from Finlay. 'I knew Elle when I was younger. We used to play together in the summer.'

He nods. 'She's a nice lass.'

'Oh my God!' I exclaim, my hand flying to my mouth.

He raises his eyebrow, a bemused expression on his face. 'Remember something?'

I nod with excitement. 'Yes! Donna used to speak about *you* when we were younger! My last Ullapool summer, when we were fifteen, and all she could talk about was her boyfriend, Finlay, who was staying in Donegal for the summer with his family. That was you, wasn't it? How could I have forgotten?'

Finlay looks flustered. 'Erm, yes. We did. You remember that?'

'She moped around all summer long talking about you. You were her screensaver on her phone! When did you break up?'

Finlay's face flushes even deeper. Lacey and Piper begin squabbling at his feet and Lacey lets out a low bark. Finlay bends down to scoop her up into his arms and she sticks a triumphant tongue out at Piper to celebrate her victory.

'We were together for six years,' he confirms. 'High school sweethearts, but she broke it off when she was about to open the salon. She wanted to concentrate on her business. And then she was with Lewis for ages. We're friends now. No big deal.'

'Could have fooled me,' I say. 'You might have broken up yesterday from the way you were dancing around each other at the launch and the pub the other night. Does it just take longer to move on when you break up with someone who's from here? Are Rory and Elle the same?'

'Ach, no, Rory and I both pined for a while after our lost loves, but we got over it. Anyway, tomorrow night's the debut of the breakup bookshop, isn't it?'

'Yes, but in the evening because of the Bank Holiday. I've got my first official day off during the day and I can't wait! You could come along, if you're free? Your "friend", Donna, will be there…'

Grinning, I wiggle my eyebrows at him.

'Ah, no thanks,' he says with a laugh. 'We don't need to take a trip down memory lane. Exes are exes for a reason, aren't they?'

'True,' I say, thinking of Seb.

'Anyway, I've got plans with your worst enemy tonight.

He's off tomorrow too, so we'll likely have a few whiskies tonight. What are you doing in the day tomorrow?'

'I'll be out exploring. I'll look at the suggestions you gave me at the pub and I'll see what's next on my hitlist.'

'I'm sure you'll find something. Speaking of walks, I'd better get these two off for theirs. See you, Ava!'

As he leaves, I revel in the new information about my friends' childhoods. I can't believe I'd forgotten about Donna and Finlay, the village's answer to Posh and Becks from back in the day. I can still picture her gazing at his picture on her phone, him with his bright red hair, and pondering whether to call him or not.

There is definitely something going on now, though. I just have to find out what it is. Didn't Donna say something about wishing she could settle down with someone right here in Ullapool? Maybe the right man has been under her nose the whole time.

And then there is Rory, the dorky teenager, who bagged the most gorgeous girl in Ullapool and managed to lose her.

Maybe that's what makes him so damn grumpy all the time.

*

Rory peers in the bookshop window as I'm serving my last customer of the day. She has been deliberating for a good hour over what to buy for a friend's birthday. I've been on my feet for hours, I'm hangry and the sight of Rory's sorry-looking face at the bookshop window almost sends me over the edge. I hope he's not here to complain or rant about something else. I can't face it, not today. I just want to close up the shop and have a (non-leaking) bath.

After the customer pays up and leaves, having picked a lovely edition of *Great Expectations*, Rory enters. I don't look up to greet him.

'You're off tomorrow,' he states.

'I am.'

'You bought me two tickets for the Summer Isles tour.'

'I did.'

'We should go together,' he says, his tone softening. It's not an apology, but it's a peace offering. 'You take the other ticket. It closes at the end of this month so you might not get another chance till next summer. If you're still here then.'

'Come with you?'

'You bought two tickets and I'm going tomorrow. I've booked up. Finlay said you're free.'

'Finlay put you up to this?' I ask, feeling a tug of annoyance in my chest.

'Do you want to come or not?'

I nod. 'I do.'

'Meet me at the dock tomorrow at ten?'

'I will.'

One of these days, I hope I understand the strange, confused mind of Rory MacGregor.

16

The sun covers every inch of my bedroom the next morning as I get ready for the boat trip. I still can't get my head around it. One minute Rory and I are head-to-head and it feels like we'll never be civil, the next he's inviting me on an expedition.

I deliberate over my outfit for a silly amount of time and end up wearing a green top and the jeans that Seb always said made my bum look good. I can still hear his voice in my head as I stand in front of the mirror. He liked seeing me in pink, which also happened to be Macy's favourite colour. Maybe she'd won him over with a flutter of the eyelashes and her collection of Barbie-inspired clothes.

I sigh. This is the problem with having a day off: it means I have – gasp – time to think. It's just as well Finlay bullied Rory into inviting me out for the day. Too much time alone would have sent me spiralling.

I'm hardly looking forward to spending the day with Rory, but I can't wait for the boat trip itself. Tourists visiting the shop have mentioned seeing dolphins jumping in and out of the water. Dolphins! It is so far removed from London life that I'm practically jumping up and down with excitement as I pack my things and set off down to the pier. Rory is already waiting by the time I arrive, first in the queue. In fact, he is the only one in the queue.

'Ready?' he asks.

I nod. 'Looking forward to it?'

'Can't wait,' he says. 'Thanks for the ticket.'

'No problem,' I say, shifting from one foot to another. 'Thanks for giving me the spare. See, isn't this nice, being civil to each other?'

Rory almost smiles. Almost. It is more of a smirk, really, but it still counts. 'Sure, we can stay civilized for one day.'

'Good. Because I want to have a good time. This has been top of my to-do list since I got here.'

'So you said.'

A few more people join the queue behind us. I recognize two of the women as the American tourists who fought over the book in my shop.

'Oh my God,' I hear one whisper to the other. 'It's *him*.'

'And you!' the other exclaims, pointing at me with an impressively long gel nail. 'You're the bookstore owner. You're *with* him? You didn't say anything.'

'Oh, no,' Rory says.

'We're not together,' I say emphatically.

They both brighten up immediately, introducing themselves directly to Rory as Lynnette and Melissa, while the tour guide starts the safety briefing.

'The safety briefing is pretty much don't fall in the water, isn't it?' Rory mutters.

Lynnette and Melissa throw their heads back, squawking like seagulls. A family with three young excitable boys joins the end of the queue. The dad struggles to fold the toddler's buggy, so the mum takes over and, even with the child on her hip, manages it with a flick of her foot. Their two older children jump up and down, asking if it's time for the boat to leave as we're ushered on board.

The white boat has seating at the back, an observation deck where a maximum of eight people can be at one time, plus a space at the very front of the boat where we are able to sit on the deck. I make my way to the front and take a seat. Rory appears behind me.

'It'll get pretty cold out here,' he warns. 'Once the boat starts moving.'

'I don't mind.' I shrug. 'It's just lovely to be here, to see the scenery and soak it all up.'

He nods, standing still. It looks like he's planning to stay here beside me. As the engine roars to life, we listen to the tour guide chatting through the loudspeaker about the islands that we are set to see and the wildlife we might catch a glimpse of on the way.

The wind picks up as the boat propels forward and, within minutes, it blasts me full in the face. I put on my sunglasses to shield my eyes, not from the sun but from the intensity of the wind, and pull my jacket closer around me.

'You weren't kidding about the wind,' I say, as my teeth start to chatter. 'Tears are being extracted from my eyeballs.'

He laughs. 'Yeah, it's a different kind of wind out here, isn't it? Feels like it's cutting you in half.'

'Too right,' I say. 'That's why we're the only ones on the front deck, I guess.'

'It'll be worth it. You've got to weather the storm to reap the rewards,' he says, pulling a flask from his bag. 'Plus, I brought coffee to keep me warm.'

'I see your cup of smugness,' I say, pulling out my own flask from my backpack. 'And I raise you hot chocolate.'

'Touché... Nice work. I see your hot chocolate,' he says, rummaging in his bag, 'and I raise you a wool blanket. MacGregor tartan, for good measure.'

I shiver as a gust of wind whips around my face. 'Does the blanket being tartan make it extra warm, by any chance?'

Over the tannoy, the tour guide points out two eagles soaring towards the mountains in the distance. Rory lends me his binoculars, and I gasp at the sight of the majestic birds. The tour guide walks around with a claw that is the same size as an eagle's, to demonstrate their strength.

As I sip on my hot chocolate and gaze out to the mountains, I sigh contentedly. I've been full steam ahead with moving, renovations and the bookshop opening. Everything has been a million miles an hour for months now. Years, in fact. During my London life, I'd barely taken the time to breathe. Looking back on it now, I'm not sure how I kept up the pace. Early starts to prepare for meetings, writing last-minute pitches, team meetings, launch nights, late finishes, and then back up to do it all again the next day. I barely had time for anything but work.

Macy had been the first to complain that she never saw me any more. Seb never said anything, but I guess they decided to take matters into their own hands. Not that it gave them an excuse. I wasn't letting them off the hook that easily. But, thinking back now, I had probably become too work-focused over the last few years as I'd climbed the corporate ladder. Verging on obsessed. And for what? The company went into liquidation, and I was more alone than when I started. I can't remember doing anything fun for myself during those four years. I couldn't even read when I got home. Instead, I collapsed into bed in an exhausted heap at the end of the day.

As it starts to drizzle, I make my way inside and Rory follows me.

'Your cheeks are rosy,' Rory says, as we sit down on a row of cushioned seats inside the boat. He coughs, a little awkward. 'It suits you.'

'A compliment? Who are you and what have you done with the Rory I know?' I ask, as I feel my fingers start to thaw. 'Are you nicer out at sea?'

'Yup, the minute we're back on shore, you're dead to me.'

He pulls out his sketchbook from his backpack, looking into the distance, and starts moving his pencil expertly around the page. Within minutes, he has reproduced the outline of the mountains.

'Wow,' I say. 'Your American fan club up the stairs will be very impressed with your artwork. I heard them say you look like a young Marlon Brando.' I wrap my jacket tightly around my body as someone opens the door to the deck area, bringing a blast of cold wind. 'I told them you've got a personality like Shrek.'

'Always around to bring me down to earth.'

'You're welcome. Although, in all seriousness, your work is very impressive. How long have you been an artist?'

He laughs. 'I'm hardly an artist. I just dabble.'

'I think you'll find that I commissioned you to paint a mural in my shop. That makes you an artist. Professional, even.'

'Well, it's not like I'm inundated with requests.' He shrugs and goes back to concentrating on his craft.

'You could be,' I say. 'If you wanted.'

He sighs. 'You've worked in The Toolbox. You can see how busy it gets. Margaret's toilet seat won't fix itself, you know. It's a family business. I can't just abandon it.'

'Family business,' I say, raising my eyebrows. 'But where's your family? Sorry, I hope you don't mind me asking. It just seems like you're doing it all by yourself.'

'I'm the youngest of eight and all my brothers and sisters have moved away. Hopefully not forever, but who knows? My mum and dad went to stay near my sister, who's just had a baby. They should be coming back in the next few weeks. Until then, I'm the last man standing in Ullapool. I have the family home and business to take care of. I can't really mess about with painting and drawing. I need to keep the business afloat.'

Here I am thinking how lucky Rory is to have a business handed to him on a plate. Watching him sketching away in his book, I realize he isn't exactly lucky. He's trapped.

'That's a lot,' I say. 'All on you.'

He shrugs. 'I like it here. The quiet. I can't imagine living in London or New York or anywhere like that. I think I'll always come back here. This is home. But I have always wanted to see a bit more of the world and maybe have some more time to draw and paint – to pretend to be an artist.'

'It's not pretending.' I nudge his knee. 'You *are* an artist. Rumour has it you planned to buy my shop?'

I say it as gently as possible. I'm so pleased with the bookshop. I know it would have stung if someone had nabbed it from me in an auction. And I had to work right next door.

'Ah, so you heard about that? Probably worked out for the best, anyway. I wouldn't have had the time to do much with it. The rest of my family are pursuing their dreams just now. I'd like to have my turn, too, at some point. My siblings are all over the world. France, Australia, even, God forbid, *Edinburgh*. Two of them are writers. My sister Ailsa, the one who's just had the baby, is an interior designer,' he says proudly.

Although he speaks of them fondly, it doesn't seem fair that Rory is the one left to keep everything ticking over while his siblings chase their ambitions.

'What was it like to grow up with so many brothers and sisters?'

'Noisy,' he says. 'But that's what I was used to, so I didn't think much of it when I was growing up. I was the one who always talked about travelling and now everyone else is doing it.'

'You miss them?' I ask. 'Or you're jealous?'

He nods, scratching his chin. 'Ach, a bit of both, I suppose. I went from a family of ten to just me in the space of a couple of years. It's been too quiet since they all buggered off. I hate the silence.'

'I grew up in silence,' I confess. 'I would have loved to have a big, bustling family growing up. I always wanted siblings, but Mum and Dad were 'one and done'. I'm not even sure they really wanted me, if I'm honest. My granny was different, though. She loved having me around. She wasn't married when she had my dad. I think it was a bit of a scandal for a while. Dad couldn't wait to leave Ullapool. He was out of here as soon as he turned sixteen.'

'No wonder your granny wanted you around, if your dad left when he was so young. She would have been delighted with your company and how you've turned out. Your parents must be too.'

I shrug. 'Nope. My parents wanted me to follow in their footsteps and work in finance. I was a disappointment for choosing marketing. They're horrified that I'm here right now. They think I'm ruining my life.'

'Starting your own business and buying your own flat? Yeah, you're pure trash. There's no coming back from that,' he says with a grin.

'I know, it's just not the way they do things. They wanted me to get married and settle down in London and I was on the cusp of it. When it fell apart, Mum was more devastated than I was.'

'You were about to get married?'

'Well, he hadn't asked me, but yes, it was on the cards.'

I don't know why I'm talking about Seb again to Rory. I wish I could keep my mouth shut.

'What would you have done with the shop? If you'd got it,' I say.

'I was going to make it into a studio and gallery to exhibit my stuff and work by local artists,' he admits. 'I thought I could paint there when my parents took over The Toolbox again.'

'I'm sorry I stamped all over your dream.'

'It just wasn't meant to be.'

'I'm still sorry.'

We sit in silence, staring out to sea, until Rory offers me a chocolate biscuit from his stash. The American tourists appear and start to chat with him, so I make my way up to the deck to look at the view. The captain offers the three young boys the chance to steer the boat and they squeal in delight.

I watch the boys jumping up and down with excitement. Seb and I had talked about having children. He wanted one child, but I wanted two. At least. Only children are lonely; I know that better than anyone. Just nine months ago, ironically, Seb asked how long we should wait to have a child. How had everything changed so drastically in such a short period of time?

Macy never wanted children. She always said it would be too much responsibility for her. I wonder if she's told Seb. Maybe it's not even an issue. Maybe Seb loves her so much he doesn't care.

I shiver, and not just because it is freezing. I can't think about them any more. As I check my phone, I realize the tour will soon end. Two hours have passed by in a flash.

'Ava!' Rory comes pounding up the stairs to the top desk, where I'm sitting alone. 'Look!'

I frown as the wind whips my hair around my face. 'What is it? I can't see anything.'

He stands behind me and leans close so his head is just above my shoulder, his breath tickling my ear, as he points out to sea. I follow his finger, ignoring the strange somersaults my stomach is doing at his sudden touch.

'Dolphins!' I gasp, as he smiles widely.

'You see them?'

I grab my phone to capture them. I yelp in delight as the dolphins leap out of the water, sending huge splashes curling into the air around them.

'I see them!'

It is the most magnificent display I've ever witnessed. The dolphins are so close that I feel like I can reach out and touch them. It is awe-inspiring. Tears spring into my eyes. Forget Seb. Forget Macy. This is why I came back to Ullapool. This is *magical*. The surprise of new experiences is cushioned by the memories and sense of belonging that stem from my summers here. As I watch the dolphins surge in and out of the vast expanse of water, I feel grateful for the time spent here.

I glance up at Rory, my mouth wide open. 'It's amazing.'

He nods. 'It is.'

I shiver, gazing out at sea, and feel his cheek close to mine. As I turn, I realize he is wrapping the tartan blanket around my shoulders. I look up into his eyes. He gazes back at me, his lips parted slightly.

He's going to kiss me. Or maybe I'm going to kiss him, I'm not sure which. I haven't kissed anyone other than Seb in years. Will it be a full-on snog, like Jen and Evan, around the back of our shops? Will I melt into him, as easily as I did with Seb on our first kiss? This is crazy. I thought Rory hated me, and now here he is, staring at me, moving closer to my lips. It's this place. Being somewhere new, on the water, far away from everyone.

As the thoughts whizz through my head, a child screams at the top of his lungs, 'I wanna swim with the dolphins!'

Rory's gaze is immediately torn away from mine as the young boy bounces at our feet, snot flying from his nose. His mother comes hurtling up the stairs and grabs hold of him by the shoulders.

'You do not run away from Mummy. Do you hear me?' She kneels down beside him, then looks up at us. 'I'm so sorry! He kept saying someone in his class swam with dolphins and he wanted to get in the water with them too. I thought he was going to jump overboard!'

'I want to swim!' he insists, as he stamps his feet and dissolves into a series of uncontrollable sobs.

'I mean, I totally get where he's coming from,' I say with a smile. 'I want to swim with them too.'

'Five minutes until we head back,' the tour guide informs us. 'Please gather your belongings.'

The moment, if there was one, has passed.

'That was... brilliant,' I say, avoiding Rory's eye.

He whistles, completely nonchalant. Maybe I imagined the whole thing. It was such an intense moment, in my head at least, but it's possible that I'd built it up into something more than it was. I'd been thinking about Seb, stupidly, and our failed future. About children. And where I belong. Maybe I was trying to convince myself, for a second, that I could move on.

I hand Rory the blanket he'd wrapped around my shoulders. I hadn't imagined that part, at least.

He nods and throws me a smile. 'It was worth it to hear you squealing like a five-year-old.'

'Ah, come on, that was incredible! We just saw freaking dolphins! Anyone who doesn't squeal like a child when they see that is dead inside. Dead! Even you looked like you loved it, and you've got a black soul.'

'Excuse me, I think you'll find it's more verging on grey,' he says. 'Like your ex's walls.'

'Verging on grey,' I repeat. 'That would be the title of his autobiography.'

He laughs at that. As we disembark from the boat, Lynnette and Melissa call a goodbye to Rory and I throw a wave in their direction before we walk back towards our shops. We stand outside, unsure how to end the day.

'Back to reality,' he says.

'At least we managed to stop arguing for a while. So that's a bonus.'

'Verging on… friends?'

Friends. Sure, that's better than hating each other. I nod.

'Right. I've got to go and get ready. The breakup bookshop is meeting here this evening. Why don't you pop your head in?'

He grunts. 'No thanks.'

'Ah, come on. I thought we were friends now?'

'Verging on friends. Anyway, sorry, I'm washing my hair tonight. Good luck with it, though.'

17

'And then Lewis told me he never liked Bonnie anyway,' Donna reveals. 'Can you believe he *said* that? How can I trust someone that doesn't like dogs?'

Beside me Eilidh stifles a laugh, and I nudge her. People's heartaches come in all shapes and sizes. While Donna's ex sounds like an utter prat, and she has more disdain for him than sorrow, she has the right to talk it through. Pete sits beside his daughter, listening intently to her rant, while Margaret mumbles to ask Fiona if there's any wine on the go.

'I mean, I should have known,' she continues. 'He refused to go out for walks with us. Said he could never pick up hot shit from the ground. I mean, it's not like I pick it up with my bare hands...'

Eilidh covers her mouth, but her shoulders are trembling by this point. She lets out a discreet cough to cover it up. The rest of the group shake their heads solemnly.

I consider pointing out that Finlay, as a dog walker, would have no issues picking up dog shit, but I'm not sure that's much of a win for Finlay. I still haven't got round to asking Donna about the weird vibe between the two of them or what broke them up years ago, when she'd been so in love. Finlay said Donna wanted to concentrate on opening her business, but somehow I didn't buy that. Donna had been obsessed with him when she was younger. What changed?

Donna takes a deep breath and passes Pete the book that we use to signal who is speaking. He shakes his head, instantly passing it back to his daughter.

'Ah, no, love,' he shakes his head. 'I'm just here for the company, really.'

'Come on, Dad,' Donna urges. 'Why don't you try speaking about Mum for a bit?'

'No, no. You talk, love. You should say how you feel about your mum. I'm just here to support you.'

'Dad, I'm here to support *you*,' Donna whispers quietly. 'I'm okay. At least, I think I'm okay. But I'm worried about you.'

Donna's eyes fill with tears as she looks into her dad's eyes. He takes her hand and squeezes it. 'I've got you, love. As long as I've got you, I'm just fine.'

Donna nods. 'Oh, I know, it sounds stupid fixating on Lewis. Honestly, I was over him before we even broke up. It's just… I'm trying *not* to think about what really matters. I think about Mum all the time. Talking about other things is a distraction, you know?'

'I know, love.'

I feel my eyes welling with tears at the short exchange. Father and daughter, both so concerned about the other that they barely think about themselves.

'Shit,' Eilidh whispers in my ear. 'Now I feel bad.'

'I don't want to speak this time,' Pete says. 'But you do it. Talk about your mum now. Say what you really feel. Go for it, Donna. You'll make me brave.'

'Okay.' Donna coughs, accepting back the book. She takes a long, deep breath and looks at the floor as she speaks. 'I've been looking through old photos. Mum's in barely any of them. That made me really annoyed at her. She's not in the pictures because she was always self-conscious about how she looked and she made sure she was taking them. And now I'm really pissed off because she's not here any more and I don't have any pictures to remind me of her.'

The whole room is still for a moment. No one knows what to say. I look up at Pete.

'I've got some,' he whispers, his voice getting louder as he continues. 'I knew she hated having her picture taken, but I took some anyway. She was so beautiful, I couldn't not.'

Tears shine in Donna's eyes. 'You did?'

'Of course I did. You should have said, love. I can show you them, if you like?'

'I'd love that.'

Pete takes his daughter's hand again, as a lump rises in

my throat. Eilidh starts to fan her face with a book, tears glassing her eyes at the exchange.

Just then, the bookshop door pushes open and Jen walks in, head down, tears streaming down her face. Donna and I jump up to greet her.

'It's Evan,' she sobs. 'He dumped me. I didn't know where to go and then I realized you were all here and—'

'Ah, Jen,' I say, bringing her in for a hug as she sniffs loudly into her shoulder. 'Come and sit down.'

'I knew you should watch out for him,' Donna rages. 'Wee eejit that he is. I never trusted him. His eyes are too far apart.'

'He told me he *loved* me last week,' Jen blows her nose in the hankie I hand her. 'Then he broke up with me tonight, right after his mum's birthday dinner. And I picked out that cookbook for him! Said he's been thinking about it for a while. How can he say that when he just said he loved me?'

'Men,' Eilidh rolls her eyes. 'No offence, Pete.'

'None taken.'

'Lads that age don't know their arse from their elbow,' Donna says, shaking her head. 'They're only thinking with one body part and it's neither of them.'

'I don't want to talk about it any more,' Jen shakes her head, blowing into the hankie. 'I just knew you were all meeting here tonight, so I thought I'd come along. I can't tell my mum – she's never liked him. She'll only say *I told you so*.'

Jen blows her nose again and passes the book to me.

'Are you sure you don't want to talk any more, Jen?' I ask. 'We're here to listen if you do.'

Jen shakes her head, clutching the hankie and patting her bloodshot eyes. 'Please, someone else be miserable so I'm not the only one. And book me in for my hair transformation, Donna.'

Donna nods. 'Yes, sweetheart, show him what he's missing!'

Jen groans. 'Right, can someone else take over now? Please?'

'Hi everyone,' I say, taking the floor to deflect attention from poor Jen. 'I'm Ava and I… God, it's harder than you think, isn't it?'

I look around at everyone – Pete, Donna, Jen, Eilidh, Fiona – and they nod sympathetically. Even Margaret seems to agree as she gives a small nod, a flicker of agreement. I'd been more than a little surprised when she arrived early, the first breakup bookshop member of the evening. She seemed reluctant to admit she'd come for the group as she casually browsed the historical fiction section. When I mentioned it, she said that, yes, she would stay, as though she were doing me a favour.

'Yes,' Margaret says. 'It's easy to listen but hard to speak.'

I swallow my surprise. Has Margaret just said something supportive? Maybe the ice queen is thawing. I offer her a small smile, remembering what Rory said about her.

She'd lost her husband. She's obviously lonelier than she wants to admit and is finding it difficult to open up. That's why she's here, and that's why the breakup bookshop is important. It can help people who struggle to admit they need help, support or company.

'Like you said, it's Chatham House rules,' Eilidh reminds me with an encouraging smile.

'What does that mean?' Jen asks.

'That we won't go around telling people what you've been saying. It's sensitive information, so we don't want to broadcast it,' Eilidh explains.

I take a deep breath. I have to set an example. This whole breakup bookshop is my idea, after all. The Next Chapter. I can't let everyone else share their secrets and feelings but refuse to open up myself. I'm just not ready to share the whole story, though. I can't talk about Macy. Not in front of everyone. I can barely admit that part to myself. It just hurts too much. Losing her as a friend seems like the biggest heartbreak of all.

So, instead, I tell them about Seb. I tell them how we met, how he encouraged me in my career, how I'd planned my future with him. Then, boom, I drop the bombshell that he cheated on me, and I moved here for a fresh start.

I smile. 'And here I am.'

My head is thumping by the time I've finished my short account of the situation, and my heart is sad and heavy in my chest. I know it is good to talk about these things out loud, but right now it feels like a long, hard slog.

'I think you're an inspiration, Ava,' Eilidh says. 'You packed up everything and moved to the middle of nowhere, where you didn't really know anyone, and started a whole new business and life. If that stuff with Seb hadn't happened, we wouldn't be sitting here talking to one another. That's all down to you.'

'Well, it was more out of desperation than bravery,' I say, and the others laugh. 'But thank you. I hope you found the first meeting useful. I've really enjoyed it.'

As the group chatter at the end of the session, I start to gather the mugs and biscuits I'd handed out during the meeting, listening to the buzz of conversation around me.

'Do you know, Fiona, I feel better after that,' I hear Margaret reveal. 'I think I'll sleep well tonight.'

'Wasn't it great?' Fiona agrees. 'We should have done something like this years ago. We're so on top of one another in the village, but how often do we actually just talk?'

I feel pride surge in my chest at the thought of helping this community I've fallen in love with. Eilidh and Donna congratulate me as they leave, both comforting poor Jen on the way out. Pete gives me a wink, then follows them out. Margaret says she *might* see me next time as she shuffles out with her stick in hand.

'I'll stay behind and help you tidy,' Fiona offers.

Granny always said that when you're part of a small community, you have to immerse yourself in it and let people in. She said your door was never really closed when you lived in Ullapool, and that people making themselves at home in your home was an honour. I think I'm feeling some of that village pride now.

'Of course, that would be great.'

Fiona picks up an empty biscuit packet to fan her face, which has started to glisten with sweat. 'These bloody hot flushes are a nightmare.'

'Take a seat. You don't need to help. We can just chat,' I say, as I offer Fiona a biscuit. She takes one, then sits down again, flapping at her face.

'You know, there are menopause support groups, there's Alcoholics Anonymous and there are grief groups, but you have to fit in a box for all of them. This group's great, because you don't need to be just one thing. So, well done, you.'

'It was good tonight,' I say. 'Emotionally exhausting, but good. You didn't want to speak?'

Fiona had remained quiet throughout the session.

'Oh, I just, well… I'm not sure about it all yet.'

'No stories to share? Good-looking woman like you, I know you'll have broken some hearts.'

Fiona laughs and shakes her head. 'It's not that. It's just, well, okay, I'll be honest. I don't like the idea of sharing my deepest, darkest struggles with the whole village. I'm here for the giving support part, but I'm not planning to ask for it, if that makes sense?'

She shifts from one foot to the other as she perches on the edge of her seat.

'I would like to open up, but I'm not sure how well people would react.'

'You can tell me, if you like. I may be able to help.'

She clutches the empty mug of tea tightly, blowing her short hair out of her face. 'The love of my life left me years ago, when I was in my early twenties, and I've not seen them since. That's my story. When I heard you were starting the support group in the bookshop, it stirred up old memories. It seems so stupid to still be hung up on it all these years later.'

'Oh, Fiona! I'm sorry. Just because it was a while ago, that doesn't make it any less traumatic. I'm sure everyone would be very sympathetic.'

She shakes her head emphatically. 'I don't know if I can. I went through too much when it happened and… I just can't go back there. I'm not sure how people here would take it.'

'What do you mean? Was he cruel to you?'

'No, nothing like that. There was no… *he*. It wasn't… a heterosexual relationship,' she says, uncertainty in her tone.

'Ah, Fiona. Tell me all about it. I'm here to listen.'

Fiona sighs, her shoulders slumped. 'I've never told a soul. I don't know if anyone would care now. But when I was young, it had to be secret. Or so we thought. Her name was, *is* – I don't even know if she's alive or dead. Her name is Lillian.' Fiona smiles wistfully, before her face darkens again. 'But her family found out somehow and they were terrible. I'm sure they moved away because of it.'

'Oh, Fiona, that's awful!'

'Her dad was the worst. He talked about Lillian as though she wasn't in the room. He thought attending church would save her. I think they joined some sort of religious group and then moved away altogether. I don't even know where they went.'

She blinks and I move forward to give her a hug. Poor Fiona. I can't imagine falling in love with someone and being ripped apart from them, never able to move on, because there was never an *end* to speak of. My split with Seb is difficult enough to manage, but I'd chosen to leave. It would be so much worse if you both still wanted to be in a relationship and loved each other dearly but couldn't be together.

'Did you ever try to get back in contact with her? Or hear anything about her?'

'I think she wrote to me. I saw my mum burning letters in the fireplace. She never told me they were from her, but I always suspected they were. My mum knew I was gay; she was fine with that. She just couldn't stand to see me upset. I cried for weeks after Lillian left. Months, maybe. I've only had a couple of relationships since – a summer fling and some dates that never really led anywhere – but I've never forgotten her. Seems stupid, now I say it out loud. But since you mentioned the support group, she's all I can think about. I hope you don't mind that I can't talk about it openly. It's just... it's a little bit complicated.'

'Oh, no, I don't mind at all!' I say. 'Have you ever tried to track her down? Online, maybe?'

'I used to look periodically, but I never found anything. She was a very private person, I doubt she'd be the kind to splash her news all over social media.'

'Ah, come on, everyone's traceable,' I say. 'Give me her full name and I'll get my detective hat on. I bet we'll find her.'

I clutch my mobile phone, ready to rush to the bins for reception as soon as Fiona gives the signal. Instead, she shakes her head.

'Honestly, I couldn't. She'll have moved on. She probably got married and had children, the way her family wanted her to. She wanted it too, but she always said she wanted it with me. I couldn't turn up out of the blue to satisfy some silly curiosity of mine.'

I nod. I don't want to make Fiona uncomfortable by pushing any further, but I can't help but think it is such an awful thing to carry regret with you for your whole adult life. What if Lillian didn't have a family? What if she was single too, living a parallel life to Fiona's, just waiting for her love to return?

Bloody hell. What the hell is wrong with me? Despite being dumped and betrayed myself, I'm still holding a torch for happily ever afters.

'Look, I better go,' Fiona says, standing up. 'I guess I wanted to say, well, thank you. You've given me something to think about with this breakup bookshop. I'd like to keep coming along, but I wanted you to know that I might not say much and why. I hope that's okay with you?'

I gather Fiona into a hug. 'Of course it is. There's no pressure to say anything, Fiona. But I'm always here to talk, if you want to.'

She nods on her way out of the door.

'And if you change your mind and want a hand with some detective work, I'm your girl!'

'Thank you, Ava. I'm so glad you came here.'

'I'm glad I'm here too,' I say with a smile.

18

My post-breakup-bookshop glow lasts for days. Everyone seems to be talking about it, and next week's attendance list is growing daily. Donna raves about it to her clients as she styles their hair, Fiona encourages her cafe clientele to come along, and Pete mentions it on his postal rounds.

Rory, to my surprise, agrees that the breakup bookshop may have thawed the ice queen upstairs. He turns up one afternoon, paintbrush in hand, declaring it's time to fix the mural in the shop that Margaret seems so taken with. My heart thuds with appreciation; I haven't even had to ask him. Verging on friends with Rory is a much better place to be. I take over The Toolbox that afternoon and the following day, until it's completed. This time, I leave him a thank you note with a cheque for the full promised payment, tucking the envelope beneath a plastic waste pipe on his counter, so he doesn't miss it.

The next morning, as I gaze gratefully up at the mural, restored to its full glory, my phone processes the updates. Somehow, overnight, I've gained a whole raft of new followers on my social media pages.

I scroll through my feed trying to make sense of it. Several people seem to have tagged me in a post. I frown, wondering what has happened.

Then I notice that the great and gorgeous Richard J. Walker has tagged me in a post. I click on it. Not only has he written a social media post praising the bookshop, he's also included it in his weekly column in the *Daily Courier*. A national newspaper. My heart thuds in my chest as I access the link. This kind of publicity is priceless.

He starts the article by saying that an 'old friend' invited him to speak at a bookshop in Ullapool and goes on to say he's been 'utterly charmed' by the village's beauty, character and residents (I am pretty sure Eilidh is the only one he actually looked at while he was here, but that's by the by). He proclaims that The Next Chapter bookshop is fast becoming the beating heart of the Ullapool community, with its quirky ideas, from the blind-date books to the breakup support group. Apparently, he's been keeping up with my antics online.

Yes! I punch the air and step back out into the courtyard to call Eilidh.

'I'm in love with your ex,' I say, as soon as she answers the phone.

'Oh, good morning, Ava, you're on speaker. I'm taking Harry and Caden to school,' she shouts back.

'Oh, sorry. Hi boys!'

They call hello as I die inside.

'They're just getting out of the car now,' she shouts, and there are some muffled reminders about lunchboxes and schoolbags. 'Okay, they're gone.'

'Oops, sorry,' I say.

'Don't worry, they were squabbling so loudly in the back I doubt they heard you. Why are you in love with my ex?'

'He's written an article in the *Daily Courier* about his wonderful visit to Ullapool and my bookshop! I will kiss him if you don't!'

'Wow. That's amazing, Ava.'

'I know! I'm sending you the link right now,' I say, pinging it over to her.

She sits in silence for a moment as she reads the article. 'It sounds like he was completely captivated by Ullapool. When Mark first came here, all he could do was talk about leaving. But Richard writes about the place so beautifully.'

'The one that got away…'

'I don't know about that. Anyway, I'm delighted he was able to come along and write about the bookshop. Job done.'

'I need all the help I can get, don't I? Can't hide from you, Eilidh, the Ullapool Savings Expert. You've seen my figures.'

'It takes every new business time to get established and start making a profit. But yes, looking at the stats, you do need all these fantastic ideas and initiatives to start paying off soon,' she admits.

I take a deep breath. 'Okay. It will happen. I'm manifesting it. We're putting good energy into the universe that Richard J.'s article is going to propel the bookshop into financial success.'

'I'll stick to the spreadsheets.'

'We all have our strengths, Eilidh. You stick to your facts and figures, and I'll continue to live in a fantasy land with my books.'

'Well done on the article. Everything he said is true, by the way.'

'Send Richard a message to say thank you! And ask him on a date!'

She laughs again. 'I am not asking him out, Ava. But I will message. Just to say thanks.'

'You can say thanks with a dinner?'

Eilidh giggles as she hangs up.

I open the bookshop early after sharing the story on social media and then wait behind the till, willing someone to walk in so I can share the joy of the article with them in real life.

But no one appears, so I roll my blind-date bookstand outside the store, glancing around for someone, anyone, to talk to. Donna's salon isn't open yet and the streets are empty, but then Rory pulls up. It's 8.56, of course.

For a moment, my face flushes as I remember the almost-kiss that I likely made up in my head on the boat trip. I'd felt so close to him – something I'd never imagined. But he hates the idea of the bookshop, the support group, everything… Which is why he is the perfect person to share Richard's article with.

'*Soo*,' I say, sidling up beside his car and leaning on it. 'You know how you said that Ullapool doesn't need a bookshop. And then you said it didn't need a support group, because we should all just go to the pub and ignore our feelings…'

'I didn't say ignore them,' Rory says. 'I said—'

'Well, you weren't exactly on board with the idea of my bookshop. Put it that way. Anyway, here.'

I thrust my phone into his hands and add: 'Read it and weep.'

'Can I get out of the car first?'

'Fine.' I step back to allow him to open the door.

He stretches out his legs, clutching my phone, and reads the article.

'A message just popped up,' he says, glancing up at me. 'Someone called Seb?'

I swallow the salty taste in my mouth. I haven't heard from Seb since I texted him on whisky night. The last message I'd had from him was a thumbs-up when I told him I was leaving the flat and had posted my key through the letterbox. Six years of my life and that was all I got – a fucking thumbs-up.

I want to snatch the phone from Rory to see what the hell Seb said, but I don't want to appear too keen. Instead I shrug, in what I hope is a nonchalant manner.

I tap my foot against the pavement. What does the text say? Oh God, what if it follows on from Macy's message that I deleted? What if they are announcing their engagement? Or a *pregnancy*? I swallow, watching Rory's face studying my phone screen. When he finishes reading, he hands it back to me.

'Well done. Great article. Seb thinks so too.'

'Is that what he said?' I frown, scrolling to read the message.

Saw the article. Congrats.

Congrats. He can't even be bothered to type out a full word in recognition of my achievements. The bastard.

'Yup,' Rory nods. 'I take it he's the verging on grey guy? The one you're running away from?'

'Something like that,' I mumble, walking back into the bookshop. The wind has well and truly been sucked from my sails.

Four words: *Saw. The. Article. Congrats.*

How can he be so flippant about it? Surely I deserve more than *that*? A response to a drunken question, for a start: *Why Macy*? Total recognition of his wrongdoing along with full admission to the arsehole hall of fame?

There had been a sort of garbled apology at the time, but I'd cut him off. I didn't want to hear whether he planned a future with Macy or where he went while I was in his flat. I'd assumed he moved into her place for a bit. The one I'd spent days, weeks, months of my life in. Where we'd hung out watching endless episodes of *Grey's Anatomy* on her sofa. Where I'd helped her build her Ikea wardrobes. Where we'd hosted regular *Come Dine With Me* evenings. I would buy the dessert and she would cook up a storm for the other two courses because she was the most talented home-cook I knew, and she made the best carbonara I'd ever had.

We were best fucking friends, Seb.

Congrats.

'Glad to see the breakup bookshop is helping,' Rory calls.

I spin around. 'What do you mean by that?'

'Just that you obviously started the support group to get some closure from him. Now you've got him texting you again and you're wandering around like a fart in a trance.'

'I'm not,' I frown. 'I have work to do.'

'So do I,' he retorts.

'Well do it then.'

'I will.'

And suddenly – after our time at sea where we'd agreed to be friends and I'd felt for a second there might be something more; after his unprompted arrival to fix the mural – normal business has resumed. Rory and I are back to squabbling.

I sit down at the till and look again at Seb's message.

The audacity of him. Seb knew returning to Ullapool was my dream. While he talked about his six-point retirement plan, I spoke wistfully about coming here one day. He shrugged it off, like it would never happen.

Why does his 'congrats' feel like such a kick in the teeth?

Bloody congrats for ruining my day. My life.

Eilidh's name pops up on my phone and I answer the call, glad of the distraction.

'Get some lippy on,' she says. 'There's a TV crew on their way.'

I sit up straighter.

'Excuse me?'

'I texted Richard to say thanks for the article, like I said I would, and he said he got a call from a contact at the six o'clock news. They want to film a piece about the bookshop this afternoon! I'll be round in ten minutes. We need to make the place look as busy and fabulous as possible. Let's turn those red figures black, hey?'

'Eilidh, I...'

'Get your lippy on!' she repeats, barking the order like a sergeant major, and hangs up.

*

I pace up and down in the bookshop, chatting to customers as normal, but my head is spinning.

First Seb, now the six o'clock news. This day is like one of my weird dreams.

The presenter had called to confirm they would conduct

a short interview with me to show on television tonight. Apparently, it would all be very casual and would only take half an hour or so. I'd laughed along and said, 'Of course,' but as I hung up, I'd headed straight to one of my gorgeous, second-hand chairs to scream into a cushion. A mixture of fear and excitement is tumbling around my insides.

As soon as Eilidh arrives, we host a mini-fashion show in the middle of the bookshop to choose an outfit that screams 'successful businesswoman'.

Fake it till you make it.

'This is going to put you on the map. You could use it as evidence in that funding application I sent you,' Eilidh suggests, as I twirl around to show her the green and white paisley midi-dress.

'I've been thinking about that,' I say, as she nods her approval of my outfit choice. 'If the application is successful, I'm going to use the funding to set up a book festival here.'

'Brilliant idea! Brings revenue to the community – tick – and brings people together – tick. Get on to it as soon as you've finished with your five minutes of fame.'

Donna brings a box of make-up with her and orders me to sit down. As she sets to work on my face, Eilidh stands behind the counter, ready to serve customers in the bookshop.

'You would suit false eyelashes,' Donna observes, as she prods at my cheeks with a blusher brush. 'They'd be nice on camera too.'

'Tried them once before. Never again. The make-up artist forgot to tell me they were semi-permanent. I tried ripping them off at the end of the night and could only get a small section off. I couldn't leave it like that, of course. I had to pull the rest of them off and ended up with baldy bits for weeks.'

Donna rolls her eyes. 'Trust you. Okay, what time is the presenter arriving?'

'We have an hour to make me look amazing.'

'You already do, lovely,' Donna smiles, leaning in for an air kiss near each cheek.

'Hot off the press,' Eilidh says, approaching us, her phone in her hand. 'The television crew is in the area. They're down at the beach asking people what they think about the bookshop.'

'Oh shit,' I say, my stomach flipping. 'I hope Rory's not there. He'll go off on a rant about what a terrible idea it is.'

'He wouldn't,' Donna and Eilidh protest at the same time.

'I thought you two were friends now?' Donna adds.

'Not sure I'd go as far as friends,' I say. 'Neighbours. Everybody needs good neighbours. He's okay. Fine.'

Eilidh raises an eyebrow. 'Methinks the lady doth protest too much.'

'They may want to ask him about his mural,' Donna points out. 'It would be good to show that the local community has been involved in the shop renovation. It looks amazing now he's fixed it all up.'

'And it would help promote him as an artist,' I say. I think back to our conversation on the boat. Rory may not be encouraging of my goals, but I can take the moral high ground and support his. He is a fantastic artist, whether he admits it or not, and it *would* look good if the whole village were shown to be rallying around the bookshop.

It also won't hurt for Seb to see Rory support me on the national news. Someone is bound to send him the clip. A big, handsome Scotsman stepping in to prop up my business venture will leave Seb wishing he'd said so much more than 'congrats'.

I pop into The Toolbox and find Rory in deep conversation with an older man about power tools. I hop impatiently from one foot to the other until the man leaves.

'Ants in your pants?' he asks.

'The six o'clock news is on its way to interview me about the bookshop. You should talk about the mural. It would be a great way to get some interest in your artwork,' I say, the words tumbling out of my mouth.

He looks up at me, then back down at the notepad he'd started scribbling on. 'No thanks.'

'They're interviewing people around the village about the bookshop anyway. People should know it was you. You might even get some recognition—'

He puts down his pen. 'Ava, look. My mum called this morning. My sister is having trouble finding a nursery for the baby, so they're staying a bit longer until she's set up. It looks like I'm in charge for a while longer. So, thank you.

I do appreciate your offer, but I won't have time to do an interview or any artwork commissions, even if they were to come. Not now. Probably not ever.'

He lets out a long sigh, his shoulders slumping.

'Oh, Rory, I'm so sorry. I really am.'

He shrugs. 'It's fine. I've just got to get on with it, don't I? But thanks for thinking of me. Just as well you were the one who got the shop in the end. Look at what you've done! It would still be a shell if it was left to me.'

'Shit, Rory. I didn't want—'

'Don't worry about it. It's just… not the right time.' His tone is different. Lighter. Appreciative. Sad.

He looks up at me. I stand in the doorway for a second, unsure what to say. I have a sudden urge to envelop him in a hug, but I resist. Rory would hate that.

'Are you still here?' He offers me a small smile. 'Go on next door and get ready to show them everything you've got. Seriously, Ava, take the credit for it. You deserve it.'

I hesitate before turning to leave. 'Okay. We can discuss this at the next breakup bookshop. You'll be first up. We can just talk all around you, so you don't feel stuck in the silence.'

He laughs.

'By the way, Ava?'

I turn to face him again.

'You don't need me to back you up, you'll be great on your own,' he says. 'You look… beautiful, by the way. Good luck.'

My whole face flushes a bright shade of pink, which thankfully can't be seen under the fifteen layers of make-up Donna has applied.

'Thanks,' I whisper.

*

As the interview comes to an end, I blink at the bright lights behind the camera. I breathe a sigh of relief.

Just as Sarah, the presenter, is packing up, the door opens.

Rory.

'Ah, here's the artist that I mentioned,' I say, moving towards Rory, as though I'd expected to see him here all along. 'He painted the mural.'

Sarah takes one look at Rory and visibly swoons.

'Hi,' Rory says, throwing her a smile. 'Sorry to interrupt. I just wanted to see if you needed any quotes from locals or shop owners about the bookshop. It's such an asset to our local area. I can say it on camera, if you need any more interviews. I work in the DIY store next door.'

Sarah flutters her eyelashes as he folds his muscular arms across his chest. Hearing him say that, advocating for me and the bookshop, I too melt inside, more than I'd like to admit.

He is here, doing this for me.

Congrats.

'I thought you were an artist?' Sarah presses.

'That's more of a hobby. I'm happy to give a supportive quote, as a local shop owner, though.'

Sarah nods. 'That would be great.'

She is thinking the same as me – this handsome Scotsman being earnest and kind about small businesses will certainly help to boost her viewing figures. As the camera turns to Rory and I look at him, really look at him, and listen to him lie to the world that, from the beginning, he welcomed the bookshop with open arms, knowing it would be such a boost to the local area, my heart pounds in my chest.

Maybe, just maybe, things are looking a little brighter.

19

My phone blows up once the six o'clock news airs and I share the content on my social media feed. According to Donna – and she is definitely an authority on the subject – the whole village is talking about the bookshop putting Ullapool on the map. There is a stream of messages and calls from people looking to join The Next Chapter's support group too.

Even my mum messages with her ever-supportive words of wisdom: *Saw the show. Make-up was a bit drag queen.* She's added a clown emoji to drive the message home. I roll my eyes. Thanks, Mum.

Eilidh's delight over the news piece is short-lived, as another unexpected bill pops through my letterbox. Something to do with a licence fee, which apparently is overdue.

'This media interest is all very well and good, Ava,' Eilidh says, 'but we do need to think about money. You need to be able to pay your bills at the end of the month. Have you filled out the funding application yet?'

Annoyingly, she is right. And no, I haven't.

'You should charge people to attend the breakup bookshop,' she suggests.

I shake my head. 'I can't do that. It was set up to help people, not to make money.'

'Yes, but it's attracting the most interest in your business. It's your USP. You need to monetize everything to start making some profits.'

I shake my head again. 'We need to come up with another way.'

Let me think about it. I know you're right, but everything should start turning a corner at some point. My social media engagement is through the roof. Look at these figures.'

I point at my weekly interaction statistics, but Eilidh rolls her eyes. 'We can celebrate when that's your bank balance, Ava.'

'I'll get there. I'll get the funding application submitted soon,' I say, more confidently than I feel. I make to change the subject. 'Anyway, what's happening with Mark? Is he taking the boys with him on holiday?'

Mark recently asked whether he could have the boys during half-term. He'd said it would be good for them to bond with his new girlfriend before the baby came.

'Well, I still want to shove a parasol so far up his arse that he can't walk for a month, if that's what you mean,' she sighs. 'But I have to think about what's best for the boys. What kind of mother does it make me if I stop them from going on holiday? They *should* be having fun. I just can't stand the thought of them going without me. Making memories without me, you know? With her…'

Her voice starts to wobble and my heart breaks for her.

'Oh Eilidh, I know. I can't imagine how hard that would be. But the boys have an amazing life here with you every day. A week away won't change that. Plus, you could take them away sometime, too, if you wanted?'

She shakes her head. 'I don't think I could right now, Ava. It is taking all my energy just to get through the day, you know? I'm in sheer survival mode, doing the bare minimum until I can collapse in bed at the end of the night.'

'I get that. You should start thinking about what makes you happy, though, Eilidh. I know you're all about the sales and spreadsheets, but don't you have a passion for something? Maybe something creative that you could turn your attention to for a bit of an escape?'

'I don't have a creative bone in my body,' she says, and I laugh. 'But the books that you've recommended are good. I'm reading constantly. It's really helping me, actually.'

'Nothing like a good murder story to cheer you up. That was Granny's advice,' I say. 'Well, you're welcome here any time. You know that. And not just so you can lecture me on my finances, either. Will I get a bill for this chat, by the way?'

'As if. You know, you're right. I might just try and book a holiday, even if it's only away to a caravan for a few days. Our camping holidays were always their favourites.'

I smile at the idea of Harry and Caden, who have everything they could ever ask for and more, with the biggest house I'd ever seen in real life, losing their minds at the idea of a caravan holiday.

Having money isn't everything.

But not having it, well, I'm realizing that isn't ideal either.

*

Finlay pops his head into the bookshop at lunchtime. 'Hey, Local Hero. Can I have your autograph?'

'You'll need to speak to my agent.'

'How did you get Rory to agree to speak on national TV? He gets embarrassed if people overhear him talking in the pub.'

'I didn't ask him. Well, I did, and he said no. But then he changed his mind.'

Finlay raises an eyebrow and opens his mouth to speak, then closes it again.

'Where are all your little dog friends?' I ask. 'It's weird to see you without your army around your ankles.'

'I know, I feel naked without them. I'm on my way to Rory's to pick up Piper just now. Then I'm going to get Bonnie, Donna's poodle. She's high maintenance.'

'Donna or Bonnie?'

'Bonnie! I can only really take Bonnie on her own or with Piper. She gets anxious and nippy around the other dogs.'

'You could ask if Donna wanted to accompany you on a dog walk sometime? Or you could come along to the next breakup bookshop? I happen to know you'll find her here.'

The looks they give each other, the awkward little interactions, their shared history. There's definitely something unresolved between Donna and Finlay. While I know logically that relationships take a lot more to work than a shared interest in dogs, I can't shake the feeling that they're meant to be together. And that optimism is really something, coming from someone who is right at the bottom of a deep, dark love-hole. It would be amazing to see them try and work it out.

'I'm trying to avoid her right now,' he confesses.

'Why would you want to avoid her?'

'She hasn't told you? I *knew* she was embarrassed about it.' The tops of his ears turn pink.

'Tell me.'

'We had been getting… close again recently.'

My hand flies to my mouth. '*Close* close?'

'Yep, after the whisky night,' he nods. 'But she's clearly embarrassed about it or regretting it. She broke up with me all those years ago. I asked her to reconsider; I would have done anything to get back with her. I told her I was ready for the works: marriage, family, everything. I guess she didn't want that with me then or now. I should just move on and let her go again.'

He lets out a long sigh. Poor Finlay. I shouldn't have pushed him to tell me all this. Donna hasn't mentioned rekindling with Finlay *at all*, so maybe he's right. Maybe she does regret it.

'I'm sorry, Finlay,' I say. 'I shouldn't have pushed it. Maybe she's just… shy?'

He lets out an indignant laugh. 'You and I both know that Donna doesn't have a shy bone in her body.'

'She seemed shy around you at the launch night.'

'Mibbes aye, mibbes no. Anyway, I'm off. See you later, Ava.'

He offers up a weak wave as he leaves the shop.

I feel for Finlay, I really do. He's clearly still into Donna, but I have a horrible feeling he may be right about Donna's feelings for him. She talked about Lewis and all her problems with him at the breakup bookshop but said nothing about poor Finlay.

After closing the shop, I wander out to the courtyard at the back of the shops to perch on my usual spot, on top of the bin. As I angle my face to catch some late-evening sunshine, my phone starts to vibrate with messages. Over and over, people ask to join the support group due to take place the following evening.

A woman originally from the Highlands who moved to London asks to dial in if I can facilitate it for her. She saw the news piece online and hearing the Scottish accents made her homesick.

A woman in her early thirties from the neighbouring

village of Rhue, who is trying to give up alcohol, messaged to ask to attend after realizing she only had 'party friends' and no one wants to hang out with her sober. She hopes to come along to the support group to strike up new friendships.

A man in his early twenties from Lochinver asks to join. He's recently lost his job and doesn't want to bring his friends down by talking about it all the time. His girlfriend also recently dumped him and, while he understood the decision, he's struggling to move on.

My heart hurts.

A series of other messages from people who ask if they can come along fill my inbox. I know they all have their own stories to share, heartache to heal or just want to soak up some company. How can I say no to that?

'Exhausted from being a media sensation?'

My heart gives a little quiver as I hear Rory's voice. The woman from London is right. There *is* something about the Scottish accent, in all its gruff glory, that makes you feel a little flutter.

'I don't know. Are you?'

'I don't mean to boast, but requests have been flooding in since my television appearance. I've even been asked to nip to Margaret's on my way home to fix a carpet that she's worried about tripping over.'

'Living the dream.'

'You?'

'I may have bitten off more than I can chew,' I admit. 'The Next Chapter has grown arms and legs – I've got too many people and not enough space. Plus, I need to start making money or Eilidh is going to break up with *me*.'

'I would offer you The Toolbox, but I'm not sure people who are weeping about their breakups should have access to drills?'

'We're supporting one another, we're not unhinged.'

'If you say so,' he says. 'We could set up a rage room in the courtyard where you can all come out and smash things with hammers.'

I jump off the bin. 'The courtyard!'

'I was joking, Ava,' he says. 'Although, I suppose it could be a good idea...'

'No, I mean, I could use both spaces. I could divide the group in two: one lot inside, where people can talk in a group setting, and one lot outside, in the courtyard, where they can mingle and chat. Then we swap over. What do you think?'

'You could,' he agrees, observing the area. 'The courtyard needs a bit of a clear-up, so we'd need to start with that. We could store the bins in my shop for the evening to give a bit more space.'

We. The two-letter word makes me want to throw myself at Rory MacGregor.

'You're going to help me?' I ask, quietly. 'Don't you have somewhere better to be tonight?'

'I was going to go to my own support group, but I can skip it to help.'

'The pub?'

He nods.

'I could buy you a drink once we've sorted here?'

'I'll hold you to that.'

Rory hands me a pair of gardening gloves from his shop and I start pulling at the weeds. He takes the floor brush and sets to work, bin bag in hand, before disappearing inside mumbling about a power washer.

Within a couple of hours, the whole space has been transformed. After adding a few garden lights from his store, Rory nips home and comes back with a sideboard that he explains might work as a pop-up bar.

'Grab the other end,' he calls, as we lift it from the boot of his car.

We haul it into the courtyard and, sure enough, it looks perfect.

'I've got some fizz left over from the launch. I can leave some glasses out here and people can help themselves as they mingle,' I say, running my hand along the tall, narrow wooden unit.

Rory nods, wiping the sweat from his brow. 'Great. Speaking of fizz, is it time for that drink yet?'

'Sure.'

'Oh, I've got a small table and chairs set in the shop,' he says. 'That could work out here. Let me get it.'

I collect a bottle of Prosecco from my flat and meet him outside, where he's set up the garden furniture. Under the twinkling lights, it almost looks romantic.

'Have a seat,' he gestures.

I sit across from him and pop the bottle open. 'I want to say thank you for helping me, even if you think the breakup bookshop is a stupid idea.'

He shakes his head. 'Look, I'm the stupid one. Everyone loves it and it's bringing people together to talk about how they feel. What could be better than that?'

'The pub?' I suggest, and he laughs as I hand him the glass.

'At least there aren't any midges in the pub,' he says, waving his hand around to get rid of the insects buzzing around him. 'That's one thing you need to watch out for up here. Hold on, I've got a citronella candle; that'll scare them off.'

Rory dashes back into the shop and emerges with a lit candle in his hand. He places it between us on the small table.

'Good timing,' I say. 'It's going to be dark soon too.'

'Were you familiar with the humble Scottish midgie from your previous visits to Ullapool?' he asks.

'My granny never swore, but she used to curse the midgies like something fierce.'

I picture Granny tearing around the back garden in her dressing gown and slippers, armed with a can of bug spray. In my mind, I'm watching her from the book nook in the back garden, all cosy in a sleeping bag under the stars sparkling in the night sky. My laugh echoes around the garden as she calls them 'wee bisums' before declaring it bedtime. The familiar pang of regret reminds me that

I've not been to see Granny's cottage yet, but I still don't feel ready. I have to swallow back the tears tonight, just from the memory of her. I can't imagine seeing the place in real life and having to contend with the flood of memories.

'They're wee bastards, alright,' he says. 'But the candle seems to be doing the trick.'

Rory stands up to observe the courtyard, just as I stand up to fetch some snacks from the kitchen. After the sudden surge of emotion prompted by thoughts of Granny and the glass of Prosecco, I am unsteady on my feet. But he's right in front of me, strong and secure. As I wobble a little, he puts a hand on each arm to steady me. My heart thuds in my chest as he looks deep into my eyes.

'You okay?' he whispers, hands still on my arms.

I try and make light of it. 'You'll need to put all of this on my tab. Seriously, the garden gloves, the solar lights, the candle, everything.'

He shakes his head. 'Don't worry. It's good to see the courtyard area come to life. I've never seen it looking so good.'

But he isn't looking at the courtyard. He leans towards me, his eyes fixed on my lips. It is like the moment on the boat all over again, but this time there is no hyper child to interrupt us. Memories of the other times we've been close flood through my mind, from the ceilidh where he led me through the steps with expert precision, to the moment when I'd embraced him at the bookshop opening. I haven't been imagining this. Rory is here, barely a breath between us, and he is about to kiss me.

His hand lightly touches my arm again and I feel my whole body spring to attention.

As soon as his mouth meets mine, I melt into him and his kiss. For so long, I'd refused to let myself think of this, but somewhere in the back of my mind, I realize I'd hoped it would happen. I wrap my hands around the back of Rory's neck as he pulls me close to him. I move my head back for a moment and he follows suit, grinning at me, before launching back into the kiss.

I haven't been kissed like this in so long, I'd forgotten how good it feels to have someone so close. So present. He presses closer to me, his hands running through my hair before they trace the curve of my spine. Right now, I am lost, so completely lost, to Rory MacGregor. Here we are, kissing in the courtyard, like the two frisky teenagers we'd chased from this very space, and I never want it to end.

'Rory?'

We ignore the voice calling his name.

'Rory!'

The voice again. Surely they will go away.

'Shit,' Rory whispers. 'It's Margaret.'

'You were supposed to come over after work,' she calls from behind the courtyard wall. 'To look at the lump in my carpet.'

'Fuck,' Rory murmurs as he pulls away from me. He holds me close, leans in again, and pecks me lightly on the lips before moving to open the courtyard door. I bite my bottom lip, still feeling the warmth of his kiss.

'I'll be right over,' he calls. 'Just had a few bits to finish up here.'

'Well, I'm usually in my bed by now,' she calls accusingly. 'What's kept you?'

'I'll be there in two minutes.'

I arch an eyebrow as he moves back towards me. I think he's going to give me a light peck on the lips again and say goodbye. Instead, he cups my face and pulls me towards him for a deeper, more sensual kiss. I sink into his arms until he pulls away.

'That's one way of killing the mood, thinking of Margaret and her lumpy carpet. Look, I've got to go,' he breathes, stroking the back of my neck with one of his fingers. 'But I'll be back.'

'Tonight?' I respond, my voice croaking.

He isn't about to leave me hanging like this, is he?

Rory shakes his head. 'I can't. I've got to get back to Piper. I'll see you tomorrow, though. And the day after that.'

I nod, while my body screams inwardly. 'To be continued.'

20

That kiss, though.

How am I supposed to run a bookshop when all I can think about is Rory MacGregor's lips? I have a business to keep afloat. Deadlines to meet. As I brush my teeth, I gaze in the mirror. And the support group? How am I supposed to wipe this manic grin from my face while I listen to people talk about their heartbreak and grief? I can't hide the damn thing. My cheeks are flushed. I barely slept last night. Rory and I were on the phone until past midnight. We even had a 'you hang up', 'no, you hang up' back-and-forth at the end of the conversation.

I haven't felt this way in such a long time.

Since Seb.

Screw Seb.

I can't think about him. I can't let myself think about the last time this happened, because that ended in the worst possible way – in a pain so intense I had to move hundreds of miles away, back to the only place I'd ever truly felt at peace. Comfortable. Happy. And now, the grumpiest, sexiest Scottish guy in the village has made everything much better – and more confusing.

I check my phone for the millionth time: 8.30 a.m.

He will be on his way to work next door to me right now. I bite my lip.

I skip, literally skip, down the stairs, grabbing my jacket to head across the street to Donna's salon, where she's just opening up.

'Morning, my lovely,' she calls. 'You look like the cat who got the cream. Something to report?'

'Oh, you know, just wanted to tell you I followed your advice and made up with Rory' – I grin – 'with a big fat snog!'

Donna's mouth forms an enormous 'O' before spreading into a wide grin. 'You did not!'

'I did! But I'm only telling you. It's a secret, okay? I don't want every person getting their hair done today knowing about it, okay?'

'Scout's honour,' she says. 'Give me all the details.'

As I dish the dirt to Donna, I keep an eye out for his car. My heart thumps in my chest.

'Speaking of secrets… Anything *you* want to tell *me*?'

Donna sighs and begins to shuffle some papers on the till point. 'You mean Finlay, don't you?'

'Yes, I mean Finlay. I'd forgotten he was your first love; you were infatuated with him when we were younger!

He thinks you're embarrassed by your recent rendezvous, though. Any truth to that?'

'He thinks I'm embarrassed? He's the one that can barely look me in the eye,' she says. 'He's a sweetheart. It's just, well, it isn't meant to be. It took so long for us to be on normal terms again after we broke up all those years ago. I just can't believe we're back to square one.'

'That doesn't answer my question.'

'Oh look.' She points across the road. 'There's your Roreo. Get it? Like, Romeo?'

I laugh, shaking my head at her attempt to distract me. 'Right, I need to go and open the shop. But this subject is not closed!'

Rory is unpacking his car and I swing out of Donna's salon to meet him.

That kiss, though.

'Hey,' he calls, as I stroll across the road.

'Hey, yourself.' I walk closer to him and whisper, 'How am I supposed to work all day next door to you, knowing you kiss like that?'

His eyes hold my gaze. 'Maybe we could catch up after the breakup bookshop tonight?'

'I'd love that. Thanks again for your help getting the courtyard ready for my extra guests. And sorry we didn't make it to the pub.'

'My pleasure,' he says. 'My night finished on a high, so I can't complain.'

'Margaret's lumpy carpet?'

He laughs. I stand at the front door of the bookshop, key in hand, while he does the same next door at The Toolbox.

'How did you know?'

*

The Next Chapter support group spills out, as I'd hoped, into the courtyard at the back of the shop. Given the popularity, people ask me whether we could hold two sessions a week, and, seeing no reason not to, I agree. People arrive early and mill around, chatting to one another. I sell a few books I'd recommended at the end of the last session. Eilidh will be pleased.

As Margaret arrives, I hear her tell Fiona that she's been looking forward to the support group all week, which makes my heart happy. Pete makes a beeline for Donna as soon as he crosses the bookshop's threshold and they hug as though they haven't seen each other in months. New faces begin to filter in too, and I tick their names off the list. I introduce the guy who lost his job to the girl who's given up drinking, and they chat easily. Finlay turns up 'to see what all the fuss has been about'. He and Donna are quickly drawn into what looks to be another awkward exchange, but, watching them from a distance, I'm not sure either of them really minds. While they giggle and stumble their way through conversation, they don't take their eyes off each other. Pete seems to get the vibe and gives them some space, wandering over to talk with Fiona and Margaret.

As the group starts, I welcome everyone along, explaining that we will follow a new format tonight.

'We have a space outside for those who would prefer to have casual chats, and here, indoors, we'll be having more in-depth discussions. We're hoping that will suit everyone, especially as we have so many new faces. There's no pressure for anyone to speak, but please do if you would like to.'

I remain in the bookshop with Margaret, Fiona, Donna and Eilidh, along with some new faces, while Pete and Finlay make a sharp exit to the courtyard with the other men. A gender split isn't the intention, but when Fiona starts to talk about how much being menopausal has affected her, and not in her usual joking terms, I'm glad if it allows her to speak more freely.

'I was convinced someone stole my car last week from the Tesco car park. Convinced. I reported it to the security guard, was about to call the police, when he pointed out my car with the registration number I'd given him. It hadn't been stolen. I'd just forgotten I'd parked it somewhere different. The brain fog is a killer.'

'Oh, yes, I remember it well,' Margaret chimes in. 'The anxiety too. I cried once because I couldn't remember if my car took diesel or petrol. I stood there with a nozzle in my hand, completely paralysed with indecision. I had to call Bill to ask him what fuel to use. It's a nightmare.'

‘I’m so glad you’re sharing your stories. It’s so important that we get to hear of your experiences,’ Donna says, with an intensity that surprises me. ‘Women’s health and wellbeing isn’t spoken about as much as it should be.’

The front door pushes open. Donna jumps up and rushes over to welcome the new arrival.

‘I’m Elle,’ the girl says, grinning around the room. ‘Hi Ava, welcome back.’

I almost fall off my chair. Elle. An older version of the stunning girl I’d been friends with as a child stands in front of me. She shrugs off her beautiful double-breasted plum-coloured coat, revealing a sleeveless black and white waistcoat, a pair of black tailored trousers and trainers. ‘Trendy’, as my granny would have said. Elle takes a seat in between Donna and Fiona and sighs with a smile, looking around the circle.

‘I’m ba-ack!’ she grins.

Donna smiles at her friend. ‘Elle’s only here for one support group. We were just talking about how hard it is to be a woman, Elle. Care to join in?’

Elle grins, taking the book. ‘Aye, it’s shite, isn’t it?’

The group laughs.

‘What’s going on for you, Elle?’ Donna asks.

‘Well, first off, thanks for having me here. I love the idea of a breakup bookshop and the group, Ava. Genius. And this place looks amazing.’ Unlike Donna’s energetic, propulsive voice, Elle’s accent has the softness that I remember, a romantic Highland beauty. ‘I’m back home for a few weeks for a friend's wedding. I'm so happy for her, but it's just made me think how behind I am, you know?'

I hear you, sister.

'All of my friends are getting married and having babies,' she continues. 'I've been so focused on my career that I haven't got round to the serious stuff yet. It feels like I can suddenly hear the ticking timebomb that everyone talks about, you know?'

I nod. Elle is a kindred spirit, feeling like a failure, even though I bet she's achieved so much in her career already.

'And then right before this, I bump into my ex here. And I realize how simple it could have been if only I'd stayed, you know?'

Oh shit. No, I don't know. Well, I don't want to know. Abort mission. I can't listen to this. I don't want to know that she wants Rory back. I want to cover my ears and sing myself a happy song to block this out, but I can hardly do that.

'And what does your ex think?' Fiona asks.

'Oh,' she blushes.

Leaning forward to hear her answer, I almost fall off my chair. Oh? What does 'oh' mean?

'Well, we were first loves, I suppose. Everyone always said he'd have me back in a heartbeat,' she reveals. 'I'm not too sure about that, to be honest. I guess you never really know. He's going to the same wedding, though. I thought I could tell him how I feel while we're there?'

Fiona nods. 'You have to! No regrets. If you feel something for someone, tell them now. Life is too damn short.'

Noooo, Fiona! That's terrible advice. Well, not for you, but for Elle!

But everyone in the circle nods in agreement.

'Definitely too short,' Margaret adds.

'What if he feels the same way and is afraid to tell you?' someone else chimes in.

Christ. I nod along, pretending I don't know she is talking about Rory. I shoot an anxious look over at Donna, but she doesn't even look like she's listening.

Maybe, just maybe, it's not Rory. Perhaps Elle has a string of exes to choose from. He hasn't mentioned anything about a wedding. He'd struggle to get cover for The Toolbox, wouldn't he? I exhale. This might just be okay. Maybe I'm jumping to conclusions.

'So, you think I should say something?' she presses, looking around the circle.

Everyone nods. I find myself following suit; I don't want to stick out like a sore thumb.

'Why did you break up?' Eilidh asks.

'I was offered a job in Edinburgh. He couldn't come with me. We tried long distance for a while, but it just fizzled out.'

'What have you got to lose?' Fiona asks brightly. 'A wedding is the best place to rekindle a romance. Love in the air and all that. Gosh, you need to keep us posted. We're invested now.'

'Oh yes! You never know, it could be us coming to your wedding next,' Margaret adds.

'Okay, I'll do it,' Elle smiles. 'I can't promise it'll end in wedding bells, but I guess you never know.'

'How exciting,' Margaret breathes, grinning from ear to ear.

Is it, Margaret? I'm not so sure.

21

'Ava!' Elle calls to me at the end of the support group. She pulls me in with a warm hug as the group says goodbye and starts filing out into the street. 'It's so lovely to see you again! I can't believe you're back in Ullapool. You've done such an amazing job transforming this place. Is it weird for me to say I'm proud of you?'

God, she's so nice. And she smells delicious, too, as I inhale a waft of her expensive perfume.

'Not weird. And thank you. Ah, Elle, it's so good to see you too! I didn't see your name on the list, so I didn't know you were coming. What a lovely surprise.'

'Oh, sorry, Donna said I should pop in if I made it back in time. I hope I didn't put your numbers out.'

'Not at all,' I say with a wave of my hand, regretting that I even brought up the list. I didn't mean to accuse her of gatecrashing.

'I've got to dash just now, but we should catch up properly while I'm home over the next few weeks,' Elle suggests, and I nod. 'Get a dinner date or something. You, me and Donna, just like old times.'

'I'd love that.'

It would be lovely to catch up. But I just don't know how to feel about all of this. Elle trying to get Rory back, while I'm trying to forget how good his kisses are.

'After the wedding,' she promises, leaning in for a quick hug. 'See you soon. And wish me luck!'

Elle waves goodbye again and strolls out of the bookshop. She peeks into The Toolbox next door on her way past, even though it's closed and Rory's not there. He told me he would be building furniture tonight as a favour to one of his regulars.

As Margaret shuffles out with her stick, I look around for Donna. Surely she hasn't left without saying goodbye? I wander out to the courtyard, where she's standing, holding a mug of tea, staring up into the sky. She doesn't turn around and grin at me like she usually would. Instead, she remains still, watching the clouds in the evening sky. I want to leap in and ask her about Rory and Elle but sense that it's not the time for that.

'Can I ask you something?'

'Of course. Anything.'

'Before you and Seb finished… Say the cheating hadn't happened. What was next for you guys?'

I sigh, pulling my cardigan around me. 'We talked about

getting married then starting a family. I'd already started to think about nursery places. Apparently you have to practically register the day you conceive to land a space at a decent London nursery.'

'And how do you feel now… now that's not happened? The family part?'

'Sad, sometimes. Relieved, mostly. Imagine I'd found out he cheated on me when I was pregnant or had his child? Look at Eilidh. She's handling everything so well, but I can't imagine how hard it must be for her.'

Donna nods slowly. 'I know. She's amazing.'

'Is this about you and Finlay? Has something happened?'

She shakes her head. 'No, it's not Finlay. Look, I've got to get going. Thanks for tonight.'

She doesn't reach for her usual cheery hug. Instead, she walks straight to the back of the courtyard, opens the door and closes it behind her.

22

I can't find the words to mention Elle's bookshop revelation to Rory.

Days fly past as we go back and forth between our shops, share coffees and sneaky kisses. We're like the two teens we chased away by the bins. Someone always seems to be about to catch us in the act, whether it's Margaret passing by with her trusty stick, a customer looking for recommendations for a good memoir or someone asking when the next breakup bookshop is going to be held, but it only seems to spur us on. I don't want to burst our happy bubble with concerns about Elle and something that might not even happen.

It doesn't stop the nagging doubts, though. As soon as Rory leaves to serve a customer or drops me home after an evening walk, the thoughts start to swirl around my head. Maybe it is a mistake to be even thinking about being romantically involved with anyone right now. I'm not sure

I'm over the whole Seb and Macy thing yet. How on earth am I meant to think about a future? And what's the point if Rory is just going to bugger off back to Elle, the love of his life he's pined for since he was a child, and leave me in the lurch again?

Ah, yes. There it is. That's the problem. Who needs therapy? I've worked it out all by myself. I'm starting to develop feelings for the gorgeous DIY guy next door, who kisses me like I've never been kissed, and I'm scared it will go wrong, like it did the last time. Give me a psychology degree and be done with it.

But Elle said it herself – without knowing she had a very interested party in the audience: Rory would get back with her in a heartbeat if he could. If that is the case, where would that leave me?

One afternoon, after I spent twenty minutes helping a mum pitch the joy of reading to a very sceptical nine-year-old who still leaves empty-handed, Rory invites me to close the bookshop for lunch.

'Close it? Altogether?'

'Yes, as in, take some time to eat.'

'That's an interesting concept. I never close the shop to eat. I just eat.'

'I know. That's why I'm suggesting it,' he says. 'Call it a date.'

My to-do list shakes its head accusingly at me, and I'm sure my bank balance is screaming somewhere, but I don't care. Rory's right. I should take the time to eat lunch. It's one of the things I promised myself when I first moved here, before I started the renovation work. Now, the bookshop is open, I can take time. Not only that, but I have a big burly Scotsman asking for my hand in lunch.

'I'd love to go on a date,' I say, running through all the things I need to do before I leave, but it really is simple: lock the door and leave. 'Let me just grab my keys.'

'Let's go to the seafood place up the street,' he suggests, as he casually reaches over and takes my hand in his.

Oh, so we're doing this. We're walking out in Ullapool, hand in hand, like a real couple.

The seafood place has an outdoor area packed with tables and wooden benches, and a large van selling food. There's also a smaller van in the corner. A gin van. How come I haven't been here before now? This is a real hidden gem, just a few hundred metres from my bookshop.

We order haddock butties with garlic mayonnaise and a portion of chips to share. I can already taste the chips with their tantalizing salty smell. The server hands us a wooden spoon and tells us to listen out for our number. Rory takes my hand again as we sit down. Sliding my sunglasses over my eyes, I bask in the early afternoon sunshine.

It's lunchtime. I'm sitting outside in the Ullapool sun with a gorgeous Scotsman. How lucky am I?

'This is bliss. How come I've not been here before?'

'Work gets in the way. I had a customer in the store

for an hour earlier, asking for tips on panelling his living room. Says he attempted it himself, but his wife almost divorced him when she saw his efforts.'

'Sounds like they need the breakup bookshop.'

'Or a joiner.'

I roll my eyes, then smile at Rory. It's not like we suddenly agree on everything.

'I had a debate with a nine-year-old about the benefits of reading versus playing *Fortnite* for hours at a time. Pretty sure I lost. We should definitely come here more often. It's easy enough just to come along and place an order. Get it? "Plaice" an order?'

'Ah, come on,' he shakes his head. 'You're not fishing for jokes now, are you?'

'Oh my cod, yes, we have to!'

'What does a fish say when he meets the love of his life?' Rory asks and I shrug, grinning with anticipation. "I've met the gill of my dreams."'

I groan, even though I love it. 'This scampi happening!'

'Och, that's terrible,' he shakes his head. 'Cod you please calm down? You're being a *reel* pain in my bass.'

Our order number is called and Rory stands up to collect it. I stretch my legs out and rack my brains for more fish jokes as he sets the haddock bap, wrapped in paper, in front of me, putting the delicious salty chips in the middle of the table.

'I've had a realization,' Rory says as he slides onto the bench.

'Is this another fish pun?' I frown, trying to think if the word 'realization' has fish connotations.

He shakes his head. 'No. It's only a couple of weeks until I remove those green tiles from your bathroom.'

I pause and look across the table at Rory. He cocks his head to one side, a tentative smile on his lips.

'Ah, yes. Victory is within my grasp.'

'So you're staying, then? No plans for that crepe shop?'

There's something serious behind the question. I've never thought about it before, but suddenly it's staring me in the face. His whole *family* has moved away from Ullapool, all seven of his siblings to follow new paths, while his parents have no return date set. Even his ex – the lovely Elle – moved to Edinburgh. Now he's asking if the flighty girl that fled London to heal her heart is serious about this. About him.

Or am I planning to bugger off and leave him too?

I take his hand across the table and squeeze it. 'You're not getting rid of me that easily, Rory MacGregor. I'm more than ready for those bloody tiles to come off.'

A smile spreads across his face.

*

I wander around the bookshop in a post-lunch happy haze, making notes of books I need to order. I can almost feel Rory next door, moving around his shop, assembling his own order list. It's so strange how quickly everything's changed since the day I arrived here. I'm starting to discover the easy-going, caring Rory that everyone loves.

I can definitely see what all the fuss is about.

As he arrives at the front door in the early evening, he closes the door behind him and walks towards me, placing his hands gently on my waist. Is his gaze always this *intense*?

'You forgot the grout,' I point out.

He shakes his head. 'Not tonight.' As he pulls me towards him, my body melts into his.

My head screams at me to slow down and think this through. I can't ignore all the doubts creeping into my mind. Seb. All the things that went wrong. Elle. Everything that could go wrong. Ignoring them will not make them go away. But the rest of my body is on another page. In fact, my body is on an entirely different chapter.

'I bought you something.'

He hands me a tartan gift bag. I glance up at him. 'What is this?'

Rory doesn't answer. I pull the gift, which looks to be a small wooden plaque, out of the bag, and turn it around. The sign is covered in illustrations of books.

A 'Do Not Disturb' sign. A *book*-themed one.

Is he freaking kidding me?

All thoughts of Seb magically disappear from my mind, any questions about Elle completely erased, as Rory leans down and presses his mouth on mine. The kiss is more urgent than in the courtyard and I fall into it completely. Utterly.

My whole body sizzles as he lifts me up and carries me across the room to the bookshop counter. I place my hand behind me, sweeping the area clear, as he stops for a moment.

'I've always wanted to do that,' I breathe, before raising my mouth back towards his. He pauses. Grins. And then leans in to resume the sensational kiss that makes my body beg for more. He dips me slightly towards the wooden surface and my back arches.

'We need to close the blinds,' I murmur. 'Or we'll be the talk of the village.'

But Rory isn't one to follow my instructions. I should know that by now.

'Fuck that,' he says as he lifts me up again and lays me on the cool wooden ground behind the counter. 'No one can see down here.'

I pull his T-shirt over his head.

I dig my nails into his back. He groans.

He squeezes my upper thigh. I gasp.

My breath turns shallow as he presses his body into mine, gazing into my eyes while we move together against the cold wooden floor. I look away, my face flushed, but he places his hand on my cheek and moves my face around to look at him, really look at him, slowing everything down for a second.

'Stay with me.'

His low, gruff voice makes it sound like an order. An instruction.

So I do. My gaze doesn't leave his and I'm lost in the strength of this feeling, being this close to and making love with someone new and different. But somehow, in this moment, it feels like I've known Rory forever. His scowls and questioning smirks have been replaced with gentle movements and tenderness. There is no doubt about this, about us, as I feel his heart thud in his chest, or maybe it's mine. We are one, lost in each other.

Afterwards, Rory continues to kiss me gently and slowly, tracing his hand up and down my arms and along my back.

'What are you doing?'

He frowns. 'I think it's called kissing.'

'I'm aware of that. But we're… it's finished.'

He lets out a low, throaty laugh. 'So you're just going to throw me out and be done with me, now you've got what you wanted? I knew you southerners were cold, but that's another level.'

I frown as he leans back in to continue the kiss.

'No,' I say, interrupting. 'It's just… You're not going to pick up your phone and start scrolling through the sports results? Or roll over and start snoring loudly beside me?'

He moves back from me, his face breaking into a grin, as he shakes his head. 'That's not how we do things around these parts.'

'Oh,' I say, arching an eyebrow. 'So explain how it works in these parts then.'

'You invite me upstairs,' he says, kissing me on the lips. 'And we repeat. Again and again.'

'I'm starting to think I should have moved here a long time ago.'

23

We talk. We laugh. We touch. We kiss. We repeat, right into the early hours of the morning. As the sun starts to stream through the blinds, I open one eye and smile at the sight of Rory sleeping soundly next to me. I study the curve of his jawline, the stubble on his chin, his muscular chest and strong arms.

My alarm begins to beep insistently, and he groans, his hair skewed to one side.

'Make it stop,' he begs.

I laugh and find myself kissing him on the forehead without hesitation. 'We have to get up. What will people say if they see the bookshop and DIY store standing shoulder to shoulder with no one in charge? The whole village will demand an explanation.'

Rory grins. 'They'd probably say, "Looks like those two finally got their acts together and admitted they couldn't keep their hands off each other."'

‘Who would say that?’ I ask, pulling his arm over my head and snuggling into his chest.

‘Finlay, for a start. He’s been on at me to make a move since you moved back here.’

‘Really? He never said anything to me. I’d forgotten he and Donna used to date. Did you know they had a recent rendezvous?’

‘Aye, one or two,’ Rory says. ‘He never really got over her. But I’m not sure what Donna thinks. She keeps her cards close to her chest when it comes to Finlay. Has she ever mentioned it to you?’

‘Not since we were young. She used to wear her heart on her sleeve. I wish she would open up a bit more. She’ll talk the hind legs off a donkey, but when it’s something she cares about, she seems to struggle.’

‘Aye,’ Rory agrees. ‘And Finlay can *be* a donkey. I overheard him delivering a TED talk about dog flea prevention to her the other day. Insightful, but not the best when it comes to foreplay. Speaking of which, how many minutes do we have until we absolutely have to get up?’

He turns to kiss me as my alarm begins to buzz again.

‘We have to get ready,’ I protest, reaching for my phone. ‘Oh, shit, hold on.’

‘Did you just roll over and check your phone?’ he teases. ‘I told you, that’s not how we do things around these parts.’

*

Rory and I pop in to see each other frequently through the day, in between customers, and go for an evening walk by the sea. I invite him to stay at my flat again.

Repeat.

We repeat for days on end. Time passes quickly and I am walking on cloud nine. I am, dare I say, happy. Happier than I've been in a long time. Longer than I can remember.

I can't get enough of him. I try to stop myself. It is far too early to feel like this. But any time doubt creeps in, he is there, standing in front of me with a cup of coffee that I didn't ask for but desperately need, or offering to fix the wonky shelf in my bedroom. Within a couple of weeks, he's practically moved into my grungy flat and has drafted a list of DIY jobs to do around the place. The green tiles are top of his list, but, even though I've now been here three months and I won the bet, he insists I have to stay longer. He wants to change the green tiles. He wants me to stay.

'What if I change your tiles and you leave me high and dry? Like that was all you ever wanted me for?'

'Is changing my tiles a euphemism?'

It's hard to keep our relationship at a slow pace with Rory right next door. I can't seem to stop myself from popping through to The Toolbox to talk, to touch and, sometimes, just to see his face. He lines up little surprises for me, from buying books I mention I like, to dropping in with coffees and the little buns he knows I love from Fiona's cafe.

We take walks after work around Ullapool and spend our nights by the cosy fire in the pub before he stays in my flat. I show him my Pinterest boards and ideas for the flat's transformation, and he helps me make lists of what I'll need for each room, once I have the money in place.

One evening, just before our shops close, a huge bouquet of flowers appears at the bookshop, with Rory hiding behind it.

'What are these for?' I ask, kissing him lightly on the lips before taking the flowers from his hands. They are a beautiful array of chrysanthemums and pastel roses.

'You are cordially invited to dine at my house this evening,' he says, puffing his chest out.

'At your house?' I repeat, swallowing.

Rory pointed out his house to me, from a distance, when we climbed up a hill one evening. It is in the same direction as my granny's cottage. To get there, we'd have to pass the lane that leads there.

I'm just... I'm not sure I'm up to it yet.

'Yes, my house. I'll cook.'

'You'll cook? I mean, I'd love to, but I can't risk it. The last thing I need is a bout of food poisoning.'

I smile, but my heart thumps in protest as panic sets in. I can't go there, not yet. I'm just not ready. As I hold the heavy flowers in my hand, I rack my brains for an excuse not to go. It's ridiculous, but I realize that by keeping the bookshop I've been trying to keep my granny alive. If I pass her house, see someone else in it, I'll know she's really gone.

'I'll have you know, I'm an excellent chef,' he says. 'Okay, maybe excellent is a stretch, but I can cook up a decent dinner.'

I shake my head. 'I can't. Sorry, Rory, not tonight. I have work to do. I need to finalize that funding application for the bookshop. Eilidh's been nagging…'

He frowns. 'I thought the deadline was next week?'

I bite my lip. 'Eilidh said the earlier the better.'

'We can have dinner tomorrow, then.'

'Or… next week?'

It's another piece of advice from Granny: if you don't know what to do, kick the ball into the long grass. Buy yourself some time. I need time right now.

He raises an eyebrow. 'Next week? Ava, we spend loads of time at your place. Why don't you want to come to mine for dinner?'

His green eyes darken as he frowns. Shit, he looks hurt. I want to explain to him, but I'm embarrassed. Imagine being an almost thirty-year-old who can't take a casual stroll down memory lane without the fear of bursting into uncontrollable sobs. I can't let Rory see me like that. Being here in Ullapool means I feel close to Granny, but I'm just not ready to face the loss of her physical presence from her cottage.

I just can't.

'I've… got a lot on my plate,' I say, my brain searching for a way to cover this up. 'The bookshop isn't doing as well as I'd hoped, from a financial perspective. And I'm not sure what I'll do if it carries on like this.'

It's not a lie. I do need to fill out the funding application. Not tonight, but now would be as good a time as any. I swallow as he narrows his eyes.

'What does that mean? What will happen if you don't get the funding?'

I sigh. 'I can't think about that just now.'

'You'll leave, won't you?'

His spiky tone surprises me.

'I didn't say that.'

'But you might?'

I frown as his face flushes a deeper shade of red.

'That's why I have to do the funding application, Rory. I can't just sit around hoping things improve. I need to make things happen. I haven't been handed a successful business, you know.'

The sides of his mouth turn down. 'What, like me?'

'Your business is well established. You don't have to worry the way I do.'

'Oh, okay, great, thanks for letting me know.'

He turns around to leave.

'Where are you going?'

'Home. You're welcome to the flowers, if you decide to stick around long enough.'

He's gone before I can protest.

Our first fight. Well, hardly our first fight.

Just the first one where it feels like a punch to my gut.

24

I toss and turn all night.

The flowers. The offer of a home-cooked meal. The invitation to his house.

Most girls would have jumped at the chance.

And what had I done? Blown it. Instead of explaining my hesitation, instead of opening up and being honest like I tell everyone else to be, I'd started to babble about funding applications. And now the possibility of this new, sweet relationship that I can't get enough of feels like it could come crashing down at any moment. I'd made him feel like having a successful family business was his fault, even though I knew he was fulfilling his family duty. Worst of all, he thought I'd gone back on my word. I'd said I was staying here and now it looked to him like I might not. God, I'd messed up.

The next morning, I wait outside his shop, the flowers he'd given me in hand. He arrives, at 8.56 a.m. on the dot. I hover, waiting for him.

'An apology,' I say, holding the flowers out to him, as he climbs out of the car. 'Can we talk?'

He looks at me thoughtfully and nods. 'Sure. Come in.'

As he opens The Toolbox, I follow him inside.

'I'm sorry about last night,' I say. 'The reason I didn't come to dinner... I should have told you. It's just... your house is near my granny's house. I haven't been there since I moved to Ullapool. I haven't had the courage. I'd be an emotional wreck. I should have told you that.'

He looks me in the eye and nods. 'Are you sure that's why you didn't want to come? It sounds like you're freaking out a bit.'

'About what?'

'Us,' he says. 'This. I know you were hurt by the verging on grey guy. You moved hundreds of miles to get away from him. That's why you started the breakup bookshop thing in the first place. You needed to talk about him so you started the group. You're not over him, are you?'

My mouth falls open. 'It's not... I'm not...'

'Ava, it's fine, you don't need to explain.' He shakes his head, unwilling to look me in the eye.

His shoulders slump. He looks even more crushed than I feel. His eyes are heavy and bloodshot too. Looks like I'm not the only one who struggled to sleep last night.

'But I want to!' I protest. 'I really want to. It's not Seb, I promise you. It's the thought of seeing... Oh, God, it sounds so stupid when I say it out loud. I want to see her house, but she won't be in it, and that will kill me, Rory. I still picture her there, even though I know she's not. And the support group… that's not just about breakups. It's about opening up about loss in general. And it's not just for me, it's for everyone.'

He's quiet. I search his eyes for a hint of understanding, but I'm not sure he gets it.

'Look, in my mind, my granny is still there making scones and jam, fixing up the book nook outside with cushions and waiting for me to come home for the summer. I know it sounds stupid, but that's just the way I feel.'

Tears spring into my eyes and he sighs, taking my hands in his.

'I really want to go there, Rory. I'd love to see it now. But what if they've changed everything? What if the cottage is completely different or the book nook is gone? I love the idea of it just down the road, exactly as she left it.'

Rory pulls me towards him, wrapping his arms around me, and kisses the top of my head. My heart thumps in my chest, relieved to feel his warmth and comfort. 'You don't have to come to mine just yet. We can work up to it, okay?'

I nod. 'I'm sorry. It sounds so stupid and childish.'

'I'm sorry too,' he murmurs. 'I shouldn't have pushed it.'

'You weren't to know.'

'Our first official couple fight,' he says with a smile, pulling back to look me in the eye.

I grin. 'Is that what we are now?'

'I think so,' he nods. 'Now let's get that funding application finished, so you have no excuse to leave.'

I nod as he leans down to kiss me.

*

The next afternoon, Rory's phone pings from its position on my shop counter. He immediately grabs it and stuffs it into his back pocket before kissing me lightly on the cheek and heading back to his shop.

I can't help the prickly sensation that creeps up my spine.

The last time someone hid their phone from me it was Seb. I hadn't even given it a second thought. Now I know I really should have. I wonder how many secret messages and clues I'd missed between Seb and Macy.

How long had it gone on for?

Had Macy been texting Seb behind my back when we'd been on nights out together, singing 'Girls Just Wanna Have Fun' on karaoke or watching Netflix crime documentaries together. It still stings. As much as I can't admit it to Rory, it hurts. He's right; my guard is up. I push it to the back of my mind, serving a handful of customers for the rest of the day. But by the time Rory returns at five o'clock, I've been spiralling for hours. I don't want to be that girl who feels jealous and suspicious every time a text pops up on his phone. I'm not that girl. But I can't help myself. In the aftermath of being let down so brutally, this appears to be what I've been left with.

Maybe he's right. Maybe my reluctance to go to his house runs deeper than I'd thought.

He grins at me, unaware of my thoughts. 'I have a surprise for you.'

'A surprise?'

'Don't worry, I won't ask you to wear a blindfold.'

'Where are we going?'

'I found out who lives in your granny's house.'

My stomach tightens. I can't. I don't want to think about someone living there.

'They're out tonight. They've said I can take you round there to see it, if you'd like to go and have a look around. I just thought, well, maybe it would be easier to see it without anyone actually being there and breathing down your neck. But there's no pressure, Ava.'

I exhale slowly. 'Who? Who lives there?'

'You want to know? You're sure?'

I nod. 'Yes, I do. Who is it?'

'It's Fiona.'

'Oh!' A smile spreads across my face. 'Fiona? From the cafe?'

'That's good?'

'Fiona lives in Granny's house. Wow, that's amazing. I can't believe it!'

'Would you like to go and see it?' he asks, tentatively.

I nod. 'I… I think I would.'

As we leave the bookshop and reach the path I've avoided for months now, the stones crack beneath our shoes. Rory reaches for my hand as we make our way along. We approach the fork in the road which leads to Granny's cottage, and he stops dead in the middle of the track.

'Are you sure about this?' Rory says. 'There's no pressure. We could just turn back and forget about it.'

I nod again. 'We'll go. To Fiona's house.'

It's unexpectedly comforting, thinking of the lovely Fiona living in my granny's house. Fiona, who loves to bake as much as Granny did, and who's been so supportive of me and my life in Ullapool. I couldn't have asked for a better new owner of my granny's cottage.

I'd always known I'd have to make this trip at some point. I want to. And it feels a million times better doing it with Rory by my side.

'You can go alone? I can wait here?' Rory offers.

I glance up into his kind eyes.

I shake my head and pull on his hand. 'Come with me.'

He nods and grips my hand as we walk together along the pathway towards Granny's cottage. My heart pounds in my chest. I feel the buzz of arriving here at the start of each summer, the relief of leaving the city behind to breathe in the fresh sea air, followed by the thrill of riding down the lane on my bike at a million miles an hour.

As we turn a corner and I catch a glimpse of the stone cottage, I feel my heart swell in my chest. It's as quaint as I remember it. Whitewashed, with a slate roof, smoke puffing out of the chimney even in the summer, just like Granny used to have it. I am home. I picture my granny waving at me from the window as she cleans the dishes – one of her favourite chores. She'd been appalled when I suggested she invest in a dishwasher.

Wash your mouth out and grab a drying cloth, Ava Campbell.

The window ledges have been painted a deep black and the curtains are much brighter and bolder than my Granny would have chosen. I smile at the red polka-dot curtains, thinking they are just Fiona's style. Granny would have hated them. But it doesn't matter. I can still feel her presence here. I inhale deeply and exhale again, proud of myself for keeping it together.

'Are you okay?' Rory asks in a low voice. 'Has it changed a lot?'

I nod. Yes, it has changed. But also, yes, it's okay.

I can handle this.

I point at the front door, which Fiona has painted a bottle-green colour. 'She would have appreciated the green, but she'd never have been brave enough to paint it that colour herself. She would bring in colour through furniture and soft furnishings, but the rooms were always painted white or cream.'

'So, you didn't get your love of colour from her then.'

I smile, for a second. My love of bright colours was shared by another person. Macy. And now she's verging on grey. I wonder if she's coming up against the same challenges with the decor that I did. Oh well, that's her problem now.

I place my hand on the door handle, the same one that I clutched with excitement every summer, and I turn it. The door swings open. I blink, taking in the surroundings.

As I gaze around the porch area, I can feel Granny urging me to come in and make myself at home, *but for goodness' sake, would you take those muddy boots off.* I can hear her voice beckoning me inside. I can smell the waft of freshly baked scones from the kitchen. I stop on the spot and close my eyes.

'We don't need to go any further,' Rory says.

'I want to,' I assure him.

Despite the change in furniture, colour and photographs, I can still picture the way it used to be. I can still see her in each room. My fear that by seeing this place I'd know she was really gone turns out to have been false. She is still with me, even now. I take her wherever I go.

'That corner over there' – I point to a slight dent in the wall – 'I can't believe it's still there! Granny told me I wasn't allowed to roller skate inside. I did it while she was hanging up the washing and crashed into the wall. I skinned my knees and tried to convince her it was from playing outside, but she knew the truth as soon as she saw the dent.'

'Were you a rebel?'

'No, I was usually good as gold for Granny. At first, I was scared she wouldn't let me stay here if I put a toe out of line, but after the first summer, I realized that she enjoyed having me as much as I loved being here. Whether I was naughty or good.'

I glance out of the kitchen window into the back garden, a place that I used to spend hours playing in.

'Oh, Rory!' I call, opening the door to the back garden. 'Come and see!'

Outside, the space is exactly how I remember it. The reading nook that Granny created for me has been repainted, but, aside from a refresh, the area is untouched. I open the nook and, sure enough, find a row of books that Fiona bought from me, from my bookshop.

'Oh, my heart,' I say, pulling him onto the chair beside me. 'This is where I used to spend hours, reading every book I could get my hands on.'

He pulls me closer to him and kisses me on the cheek.

'No funny business in Granny's garden,' I warn him.

He nods with a smile as I look around, soaking it all in, from the long stretch of green grass to the view of the mountains in the distance that always made me feel so small. I remember looking at them from this exact angle, feeling so insignificant, while my granny made me feel like the most important person on the planet.

I feel my eyes fill with the inevitable tears. God, I *miss* her.

Rory pulls me in towards him, stroking my hair as the tears land on my cheeks. He wipes them away and kisses me gently. 'I know it's hard.'

'But it's also happy,' I sniff. 'My happiest childhood memories are right here, in this garden. Granny would be so happy to know that I'm back.'

'Do you think she would approve of me?'

'She would,' I whisper in reply. 'I know she would.'

We sit there for hours, watching the sun set over the mountains.

I feel at peace.

*

As we follow the road towards Rory's house, lights spring to life, illuminating the path.

'Sensors,' he explains, as we traipse up the gravel walkway. At the end of the path, we turn a corner to see a large detached home surrounded by an immaculate sprawling lawn.

'You didn't tell me you lived in Downton Abbey,' I gasp, gazing up at the huge windows.

He laughs. 'It's the family home, remember, not just mine. And for eight kids.'

'So you're not filthy rich, just your family?' I ask, squeezing his hand. 'God, now I'm embarrassed. You've slept over in my tiny flat with tiles falling off the walls and a lounge the size of a shoebox. My whole flat could probably fit in your living room.'

'I love your flat,' he protests, taking his house key from his pocket as we enter the large, tiled porch area at the front of the house.

'Do you have a title or something? Oh my God, am I sleeping with the Duke of Ullapool?'

'You'd better wipe your feet,' he warns. 'The serving staff hate it when we bring dirt in from the roads.'

'You have *serving* staff?'

He pushes on the brass door handle. 'Nah. I usually let them have a few weeks off after a busy summer of soirées.'

Judging by the house's interior, I'm not even sure he's joking. A grand staircase sits proudly in the middle of the entrance hall, its grey tartan carpet contrasting with the bright white panelled walls. There is even a chandelier hanging proudly above the staircase, with paintings adorning the walls.

'Your paintings,' I breathe, gazing up at them.

He nods. 'How did you know?'

'They're like the shop mural,' I say. 'On speed.'

'I spent a bit more time on these,' he nods. 'As the house got quieter, I found myself painting more. It made it feel less empty.'

I nod, gazing up at his artwork, landscape paintings with the vibrant colours and intricate details that have become so familiar to me. If I didn't know it before, it's obvious that Rory is a true artist. His paintings are at home here, surrounded by all this decadence. This is what he is supposed to be doing with his life. The Toolbox is great, as a family business, but Rory should be selling paintings to people who admire his work.

'You're so talented, Rory,' I tell him. 'You need to make more time for your artwork.'

'Ah, shucks. You're making me blush.'

'Seriously, though,' I say, following him through the hallway into an enormous open-plan kitchen. 'And I can't believe you live here all by yourself.'

'Well, I do just now,' he says. 'Sit down and I'll rustle up some dinner. I prepped it this morning, so it shouldn't take long.'

But I can't sit down. As Rory sets to work, throwing vegetables in the pan to make a stir-fry, I take the chance to explore the vast space. I am particularly drawn to the family pictures that adorn every wall in the kitchen and dining spaces, from his parents' wedding pictures to graduation photographs, family shots and holiday snaps.

'Where are you?' I ask, peering up at the wall. 'I can't pick you out at all.'

'It's a bit like Where's Wally, isn't it?'

I peer more closely at a picture of the family of ten, where Rory is presumably the baby on his mum's knee.

'Aww, so cute!' I tease him, walking up to grab his face. 'There's Wally. You've got such chubby cheeks!'

He leans down and pops a kiss on my forehead. 'Don't tease me when I'm working with a hot stove.'

I grin, walking back to the photos, and frown at the picture that features a group of young people down at the seafront on a gorgeous, sunny day. I spot Finlay's bright red hair straight away. He's younger, sixteen or seventeen. The age he was when he was the love of Donna's life. A tall, lanky, awkward-looking teenager stands beside him, wearing thick-rimmed glasses. His brown hair is long, down to his chin, and he glares at the camera.

'Mackie!' I exclaim, pointing at the picture.

Rory's head shoots up. 'What did you say?'

'That's Mackie! I used to see him in the summer when I visited my granny. I don't remember seeing Finlay, but I remember Mackie. We used to skim rocks into the sea together. What's he doing here?'

Rory switches off the pan. His eyes dance between me and the floor. Several seconds pass. I wonder what I've said. He looks up, gazing at me over the long kitchen island.

'You remember that?'

'Yes, of course. We used to have these amazing conversations about life and travel. I told him how much I wanted to live in Ullapool, then my plans to move to London and study marketing, while he would talk about wanting to go backpacking. Wait, he's not one of your brothers, is he?'

Rory stops, completely still for a moment, a flash of something crossing his face. I'm not sure what's happening here. Who is Mackie to Rory? Why does he seem so thrown that I know him?

'Ava, that was me. I'm Mackie,' he says finally.

He looks crestfallen as I frown, confused. 'No. Wait, what?'

'We had a handshake one year,' he says. 'Do you remember? We used to practise it down by the sea the first day you came back.'

'Oh my God,' I gasp. 'How can you be Mackie?'

'Short for MacGregor,' he says, his face turning pink. 'It's what my friends called me when I was younger.'

'Why didn't you tell me? Wait, do you remember me from back then?'

His cheeks flame as he starts to pile the food on the plates, avoiding eye contact with me. 'Of course I do.'

I walk towards Rory and put my hand on his arm. He flinches. And suddenly I see him, I see Mackie. In the concerned crease of Rory's brow, in the vulnerability in his eyes, I see the boy I spent my summers with.

'Why didn't you *say* anything?'

He doesn't look up.

'Rory!' I urge him to meet my gaze.

'I was going to,' he says, reluctantly. 'On that first day. Then you got all stubborn, insisted you didn't need help and stomped away in a huff. And it was obvious you had no idea who I was, so I thought it best to leave it.'

'You should have said! Rory, I can't believe this.'

'Having to remind someone who you are is pretty embarrassing. And I've still got that gawky teenager inside me sometimes, you know?'

I swallow, watching as he picks up the plates and carries them to the dining table.

'In my defence, Mackie,' I say, following him over, 'you look pretty different now. You've had a bit of a glow up.'

Rory's eyes darken as he walks across the room and sets the plates down on the long dining table that looks like it can seat fifteen people. We sit down, just the two of us, and he sighs. 'Look, I get that I've changed. I barely opened my mouth for two years because I was so embarrassed by my train-track braces. I was ashamed of myself, of Mackie. I begged people to start calling me Rory because I wanted to be someone new. You didn't like me then and you fancy me now. I get it. It's fine.'

'That's not true. I *did* like you then. My friend back home even teased me about it… About you. I just wish you'd told me before now, Rory. I wish you'd said something.'

'Yeah, well, I didn't.'

I swallow hard and take a seat across from him.

This is why Rory has blown hot and cold with me. He's been embarrassed that I didn't recognize him. He'd thought of me as this big-shot city girl with all the confidence in the world, who completely overlooked him. And can I blame him? I think of how I would have felt if the scenario had been switched and it was Rory – Mackie – who didn't recognize me. I'd be upset.

I place my hand over his at the table. 'Look, I'm really sorry I didn't recognize you. But I do wish you'd told me.'

I exhale, feeling my legs shake. It's so confusing. Rory's been keeping this a secret from me while he calculates ways to annoy me? The cutting comments, the junk mail, the hole in the wall. Why? To make me like him? He doesn't say a word.

'You should have said something, Rory,' I say again. 'I'm sorry I didn't recognize you. I know that will have been hurtful. But you've hidden this from me and now, for some reason, you're the one that's angry with me?

You're the one who's been keeping secrets. I genuinely had no idea who you were, while you've known who *I* am the whole time. You knew my granny, too, didn't you?'

He pauses for a moment, before his voice cracks. 'I'm sorry, Ava. I should have said something. I just felt so stupid.'

Suddenly I don't feel hungry.

'I don't like secrets,' I whisper, taking a sip of water from the glass on the table. 'This could have been something lovely, Rory. I don't have shared memories with many people. It would have been amazing to be welcomed with open arms to Ullapool, instead of thinking for weeks you didn't like me.'

He places his hand on mine. 'I never disliked you. Far from it. I… I'm sorry I made you feel like that.'

We eat our dinner in silence.

25

As I glance out of the car window on the way home at the dark night stretching in front of us, I feel deflated. Rory could have opened up to me, but instead he'd stomped around making a fuss about every little thing. Every interaction had been laced with tension when we'd first met. Now I know why, and it didn't have to be like that.

As he pulls up and stops outside the bookshop, I turn around to face him. 'The trip to my granny's house was special. Thank you for organizing it.'

'I'm sorry the evening didn't continue that way. I was embarrassed that you didn't recognize me. I felt like I was that awkward teenager all over again.'

I sigh. 'I just can't get my head around it.'

He nods. 'Look, you'll have a few days to clear your head while I'm away at the wedding. We can talk about it when I get back. Maybe we'll feel better then.'

I frown. 'The wedding? What do you mean?'

'The wedding,' he repeats, without skipping a beat. 'Remember, I told you?'

He hasn't told me. I've been on high alert for any wedding discussion since Elle dropped the bomb at the breakup bookshop. I can assure Rory that he hasn't mentioned any wedding.

'No, you didn't,' I frown. 'Who's looking after the shop?'

It's not the question I want to ask, but my head is completely scrambled.

'Pete. Someone from the post office is helping with his shifts for a few days.'

'You're going for a few days?' I repeat.

Stop sounding so shrill, Ava. Calm down.

'Sorry, Ava, I thought I'd told you. An old friend is getting married in some fancy hotel in Inverness. I'm a groomsman so I need to drive up first thing tomorrow to help my mate with a few things at the hotel before the rehearsal. I would have asked for a plus one, but we're so new together and I didn't want to put that pressure on you.'

He didn't want to put pressure on me? A million questions run through my mind. I can't tell Rory about Elle's confession. What happens at the breakup bookshop stays at the breakup bookshop, after all. Chatham House rules.

My stomach churns at the thought of them together. Rory's so casual about it all. I want to demand to see a full itinerary, broken down by the hour, but I need to keep my cool.

'Who else is going?' I ask. 'Finlay?'

I'm trying to appear nonchalant, but I want details. Does he know Elle will be there?

He shakes his head. 'Finlay couldn't make it. And he's looking after Piper for me. I was sure I'd mentioned that too. God, where has my head been? Elle will be there. She's a bridesmaid, I'm sure.'

A-ha.

Yes, she is going to be there. And she's going to confess that she still has feelings for you.

My heart drops into my stomach.

I can't think straight.

I want him to know how disappointed I am that he lied to me or withheld this from me, whatever he wants to call it. I want to pour out my heart to him, beg him not to go, warn him that Elle is going to make a move on him and plead with him to say no.

But what good will it do? Not much, not really. Maybe he's right. Maybe a few days away will be good for us. Maybe he'll realize it's Elle that he's wanted all along. At least then I'll know and have none of the uncertainty.

I guess now I have to be prepared for that. It's not like I can grab his ankle and beg him not to leave.

'Okay,' I say evenly, even though there are so many other words flying around my mind. 'Well, have a great time then. I'll see you when you get back.'

I open the door and leap out, trying to stifle the tears in my eyes.

'Ava!' he calls from the car. I turn around. His arm is draped over the side of the car, the window wide open. His eyes shine earnestly in the moonlight as he says, 'Look, we'll talk about it when I'm back, okay? All of it.'

I pull out the keys from my bag and nod, unable to meet his eye as the window closes. He speeds off into the night.

26

My head is all over the place following Rory's departure. I find myself checking my phone every five minutes and spend an unhealthy amount of time hovering around the bins, to see if a message will pop through. But, so far, nothing.

I've never been one for moping around. Even when Seb cheated on me, I lost my job and felt like my world had imploded, I started to make my escape plans. But this feels different. Even though Rory's away, I feel like I'm surrounded by him. Pete whistles away in the shop next door, while I catch sight of Finlay taking Piper up the hills for a walk. Every time the bookshop door opens, I expect to see Rory popping through for a chat, or a rant, or a cuppa.

I miss him already.

By the morning of the wedding, I am contemplating a trip to Inverness, to halt the wedding just to take the handsome groomsman off their hands and claim him as my own. I'm in countdown mode, wondering when the ceremony will finish, where the pictures are being taken and when Elle will take her chance to drop her love bombshell on Rory. It is the perfect night for The Next Chapter support group and, desperate for company, I'm ready to welcome everyone with open arms. I won't even care if Margaret complains that the toilet's not flushing.

I'm in good company too. Eilidh is glued to her phone as she arrives, awaiting updates from Mark. She eventually agreed to the boys travelling abroad to Spain and has come along to the bookshop early, for some company, to keep her mind off things. She curls her long red hair around her fingers.

'You're almost as bad as me,' she says as I hover with my phone in the air near the bookshop's front door. 'I just want the text that says they've arrived safely. What are you hoping for?'

'A bloody miracle,' I say, explaining the whole situation to Eilidh, from start to finish.

'No way, so Elle was talking about *Rory*?' she says. 'Are you sure? I don't even remember them being together. It can't have been for long. Maybe she has more than one ex at the wedding?'

'I tried to tell myself that it wasn't going to be Rory. But that would be a pretty big coincidence. And he "forgot" to tell me he was going to a wedding. Who forgets to tell someone something that significant?'

'He's been single for a long time,' Eilidh reasons. 'He's probably not used to keeping someone in the loop.'

It may be true, but it still stings.

'If I hadn't known Elle's plans, I probably wouldn't even care that he forgot to mention the wedding. But we didn't part on good terms. I just can't believe he has known me this whole time but didn't tell me. I don't like that he's been lying to me. Or that we had the fight when Elle is about to confess her undying love for him. Most of all, I hate the bloody wedding. I just want it to be over and done with.'

'He'll be back before you know it. I know it's not an excuse, but I can see why he was embarrassed. Rory was painfully shy as a teenager. He really struggled with his confidence.'

'But he's changed so much. Surely I'm not the first person not to recognize him since his glow up?'

Eilidh shakes her head. 'I doubt it, Ava. You've got to remember, Rory has never really left Ullapool. It's all he knows. It's not like he's meeting new people all the time. When you change here, people don't notice. They see you every day, so the process is so gradual that it's hard to recognize it, even if it's big. I'm not sticking up for him, though. I'm on your side, I promise.'

'Well, Elle clearly likes what she sees. Anyway, enough about me. Have you heard from the boys yet?'

'Not yet. They arrive tonight and they'll call tomorrow morning. I keep wondering if they're okay. What if they miss me? Even worse, what if they don't?'

Eilidh sighs. I pull her in for a hug that I need just as much. 'Of course they'll miss you. You're their mum.'

'I can't stand the thought of them being sad without me, you know? Oh, screw this. I hate being a single parent. I hate Mark for putting me in this situation. It's shit.'

'I know, Eilidh. But they'll be back next week and things'll be back to normal.'

'Yes,' she grumbles. 'I have the school to sort out, the activities to organize. All the boring stuff, while he gets the holidays and the fun. I don't mean to sound like a child myself, but it's bloody well not fair.'

'Book the caravan holiday,' I remind her. 'Don't let yourself feel like that. You can be the fun parent too.'

She nods. 'I can be the fun parent. I will. I'll book the caravan break.'

'Good,' I say with a smile.

I start to set up the chairs and tables for the breakup bookshop, reviewing the list, as Eilidh pops out to check her messages. I don't want to mention it – not that there's any hiding from Eilidh – but shop sales have dipped this week. Any moment now, she's likely to get back on my case about charging people for the support group. At least I managed to submit the funding application. I just have to pray that it's successful or it could spell the end of my business.

I must focus less on emotions and more on finances if I want to save my sinking ship.

*

I don't mean for the attention to turn to me at the breakup bookshop.

I'd planned to stay extra quiet tonight. I don't trust my own emotions and I hadn't wanted to say something to the group that I would regret. But I can't seem to halt the thoughts of Rory and Elle together in my mind and somehow the floodgates just open.

Margaret's jaw almost hits the floor, as I find myself recounting the moment I walked into my London flat or, more accurately, Seb's, to discover my best friend underneath my bedsheets.

'I never expected it,' I say, my lip trembling. I stare at the legs of one of the chairs, not trusting myself to look at anyone directly in case it throws me off. I have to talk about this now; it is time. 'Not in a million years. Macy and I had been inseparable since I met her in high school. The teachers always said we were a "two for the price of one" deal, and we were until this happened. She was the last person I ever expected to hurt me. Macy wasn't just a best friend, she was like a sister to me. Seb hurt me, but Macy... she's the one that broke my heart.'

The whole room is silent as the tears land on my cheeks. Donna envelopes me into a tight hug as I finish, while Eilidh hands me a hankie.

Donna squeezes me a little tighter. 'That can't have been easy to talk about.'

'You've never even mentioned Macy,' Eilidh says. 'You poor thing.'

I nod slowly. 'I've not been able to talk about it for so long. It's been months now and I haven't opened up about it to anyone. I've gone through all the emotions with it, but I guess the real reason behind the breakup bookshop wasn't because I'd broken up with some guy. That was horrible, but I think the thing I've really been struggling with is mourning the end of such an important friendship. That meant more to me than one hundred Sebs.'

'Euch.' Donna shivers. 'One hundred Sebs – no thank you. One sounds bad enough.'

I shrug. 'Seb was great, until he wasn't. It's losing Macy that I've struggled the most with. I don't feel like I'm over that yet.'

'You know what I say to Macy?' Margaret interjects, her small eyes looking like they might pop out of her head. 'Fuck her.'

The whole support group looks at one another in surprise. Everyone bursts into laughter, including me.

'Margaret!' Eilidh laughs.

'Ah, come on now,' Margaret says. 'We women should stick together, shouldn't we? If anyone ever made a move on my Bill, I'd have knocked their block off.'

Pete shakes his head, sadly. 'Your Bill never had eyes for anyone but you, Margaret.'

'I bloody well know that, and nor should he have. Nor should anyone in a relationship, truth be told. You don't settle for these silly men, do you hear me, ladies?'

The group, including Pete, nod in unison. Margaret is right; we shouldn't settle for less. I love her words of wisdom. I am pretty sure, minus the swearing, that my granny would have said the same thing.

My sudden confession, and the unwavering support, makes me feel lighter. If I am finally opening up about Macy, it means I am healing, doesn't it? I look around the circle, wondering how many others are keeping their real battle hidden. My eyes land on Donna. She's back to her usual cheery, supportive self, but I've not forgotten her faraway look in the courtyard that night. I know she's concealing her own secret. I'm just not sure what it is yet.

Eilidh lets out a long sigh as I pass the book along to her, signalling her turn to take over.

'Well, I can't imagine ever feeling like I'm over Mark's affair, but I know everyone is different.'

'Ah, come on, Eilidh, you and Mark were married with two kids and now he's having a baby with someone else,' I point out. 'No wonder you're not "over" it.'

'I want to be, for the sake of the boys.' Her voice cracks as she looks around the group, who nod sympathetically. 'I can't keep holding on to this anger, you know?'

It is the most emotional breakup bookshop meeting yet. Fiona even starts to open up about her long-lost love and, while she doesn't 'come out' to the group, she talks fondly about her relationship and the devastation she faced when it ended, keeping the pronouns firmly gender neutral. Margaret reminisces about her husband Bill, revealing that, while they'd been lucky to have so many happy years together, they'd never been able to conceive the child they wanted so desperately.

'I think we used up all of our luck getting each other,' she says with a smile, her eyes crinkling.

That starts everyone off again. Donna seems completely thrown by the comment. Her eyes well up and she excuses herself with a trip to the bathroom. She eventually returns to the group with red eyes and a wobbly, apologetic smile.

We are way past the finishing time of the group, but no one cares. It feels important that we keep talking, keep the flow going, so everyone gets their chance to speak.

Pete clears his throat and holds some pictures in the air.

'I just wanted to say that these are the pictures I showed Donna after she said at the first session she wanted to see more pictures of her mum. I genuinely don't think she'd have told me that without this group. It really is helping people in our community and that's bloody brilliant if you ask me.'

'Hear, hear Pete!' Margaret agrees and the group offers up a round of applause. Donna chimes in with a 'whoop whoop', followed by a loud whistle.

'God, you'll start me off all over again,' I say, my voice cracking slightly. 'Thank you, everyone.'

'We should meet again tomorrow night,' Donna suggests. 'It feels like we've had a breakthrough tonight. We should run with it.'

Everyone nods in agreement, and I smile. This is what it's all about – being there for one another. The pit of doom in my stomach feels much lighter and everyone else feels the same. As we all say our goodbyes, there are hugs and well wishes all round. I catch sight of Fiona as she picks up her bag to leave and call after her.

Fiona beams at me and I envelop her in an embrace.

'I just wanted to say thank you for letting me see your house,' I say, rubbing her back. I hold on to her hands as I pull back. 'My granny's old house. It was so special for me.'

Fiona smiles. 'I only bought the cottage last year. I didn't realize your granny lived there. Rory and I agreed you'd want to take some time in the house alone, but please come and visit while I'm there next time. I'll make us some tea and scones. You can tell me all about your childhood memories of the cottage. I'd love to hear them.'

'Honestly, I can't think of anything I'd like more. Thank you.'

'I'll hold you to it,' Fiona says. 'Now, can we please address how sweet it was of Rory to organize it for you?'

I nod. 'Yes, it was. It really was.'

'When you find a good one, you hold on to him,' she says, her eyes twinkling. 'Or her.'

'Or her.' I smile as Fiona waves on her way towards the door. 'See you for scones soon!'

Donna and Eilidh promise to stay behind to help me clear up, but after the group have left, we remain firmly in our seats.

'I'm emotionally exhausted after that,' Donna exclaims. 'I feel like I've been through an exorcism.'

'I'm the same. In the best way possible,' Eilidh says with a smile. 'There was something in the air tonight, wasn't there?'

I nod. 'We got pretty heavy. I suppose it's because the first few weeks were us getting to know one another. It really feels like we're getting somewhere now, doesn't it? Great idea to continue tomorrow night.'

'Everyone's starting to feel comfortable with one another,' Eilidh says. 'Even people that have known one another for years. I've been to Fiona's cafe, spoken to her a million times about the weather or whatever, but never gone any deeper than that. A lot of the time we co-exist with people in our community without getting to know them properly. Pete's right, this bookshop has brought us all together.'

'We should celebrate,' Donna grins. 'Toast the success of The Next Chapter bookshop with a night on the town.'

'Not sure we can call it a success right now. My bank balance suggests otherwise. But if my funding application for a book festival is approved, then we can break out the champers. Or, more likely, the English sparkling wine.'

'Ah, come on,' Donna urges. 'We need a good girls' night out! It'll help you take your mind off your finances and stop Eilidh thinking about her twat of an ex parading around in his Speedos.'

And keep my mind off Rory receiving a declaration of love at the wedding. It could be happening right now. Elle could sidle up to him at the bar, compliment him on his kilt and whisper in his ear…

'Okay, I'm in,' I agree.

We make our way over to the pub and place our orders. A large group of men dressed in Scotland tops and kilts gather around one of the tables.

'Is there a Scotland game on tonight?' I whisper to Donna.

'Worse than that,' she whispers back. 'It's a stag do. I recognize a couple of the lads here.'

'Alright, Donna!' one calls. 'Do you ladies fancy joining us?'

'Christ, we've only been in the door five seconds and you're already pouncing,' Donna says with a roll of the eyes. 'We'll be keeping it quiet over in the corner. Maybe later, okay?'

Famous last words. One gin turns into two, before we agree we'd be as well sharing a bottle or two of wine. Within a couple of hours, we've put the world to rights and Donna is trying to persuade Eilidh to approach one of the men on the stag do.

'I'm telling you, Eilidh, he's perfect for you,' she says, slurring her words.

'What do we have in common exactly?' She raises an eyebrow towards the group, who are cheering one another on in a game of beer pong on the pool table.

'Who cares?' Donna retorts. 'You just need some love. Unless, oooh, did you finally take up Richard J.'s offer of a good time?'

Eilidh's cheeks flush. 'No. I mean, maybe. I don't know. We've spoken on the phone a few times since he was here.'

'Talking on the phone,' Donna says, flicking her wrist dismissively. 'Just throw yourself in at the deep end and be done with it.'

Donna starts to sing 'Come on, Eilidh' to the tune of 'Come on Eileen'. The stags overhear. The next thing we know, they are singing at the top of their lungs. Eilidh's cheeks flush bright pink, while Donna and I take turns twirling her around the circle they've created. No one really knows the words to the song, aside from the title, so it turns into a drunken, not-particularly-tuneful chorus as Donna picks us up some shots.

I order a drink every time I check my phone and hear nothing from Rory, which makes for a boozy evening. The last time I was in the pub, Rory swept me off my feet. Now, I'm on the edge of my seat waiting for some kind, any kind, of update from him.

Stop thinking about the wedding. Concentrate on having fun with your friends, Ava, I tell myself in the bathroom mirror.

Oops, I am drunk. Shit. It has been such an emotional, evening, and now it's spiralled out of control. One minute Eilidh is having a deep and meaningful chat about Mark, the next we are joining the stag do's conga line.

By the time we leave at closing time, one of the stags is in deep discussion with another about changing career at the age of twenty-five, as if they are eighty-five.

I spot Finlay on a late-night dog walk with Piper as we wait outside for Donna and Eilidh's taxi to arrive.

I slur slightly, nudging Donna in the ribs. 'There's Finlay. Why don't you go speak to him?'

She seems to consider it before saying, 'No, I can't. It's bad enough trying to talk to him sober. I'd be all over the place tonight.'

'You still like him, don't you?' I ask gently.

'It wasn't meant to be with Finlay. I can't… It wouldn't work.'

'What doesn't work?' Eilidh asks, with a frown. 'Oh, God, you don't mean—'

'No,' Donna giggles. 'No, that works fine. That works well, actually. Very well.'

'What then? What doesn't work?' Eilidh presses.

'I don't. Finlay wants a huge family. I broke up with him when I found out… That's not possible for me. Because I can't have children,' she says in a matter-of-fact tone. 'It's a medical thing. Early menopause that started in my early twenties. I broke things off with him when I learnt about it.'

'Oh, Donna!' I exclaim, my heart hurting for my lovely friend. 'I'm… I'm so sorry.'

'Thank you. I decided not to tell him about it, for lots of reasons. I know he's always wanted to be a dad, and I wanted to give him that chance. Then I stupidly let my guard down again recently. He's just so kind and thoughtful and really looked after me and Dad after Mum died. But

I shouldn't have done that. I've hurt him all over again.'

There are so many things I want to say to Donna, beginning with: wouldn't it be better to tell Finlay and at least try and work it out? If you want to have children, can you look at other options? But I doubt I'm the best person to be dishing out advice when my own love life is in tatters. Eilidh obviously feels the same way, as she stays quiet too.

Instead, we gather Donna into a hug.

'Ooh,' she giggles. 'I've never had a three-way before.'

'Donna!' Eilidh exclaims.

'Well, if you don't laugh, you'll cry,' she says with a shrug. 'And I'm past the crying stage, you know?'

'It's obviously your decision,' I say, carefully, 'but can't you at least think about telling him this?'

'I could,' she says, rubbing my arm as though she's coaching me through the situation. 'But he would stay with me, out of a sense of duty. I don't want that, never knowing if I'd caused him disappointment because I can't give him what he really wants.'

As Donna and Eilidh's taxi pulls up, Donna gives me a quick kiss on the cheek, tells me not to worry about it and that we can talk again soon, and jumps into the back seat. Eilidh says goodbye too, following her into the taxi. The window opens and Donna leans out as the car speeds away, calling on me to text them when I'm home.

I stand rooted to the spot, my mouth hanging open. The boozy haze and sudden emotional conversation make my shoulders feel heavier as I head for home.

I won't tell Rory. I won't tell anyone. It's Donna's decision not to let Finlay know and it's not my place to talk about it, but I just feel so sad for her, for Finlay, and what could have been. The weight of Donna's confession weighs on me. She appears so happy, so carefree, but this has obviously been on her mind for a long time. And not having her mum to talk to about it any more, that must hurt too.

'Ava!' a voice calls, interrupting my train of thought. I gaze around to locate the voice. It can't be Rory, he's away for the wedding. Besides, it's too English.

I turn around and there he is, standing at the door of his cobalt-blue BMW, which gleams even in the darkness.

Seb. Seb is here in Ullapool.

What the fuck?

27

'Ava,' he repeats, in a low voice. 'Can we talk?'

I frown as he leans against the BMW, his pride and joy, wearing the dark grey suit he bought after his latest promotion. He looks good. He always looks good. But who wears a suit for a ten-hour drive? His bright blue eyes regard me playfully, like this is one big joke. His dark hair is slicked back into his favourite style, and his dark-rimmed glasses are as on-trend as ever.

'Nope,' I say, fumbling in my bag to locate my house keys. It's a struggle. My shaking hand fishes around in its mass and finds nothing. Seriously, there is nothing in the bag except my house keys and phone, how can I not find them?

I glance up and frown at the small drops of rain that start to spit from the sky. Great timing. I hope it pisses down on Seb.

'Need a hand?' he asks.

'Not from you.'

Keys. I'm drunk. I need to find the keys and get the hell away from Seb and his stupid fancy car. I don't want to look at him for too long. I don't want this to be real. I don't want to see Seb here, in Ullapool. This is my happy place, my peace, and he is ruining it.

'Oh, come on, Ava. I've come all this way.'

Seb's self-important tone vibrates around the narrow streets. His accent sounds weird here too. Posh and pretentious. Did I really listen to him for six years?

'I brought a few things you left at our flat,' he says, trying to lure me into conversation.

'Your flat.'

Bingo! I want to cheer out loud as I finally find the keys. I push one into the front door, but it's stiff. I give it a shuffle but end up shaking them out of the door again. I close one eye, staring at the lock.

'Have you been getting this pissed here every night? That text. You sent me that when you were pissed, didn't you? At half one in the morning.'

'The one you didn't bother replying to?' I say indignantly, as he moves in front of me and turns the key in the lock.

'There you go.' He stands back to let me walk in front of him. Into my own house. The twat.

'Fine, bring me my stuff, dump it in the bookshop and go. Please.'

'It's after midnight,' he points out.

'Great to hear you can still tell the time. Well done.'

'Where am I going to go?'

'Seb!' I turn around to face him. He stands in the doorway, giving me his best puppy dog eyes. 'I don't care where you go. I didn't invite you here.'

'Just give me a second,' he says, rushing back outside to the car.

I flick my shoes off and they tumble into the corner, stopping with a thump.

Fuck this. Fuck Seb.

I don't need his shit.

He returns to the front door clutching a book. I recognize it straight away – my granny's cookbook. The one I thought I'd lost in the move. My heart swells at the sight of it.

'I saw the news interview,' he says. 'There was a close-up of your granny's recipes displayed in your bookshop. Then I remembered you'd left this in the cupboard. I'm pretty sure it was your granny's too?'

I take the book from his outstretched hand. 'You turn up here at midnight to give me a book?'

He shrugs. 'Thought you'd like it.'

I hug the book close to my chest and inhale the scent of the pages.

He speaks again, more softly this time. 'I wanted to see you. I want to apologize.'

I fold my arms across my chest. 'Why now? It's been months. I was living in your flat for days after the little show you put on with Macy and you didn't come once to apologize. You had a key. You could have come whenever you wanted. Wait, did Macy dump you?'

He blinks twice, as if astounded at the suggestion. 'No. If you must know, I broke things off with her. It's you I want, Ava.'

I pull myself up to sit on the till area. The memory of the time I was hoisted up here by Rory flickers through my mind. It's past midnight at the wedding too. I wonder what Rory's doing. Is he toasting his friend's marriage with a few drams at the bar? Is he spinning Elle around on the dance floor?

I shake my head.

'So you and Macy aren't together?' I demand, crossing my leg over the other.

'No, that was all just a stupid mistake.' He releases a dismissive sigh, as though we've already talked about it a million times. 'It was never going to be a real thing.'

My heart thumps in my chest as tears suddenly spring to my eyes as I think of my friend. My best friend. 'I don't want to hear that, Seb.'

'Seriously?' He frowns. 'I thought that's exactly what you'd want to hear.'

'What, that you and Macy threw away everything we had for nothing? I'd rather you lived happily ever after. At least then there would have been a point to the whole thing.'

'I'm sorry to disappoint,' he says. 'Look, I drove all the way up here to the fuck-all of nowhere to speak to you, in my BMW, which I never drive long-distance, as you know. I want us to try again.'

He moves slowly towards me, creeping along the edge of the till. I fold my arms more tightly across my chest. If he thinks I am this easily manipulated, he has another thing coming. He hovers his hand above my knee, en route to touching me, but I bat it away.

'Hands to yourself,' I warn him, narrowing my eyes.

'I really miss you, Ava,' he says. 'I watched your TV interview over and over like some sad sack. I can't believe what you've accomplished here. I'm so proud of you.'

'I don't need you to be proud of me, Seb. No, you don't get to be proud of me. There are lots of things I've needed from you in the past, but I stopped needing anything when you slept with Macy behind my back.'

'Look, Ava, we can go over this and over that, but I have driven for hours to get here. Can't we get some sleep and talk about it in the morning?'

'And where exactly do you plan to sleep?'

His sheepish expression tells me all I need to know about his plans. He has to be joking. He cannot seriously expect that I will allow him to stay with me? After everything he's done?

'Look, I've taken some time off work so we can talk things through,' he says. 'David encouraged me to come and win you back because I've been off my game for months without you. That tells you everything you need to know.'

David, his boss, is a workaholic and expects everyone to follow suit. We used to laugh about that, but Seb lost that privilege. Doesn't he get that? Plus, I don't care if he's been 'off his game'. Maybe being a manipulative cheat keeps Seb up at night, but that's not my problem.

'How much time have you taken off?'

He puffs out his chest like a proud peacock. 'Three days.'

I roll my eyes. Three days. That's all he'd decided it would take to lure me back to London. Three bloody days.

'I don't think you're fully grasping the issue at hand here, Seb. Even if I was ready to overlook the fact that you slept with my best friend, which I'm absolutely not, I am set up here now. My business is here. I *live* here.'

'Ah, come on, Ava,' he says, glancing around.

'What does that mean?'

'You put your money where your mouth is with your social media strategy and you're smashing it. You've proved your point, but you don't need to stick around here any more. Come back to London with me. You'll walk into one of the big agencies and start earning real money again. Don't tell me that selling second-hand books is profitable. You must be earning a quarter of your previous income, if that. Am I right?'

I'm not about to open up about my current financial status to Seb. No chance. I'm only getting angrier the longer I talk to him. Who the hell does he think he is, coming here to tell me to pack it in and admit defeat? He has no idea what I've achieved here.

Rain starts to batter against the bookshop window as the wind picks up pace. A strong gust makes the door rattle in its hinges. Seb throws a disparaging look in my direction.

'Is it always like this? I left twenty-five degrees for this.'

'No, it's not always like this. It's been beautiful for the whole summer up until you arrived. Surprise, surprise.'

'Your flat,' he says. 'Let me see it.'

It's not even a question. I used to love Seb's assertiveness. He has balls. He hadn't just climbed the career ladder, he'd skipped a few rungs along the way, negotiating his salary upwards with every move. He'd encouraged me to do the same; in fact – and I blush at the memory – he'd guided me through it. He took charge of every situation, from sending back a dish in a restaurant that wasn't cooked the way he liked it to surprising me with an upgrade during a weekend hotel break. He'd coached me in time management, reviewing my schedule so I could 'work smarter, not harder', even though I ended up working all hours under the sun anyway.

Aside from the whole cheating-on-me-with-my-best-friend thing, he had been there with me every step of the way.

I walk towards the staircase. 'It's not been renovated yet, so lower your expectations.'

He quickly follows behind me. 'I can help you with it. The flat renovation.'

A laugh escapes my mouth as I climb the stairs. 'Seb, your toolbox has never been opened. I'm pretty sure it's still sitting in the bag with the receipt from three years ago. And remember that time your fingernail got into a fight with a hammer and lost?'

He laughs too. 'Of course, Nurse Ava was there in a jiffy, with her reassuring words of comfort: "You'd better not get any blood on the white walls."'

'Shame. We could have used some blood splatter as a distraction from the fifty shades of grey in your flat. Anyway, here it is.' I sweep my hand around the small space. 'Home sweet home.'

He looks around, taking it all in with a shake of his head as though he can't quite believe it. He moves forward, peering around the door into the bathroom, staring at the green tiles. 'My eyes. My eyes!'

'Yes, I know, they'll be the first to go. You need to have an open mind here. Think about the potential.'

'We could get you a good return on your investment, if you decided to rent it out now,' he observes, as he wanders around. 'Given all the media interest. You should capitalize on it. People would love the idea of staying above a bookshop for a week or two. How romantic, et cetera. You'd make your money back and more, Ava.'

It is the one piece of financial advice that Eilidh has

avoided giving me, even though we both know it would make sense.

'I'm not renting it out, Seb. I live here.'

God, I wish I could sound more confident. Does my voice give away just how in the red my spreadsheets are right now?

'Come on, Ava.' He walks ahead of me to peer into the kitchen and makes a face at the small space. 'Now's the time. You've proved your point. Let's learn our lessons and move on.'

I shake my head and yawn. I don't have the energy to think of twenty new ways to say 'no' to him.

'I need to go to sleep, Seb,' I say. 'You can crash on the couch in the bookshop.'

'You're kidding,' he replies, as I hand him a cover and pillow from my bed. 'I'll be like Buddy the Elf on that thing.'

'It's either that or your car. You're not sleeping with me.'

'Fine.' He turns around to stomp downstairs. 'We can continue this conversation tomorrow.'

I roll my eyes as I brush my teeth in the bathroom. This evening has been a roller coaster of emotions and the beginnings of a hangover are already starting to creep in.

I've been doing fine without Seb. In fact, I've been doing well. Now he is back and pretending it never happened, in a ploy to lure me back to London. He knows which strings to pull, too, talking about financial sustainability and all sorts of corporate mumbo jumbo that I've tried to block from my memory.

As I climb into bed, my body and mind feel utterly exhausted. I'm not thinking clearly. Things will be clearer in the morning. They have to be.

28

The smell of bacon and eggs wafts seductively through the air as I wake up with a dry mouth and a sinking realization.

Seb is here, in my kitchen, making me poached eggs just the way he knows I like them. I have to put a stop to all this. I can't have him parading around, pushing my panic buttons, making me doubt my life choices. I am perfectly capable of doing that all on my own.

The wedding is over after what felt like the longest day and night in history. I check my phone, but there's nothing from Rory.

'Breakfast's ready!'

I groan, slide out of bed and walk into the kitchen. Seb stands there, dressed in his boxer shorts and the white shirt he'd worn the night before, nudging the bacon around the pan before switching off the gas. He'd set up the folding table, placing a small flower in the tiny vase that had been empty since I arrived.

'*Voilà*, m'lady,' he says, dishing it up as I take a seat. 'Breakfast is served. God, it's tight in here, isn't it?'

'It's not any smaller than your flat in London.'

'Our flat,' he says.

I groan.

'So, guess what? Red Letter has an opening for a social media strategist,' he says with a smile. 'And they want you.'

I stop and put my fork down, my mouth hanging open. Damn Seb. He's always known how to push all the right buttons.

'What do you mean they want me? How do they know about me?'

'I sent them your CV,' he says. 'I had it saved on my computer. They think I'm a recruitment agent working on your behalf and replied to my email this morning. The salary is insane, Ava, much better than what you were on at the last agency. You have an interview this afternoon for the senior strategist job.'

I take a sip of water, trying to steady my nerves. I've always wanted to work for Red Letter. I applied for a junior role there when I first started out but didn't even get an interview. Then, when I had some more experience under my belt, I sent my CV in for consideration if anything came up but didn't hear a thing. They are renowned in the industry for excellent pay and benefits, but, more importantly, they have the best clients on their books, including some high-profile authors and literary festivals.

Here I am, trying to get my own bookshop off the ground, praying for the funding application to be approved so I might just be able to pay my mortgage, when I have the chance to walk into a senior role running the social media for the people and organizations I admire most.

Trust Seb. He never forgets, like a bloody elephant.

I swallow.

'Well, that's an annoyingly tempting offer,' I say.

'You're welcome. I could get you an extra few grand on your salary too. They've seen what you've done for the bookshop here. I sent them a link to your news interview. This is what I mean, Ava, you can capitalize on your success. You made a splash here, which is great when it's all new and shiny, but that's not sustainable. I know you won't be making anywhere near the salary that's on the table at Red Letter.'

'What's the salary?' I whisper.

He tells me the figure and I have to fight to stop my eyes from widening. It's an enormous sum. I think about my poor bank balance and the work still to be done in this flat. The seemingly endless supply of bills and envelopes with overdue stamps Pete pretends not to notice as he hands them over with a sympathetic smile.

'I'll do the interview. But I'm not promising anything, Seb.'

'You can move back into our flat,' Seb says, as he reaches across the table and squeezes my hand. His touch feels cold, strange, like a wet fish. 'I'm ready to give this a proper go this time, Ava. No bullshit. It's you I want; I know that now. We could settle down properly. The ring, the wedding, the honeymoon, whatever you want. We'll take it all at your pace. You're in charge.'

It is everything I'd wanted, laid out on a plate in front of me, with perfectly poached eggs on the side. Not a proposal, as such, but a proposal of a proposal.

And things with Rory have taken a turn. I like him, I really like him, but I can't let him off scot-free. Pardon the pun. Seb's not the only one who's lied to me, after all. And there's the gorgeous Elle. What did Rory say when the former love of his life asked to try and give things another go? Finlay said Rory was always pining after some girl he couldn't have. Now, he could have her. Maybe I've never stood a chance with him.

'I'll do the interview and think about it.'

Seb grins. 'You won't regret it.'

*

Seb takes charge of the bookshop, urging me to take some time out to prepare for my interview. As I look through my CV and write responses to standard interview questions, I sit in the corner of the bookshop and listen to him chatting with the bookshop customers. Seb isn't much of a reader, but he is making an effort.

I still haven't heard a peep from Rory. No messages, no phone calls, this whole time. I've been checking by the bins periodically for updates, but there's nothing.

'Hi, is Ava here?' I hear Fiona's voice ask from the front door.

'I'm here, Fiona!' I call from the couch in the corner. 'Come over!'

'I thought you might be lying in a pile in the middle of the floor begging for a caffeine hit. You've not been in this morning. And who's that behind the counter?' She hands me my usual coffee order. God, I love Fiona.

I'm not ready to out Seb to everyone just yet, but I don't have much choice. All six foot of him is standing behind the till and it's not like I can hide him away.

'That's my ex-boyfriend, Seb,' I whisper.

Fiona's hands fly to her mouth, and she looks at him with disgust. Seb, completely oblivious, is busy talking to a customer. 'He's got a cheek. Why is he serving in your bookshop? Tell him to sling his hook.'

'It's a long story. I will tell you about it, but not just now. I've got to get my own head around things first, okay?'

Fiona shakes her head firmly. 'Don't go back to him, Ava.'

I swallow the emotions that threaten to rear their ugly head. Hurt. Anger. Embarrassment. But I have to prepare for the interview and weigh everything up. Make an informed choice.

'Anyway, listen, I don't just come bearing coffee. I have some news,' Fiona says, her face lighting up as she speaks. 'It's Lillian. I'm in touch with her again.'

'What?' I squeal. 'Oh, Fiona! That's amazing news! How? Tell me everything!'

Fiona's face flushes as her grin widens. 'It's all down to you, you know. I buried all those feelings in the past, but your breakup bookshop, listening to everyone's stories and talking about living life with no regrets, led me to seek her out. I found her on Facebook after a bit of digging. I pinged her a private message.'

'Oh my God, Fiona!' I squeal. 'And what did she say?'

'We chatted back and forth for ages. She's working as a high school English teacher in Perthshire.'

'I can't believe it – this is amazing news. Is she single? Are you going to meet up?'

'Oh, we've not got that far yet. I'm just enjoying being in touch with her again. I'm like a giddy schoolgirl, checking my phone every five minutes to see if she's messaged.'

'This is so exciting! What have you been talking about?'

'Life. What's happened since she left Ullapool. And we've been reminiscing about old times.'

I squeeze her hand. 'Oh, Fiona, I'm so happy for you. That's great news.'

'All thanks to you. Listen, I've got to run, I've left Jen in charge of the cafe. I just had to come and tell you about it. Remember what I said about Seb, Ava. Don't go back the way.'

With that, she stands up, her face still beaming, and practically bounces out of the shop. She doesn't acknowledge Seb as she saunters past him.

'Was it something I said?' he calls.

'You've been mentioned on more than a few occasions,' I say. 'People don't just forget things.'

He leans forward on the work surface and lowers his voice conspiratorially. 'They have a real village small-*mind* mentality here, don't they? This would be forgotten in five minutes in London, where we actually have lives of our own. Here they're practically digging out their pitchforks for a witch hunt, right?'

'We care for one another here. Fiona's my friend. She's looking out for me.'

He shrugs it off. 'Friends let you make your own choices and decisions. Anyway, I've got a Teams call in five. Can I borrow the sofa? I feel like it's practically mine now, given how intimate we got last night.'

Seb's still astounded that I didn't just let him hop into bed beside me. As if that would ever happen.

I nod, stepping behind the counter with my laptop as Margaret walks into the bookshop.

'Ava, dear, I just wanted to say thank you for that book you recommended to me. I thoroughly enjoyed it from start to finish.'

'Which one was that, Margaret?'

'*The Hating Game*. I just devoured it, could not put it down. I sat up until all hours last night to finish it. They can't stand each other – Lucy and Joshua – and they're battling it out for promotion. Have you read it?'

I nod, smiling at Margaret. 'Yes! I loved their banter. It's a great enemies-to-lovers book.'

'Oh, it really did brighten up my day. I used to love curling up with a good romance but found it difficult when Bill passed. Now, I feel like I'm ready again.'

I should have known fiery Margaret would be up for a good enemies-to-lovers story. She isn't one to shy away from a bit of confrontation, but I'm slowly but surely getting her on side, book by book.

'Good for you, Margaret. I have another book in stock by the same author, let me find it for you. I think you'll enjoy it.'

Seb's call is starting as I pass him, scanning books on the shelves. He grins manically while greeting his colleagues.

So much for taking three days off work.

'Ah, here it is,' I say, picking it up from the shelf and carrying it over to Margaret.

'Lovely.'

'Yes, hello,' Seb's voice bellows around the shop. 'The reception here is terrible. They're stuck in the Dark Ages. If I cut out, send a pigeon carrier, it would probably be quicker.'

He lets out a loud chuckle.

I want the ground to swallow me up. Margaret pretends not to hear; she says nothing as she taps her card on the reader to pay for the book.

Seb continues: 'Anyway, why don't we circle back a bit? We need to think outside the box with this project and forge ahead with breaking down silos, don't we?'

Margaret leans forward and whispers, 'Is he speaking a different language?'

'He's bilingual, Margaret. Fluent in English and corporate jargon.'

Margaret grins, picking her book up from the counter. 'He sounds like a bit of a twit. Okay, I'm off now. Thanks again for the recommendation. I hope you manage to drill down and move forward.'

I laugh as Margaret leaves the bookshop, shaking her head.

'Let's put a pin in that,' Seb continues. 'There's no point in trying to reinvent the wheel. We'll run the numbers, see what works. We can take it offline, can't we? Let's get to the next point in the agenda.'

I don't know whether to laugh or cry. I've heard Seb in many business meetings over the years but never really noticed until now how ridiculous he sounds. So many words without saying anything. I picture Rory's face listening to Seb in full swing. He would die laughing.

I sigh, checking my phone again. Nothing from Rory. Not one message the whole time he's been away.

Pete opens the door of the bookshop, whistling at the top of his lungs. I watch annoyance flicker on Seb's face at the intrusion, but Pete doesn't seem to notice him.

'Morning, morning!' Pete calls, ducking down when he sees me, bracing himself for impact and standing back up again. He laughs loudly to himself, and I smile along. The joke really never gets old. 'I come bearing post.'

'Ah, thanks Pete,' I smile, taking the letters from his outstretched hand. 'I thought you were on DIY duty today? Aren't you in charge of The Toolbox until Rory's back?'

I'm trying to subtly dig for details on Rory's return, since he didn't exactly give me a breakdown of his itinerary. But Pete doesn't take the bait.

'Yep, just taking a quick break to do the rounds.'

Seb's loud voice continues to fill the whole shop with his Teams call. 'I'm glad we're on the same page. I know you've gone above and beyond for this project, taking on things that are above your pay grade. Let's just say, it's been noted. Look, I've got to hop on another call here, but I'll ping you a message later, okay?'

The meeting seems to continue, despite Seb trying to wrap it up.

'Who's the suit in the corner?' Pete asks in a low voice. 'He sounds like a news presenter.'

'You don't want to know. Anyway, how's The Toolbox been?'

'Busier than I expected. I'll need a lie down by five o'clock.'

'I have someone at a loose end,' I say, gesturing at Seb, who is still trying to finesse his way out of his call. 'You could take him off my hands, if you want.'

'I think I'll pass, love. Sounds like he's got a screw loose himself. See you later.'

After Pete leaves, Seb approaches the counter, folding his arms. 'Your postie's a bit of a prat. Could hear him whistling the whole way along the street before he even arrived. Doesn't he know people are on work calls at ten in the morning?'

'Most people around here aren't,' I point out, absent-mindedly. 'The fishermen have been up for hours and the shops are busy with customers.'

'Fishermen? Is that an actual job? Like outside of children's books.'

I glance up, biting my lip to stop myself laughing. 'How do you think they get the fish from the sea?'

'Ah, bloody hell, Ava. We need to get you back to reality. This place is great to visit, I get that. But it's too slow-paced for you. You love the city buzz and the lunchtime shopping! What can you buy around here at lunchtime? A hammer from the guy next door?' He laughs, rolling his eyes.

Oh, if he only knew what the guy next door had to offer.

'Actually, I don't. I'm happier in my bookshop than I ever was working in the corporate world. I don't care about shopping either. I'm perfectly happy without it all.'

It's true. Hearing Seb and all his nonsensical lingo has made me realize how much I *don't* miss all that.

'But, Ava, come on. You've had three customers this morning, including your friend and a postman. You've sold one book, as far as I can see. You must have only earnt about eight quid. That's not sustainable.'

My heart thuds in protest. Seb's right. I hate that he's right.

'It isn't all about the money. Plus, I've put in a funding application for a book festival here. If it's successful, it could really turn things around,' I say, although the nagging doubt that I had stuffed to the back of my mind is certainly rising to the surface with Seb around.

I'm not even convincing myself here. How can I be happy without *any* money? I can't live on fresh air.

As I set my chair up for the interview at the back of the bookshop, I check my phone. Still nothing from Rory. It feels like we are on some dating show on TV, where we are both being tempted by our exes and have to see who'll crumble first. After the way we left things, it's a real possibility that Rory and Elle could come back to Ullapool hand in hand, while I'll have turned Seb down, as well as a job and a life back in London. Seb is offering up everything I'd wanted on a silver platter. Six months too late, but still. All I have to do is accept that he slept with Macy and we can move on.

But things have changed so much in the last few months.

I've changed.

As the screen flickers and my interviewer joins the call, I plaster the biggest smile I can muster on my face.

The interview starts well. I answer with ease questions about past successful social media campaigns, my management style, dealing with challenging work scenarios and even the dreaded question about my greatest weakness.

'That's great, Ava,' the interviewer continues, with a wide smile. 'So, tell me, what are you passionate about?'

I pause. I know what my answer should be. I think back to my London life: juggling client needs and expectations, feeling exhausted and empty at the end of the day, only to have to search for the strength to start all over again the next morning. And everyone around me in the same loop. Endless meetings that leave your social battery flat, nothing left for personal relationships. Listening to Seb's Teams call and bad business patter have made me realize corporate life is *not* where my passions lie.

I look around the vibrant colours of The Next Chapter bookshop, from the canary-yellow cabinet to Granny's recipes on display, the mismatched furniture, the shelves lined with books I love. I blink in disbelief as I really see the space that I have created.

This is what I am passionate about. My bookshop. My home. The excitement of my deliveries every day. The pleasure I get from someone telling me they love a book I've recommended. The connection, the *real* connection people here have, forged through the breakup bookshop sessions.

My eyes land on the colourful mural of Ullapool created by Rory. It's a head versus heart decision and, right now, I'm not sure which to follow.

29

Granny always said your choices should reflect your hopes, not your fears.

Seb is in my ear as soon as the phone call ends. He follows me around as I organize books on shelves, pitching my old life back to me. He mentions making a reservation at a sensational new Thai restaurant that has taken TikTok by storm, with queues around the block every night. When I suggest he takes a walk to see some local attractions in Ullapool, he snorts and declares he'll organize a tourist day for us in London, where we'll take in all the sights together. There's talk of breathtaking views from the Sky Garden, and I urge him to walk out of my front door and open his eyes. When he refuses, I decide to go myself and leave him in charge of the bookshop. May as well take advantage of his presence, after all.

As I meet with Eilidh and Donna for the emergency walk down by the seafront, the cold sea air blasts my face. The wind whips my hair as I fill them in on Seb's proposition that I move back to London.

'You can't go back, Ava!' Donna gasps, as her hand flies to her mouth. 'And you definitely can't get back with *him*! What is Seb saying about sleeping with Macy?'

I shrug, as I exchange glances with Eilidh, who keeps quiet. 'Not much. Just that he broke it off. They're finished.'

'Wait, did you just say he applied for a job for you?' Eilidh adds, scrunching up her face. 'What is this, the 1940s?'

'It sounds weird, but he saw an opportunity somewhere I've always wanted to work.'

Donna shakes her head. 'That's creepy and controlling, Ava.'

I sigh. 'I'm not saying I'll go. I just… I'm thinking it through. The bookshop is wonderful and I love it, but it's not exactly been an overnight success financially. The job at the agency is stable. I'd be heading up my own big department. I mean, I'd need to leave the Christmas party early because I'll be the boss and they'll all want me to go so they can start having a good time, but that's only once a year. I could go home and count my money. Throw it in the air with an evil laugh.'

'You'd miss out on all the fun with that job,' Donna says. 'You'd hate that. You like being right in the middle of everything, Ava. Look at the breakup bookshop: imagine you brought everyone together and had to leave us all to it. You like being with people, not managing them.'

'I could *buy* a support group,' I say, with a small smile.

Donna laughs, while Eilidh nudges her in the side. 'Don't encourage her.'

'What about Rory?' Donna asks, glancing over at me. 'Are you really ready to give that up?'

'I like him. I really do. But he lied to me, too, Donna. He could have told me he remembered me from our childhoods together, but he didn't. I know it doesn't seem like that big of a deal, but it is to me.'

'I tried to persuade him to tell you,' Donna says. 'That first day I got back from my holiday, I remembered the two of you had been close when we were younger. But he was mortified you hadn't recognized him.'

'But then there's also Elle. Finlay told me Rory lost the love of his life when he was younger and never got over it. Who am I to stand in the way of their true love?'

'True love, my arse,' Donna says, making a face. 'Elle and Rory were not a good match, no matter what she's saying. They were like chalk and cheese. They didn't want any of the same things. I love her to bits, but she's got rose-tinted glasses. I've told her that, and not just because of you. Trust me.'

I do miss Rory. He's at his happiest helping people, picking up a paintbrush and exploring Ullapool and the world around him. What does he envisage for his future now? It won't be climbing the corporate ladder, saving for a pension and sending your child to private school, like Seb, that's for sure. He will make his choice, and I'll make mine. If, by some miracle, the stars align and we both avoid ex-temptation, then we can have that discussion. For now, it isn't looking likely. He hasn't even messaged me. The jury is out on my feelings right now, but he's made his perfectly clear. The silence is deafening.

'I'd better get back,' I say. 'Can't leave Seb in charge for too long. He'll probably have the place on the market by closing time.'

Donna and Eilidh hug me goodbye, and I promise to keep them posted.

As I walk back towards the bookshop, my head is in a spin. I take a big, deep gulp of breath, readying myself to face Seb and be bombarded by his questions and opinions all over again. He'll probably have come up with some brand-new argument to add to all of his reasons why I should come back to London. I won't be surprised if he gets my parents on his side next.

I stop dead in my tracks as I see her standing on the pavement, looking down at her phone, her face confused, as she checks the street sign on the side of the building.

My heart stops. For a moment, before my brain catches up, my heart is overjoyed to see her, but then I remember what she did.

Macy. I can't believe Macy is here.

30

I take a deep breath and consider bolting past her, but she looks up and catches my eye. I lower my head, feeling her watching me.

'Ava,' she calls gently.

I look down at the ground and start walking towards the bookshop. I don't want to do this with her. I have everything and nothing to say all at the same time. Nothing nice, though. And what did Granny always say? If you've not got something nice to say, don't say anything at all.

'Ava, please, can you talk to me? Just give me a second. Please,' she pleads as she approaches me.

She looks different. Her usual wide, smiling face is gaunt and pale. She's dressed all in black, like she's attending a funeral. Macy never wears black. My hearts squeezes in my chest as I try to stop the voice in my head reminding me how much I've missed her.

'He's in the bookshop,' I say, avoiding eye contact. 'I can take you to him.'

'I want to talk to *you*,' she says. 'Please. Can we sit down somewhere?'

I want to say no, but I can't.

'Follow me.'

We take a seat on a bench by the beach and look out to sea. I sneak a look at her face again. She looks awful. Drained. Exhausted. Despite everything, I feel sad for her. I never wanted to see her like this. I have to stop myself from wrapping my arms around her and telling her that everything is okay, because it's not. I'm not sure it ever can be.

'You were right about Ullapool,' she says with a sad smile, gazing into the distance. 'It's beautiful here.'

'So, you've come to get Seb. Why waste time with me?'

'It's not just about Seb. I'm so sorry, Ava,' she says. She shakes her head from side to side, wiping the tears away with trembling fingers. 'I'm a mess. Seb – he just left without saying a word. I went to work, came back and he was gone.'

I've never seen Macy cry before. Ever. She's always been the life and soul of the party, swinging from the chandeliers on every night out, singing karaoke at the top of her lungs, dancing into the early hours.

But now Seb has broken her too.

'He finished with you,' I whisper.

She turns to look at me, appalled. She shakes her head. 'No. He didn't. Oh God, I knew he'd say that. You probably think I deserve this. I guess it's called karma.'

Bloody Seb. Of course he hasn't broken up with Macy. He's back here to try his luck, hedge his bets. I should have known.

She turns around on the bench and looks me in the eye. 'I want you to know something. I've been in love with him for years, Ava. I tried to block it out, to stop myself from feeling that way about him. He wasn't interested in me, not like that. And I was glad, because of you.'

I swallow, unable to compute what Macy is saying. She'd been in love with Seb the whole time we'd been together?

'I tried going out with different people. But he was always in the back of my mind. I was on my Christmas night out at the end of last year, and he turned up at the same bar. I know I should have resisted, and I tried, but I just… I couldn't. I'd been suppressing the feelings for so long. I should have stopped it. God, Ava, I wish I'd been able to stop it.'

Tears fall onto her black trousers as she continues. 'I never wanted to hurt you. You've been like a sister to me. A soul sister, remember? But he filled my head with all these promises. I thought he would be different with me. I guess… I was wrong. I wish I'd had somewhere to go, someone to talk to about it, but I felt so lonely. It's been so lonely without you.'

Macy's whole body shakes. I think of the breakup bookshop and how much it has helped everyone who's crossed its threshold. Macy doesn't have that. She's lost me, she's lost Seb, and she's left with no one.

'You could have talked to me about it, Macy,' I say, carefully.

'What good would that have done?' she asks, wiping her eyes. 'He loved you. He wanted you. He still does. That's why he's here. He never wanted to be with me. I was just a bit of fun that you were never meant to find out about. God, I feel so stupid. I'm so sorry, Ava.'

'And when he left, you knew he'd come here?'

She nods. 'I knew he wanted to get back with you. He told me after our last fight. I begged him to keep trying to make us work, but his mind was obviously made up. I gave up our friendship, the most important thing to me, but it wasn't enough.'

'So, you're here... why? To try to bring him back to London with you?'

She shakes her head. 'I don't know. I'm not expecting you to forgive me, I just wanted you to know that he wasn't just a whim for me, the way I was for him.'

We sit in silence, looking out to sea. I sigh and reach across and pat her hand.

'Macy, you deserve so much better than Seb. We both do.'

*

As we walk back to the bookshop, I keep Macy close beside me. I know she's hurt me in the worst way possible, but

I can't help but feel protective of her. She's been blinded by Seb and all his promises, like I was once upon a time. I hope she can move on from this, from him.

I hear raised voices up ahead. I look across at the hairdresser's, where they're all at the window gazing over at the bookshop, like the day I arrived. I wonder what they're all looking at. Shit, what have I missed?

I blink as I see Seb come crashing out of the bookshop, falling to the ground. What the hell is going on? I rush forward, leaving Macy open-mouthed behind me.

'Ah, fuck,' Seb says, rubbing his elbow. 'Do you know how much this suit cost? You'll be paying for the dry-cleaning bill, you mark my words!'

I look up as Rory comes charging out, his face bright red, his fist clenched.

'Dry-cleaning bill?' he snorts. 'Away and boil yer heid.'

'Rory, what the hell?'

He turns to face me and points to Seb, who's on the ground brushing dirt from his elbow. 'This is him? The London guy who cheated on you? You let him stay here?'

'No, Rory, I…'

'Did he stay here last night, Ava?' He doesn't wait for an answer. 'He's talking about taking you back to London with him. I guess the summer's really over this time, isn't it? God, I've been so stupid!'

He paces up and down in front of me as my face flushes. This is bad. Rory knows that Seb has stayed here. Why did

I even let that happen? I should have flung him out, like my instincts told me. Yet again, I've allowed Seb to worm his way back in, and now he's caused a divide between me and Rory.

I swallow. 'Rory, no, it's not...'

But he doesn't listen. He turns on his heel, walks past The Toolbox, and jumps into his car, speeding off into the distance. I want to run after him and beg him to stop, but I find myself rooted to the ground. I can't seem to make my brain catch up. It's all too much; Seb's here, Rory's back early and Macy is shaking beside me.

'Macy?' I hear Seb's small voice say, as my hands shake.

She is in floods of tears. Full, uncontrollable sobs. I can't abandon her, not when she's like this. I need to help her fight back and stick up for herself. She needs me.

Seb sighs and puts one hand on his head. 'Jesus, Macy, you followed me all the way here?'

'What else was I supposed to do?' she hiccups.

I usher them both into the bookshop for a more private conversation, away from the eyes of the salon's clients.

Seb lets out a huge sigh before turning to me. 'You're not coming back to London, are you?'

I shake my head. 'I'm not. Not with you. And I'd like you to leave.'

He rolls his eyes at the inconvenience of it all, without a glance towards Macy to see how she's feeling. Hedging his bets, as usual, wanting us both but not enough.

'I'll go upstairs then. Grab my stuff.'

I nod, left alone with Macy in the bookshop. She glances around, taking it all in. The vibrant colours, the shelves packed with books, the warm lighting that creates the perfect reading ambience.

'It's beautiful, Ava,' she sniffs. 'I can't believe you've done all this. Congratulations.'

'Please tell me you're not going to get back with him, Macy.'

'I don't know what I'm doing. I just knew I needed to come here. To see you.'

'It wasn't really to see me, though, was it? You wouldn't have come here if he hadn't. I always wanted to show you around Ullapool, the place I always talked about. I talked about it to both of you. And now you're both here, but everything's changed. I hate that, Macy.'

'I'm sorry,' she says again. 'For everything. I've missed you so much. I wouldn't have done this if it hadn't been him. I want you to know that. It sounds stupid now, but for me it's always been him.'

Seb reappears with a bag in his hand, swaggering towards the front door. He barely looks at me or Macy. 'Can't wait to get out of this hellhole,' he mutters. He turns to Macy. 'Let's get back to London. Quickly.'

Macy remains tight-lipped as he pulls open the shop door and presses the button to unlock his BMW. She glances at me and whispers, 'I'm sorry, Ava,' before she follows him outside.

What was it Granny used to say? You can lead a horse

to water, but you can't make it drink. Macy looks like she's set to be parched for a long time to come.

As the car speeds off, I want to stop her. I want to tell her Seb's just going to hurt her again, but within seconds, the car is gone. Instead, I go out into the courtyard to call Rory. I need to track him down as quickly as possible. As I stand by the green bin, my phone starts to vibrate. Over and over again.

Rory: *Just arrived. Hotel's lovely, phone reception shit. Miss you! x*

There's a flood of messages from Rory, Rory, Rory. Missed calls too. I frown. What the...

Rory: *I'm sorry. For everything. Can we talk?*

My eyes widen as realization dawns on me. The messages date from when Rory left to just a couple of hours earlier. My stupid phone hasn't delivered the messages. A series of pictures follow in quick succession. The beautiful ceremony, hosted under an archway with a lake serving as the backdrop, a picture of the bride and groom cutting the cake, a few other wedding reception pictures.

Then, the *pièce de résistance*: a selfie of Rory in his kilt, accompanied by a long line of kisses.

Rory *had* contacted me; the messages just hadn't been delivered. And now it looks like I'd ignored them, ignored *him*, while allowing my ex-boyfriend to stay with me.

Fuck's. Sake.

31

I look everywhere for Rory. First, I check his personal support venue, the pub, and then I head to his house. He's not there. I spend the evening wandering around the village. I periodically check he isn't secretly hiding under the counter at The Toolbox but, again, nothing. I ask Fiona, Pete and Donna to let me know if they see him while I'm doing my rounds in the village, but I don't hear anything. I try calling him, but it goes straight to voicemail.

A horrible thought, which I can't seem to shake, parades around my mind: maybe he's with Elle now. Maybe my radio silence sent him straight into Elle's comforting arms. Seeing Seb here would have only confirmed his decision.

I want to be with Rory more than ever, but I've well and truly blown it.

As I walk down to the seafront to check Rory isn't skimming stones, I receive an email with good news. Great news, in fact. My application for funding for the book festival has been approved. The cover email says the funding body was particularly impressed by my growing social media following and strategy, my stakeholder and community engagement (I'd name-dropped Richard J. Walker and highlighted the breakup bookshop sessions) and my business plan. They can't wait to see the book festival come to fruition.

I swallow as I spot the amount that is due to be deposited into my bank account. It is an even bigger sum than I'd anticipated. Eilidh had encouraged me to apply for the full amount but said I'd likely receive a smaller grant. But they've awarded me the full thing. Every penny. I am out of the red. I am back in business. Somehow, along the way, everything I've worked for has come together. Now, if I want to, I can move forward.

Alternatively, I could still sell the business. I would definitely make money from it, especially with funding and permission in place to go ahead with the biggest book festival Ullapool has ever seen.

Turning back to the bookshop, I'm not sure whether to laugh or cry. I can't wait to give Eilidh the funding news. She'll be so pleased. But I also know that if I tell her, there will be an expectation I'll stay in Ullapool. Without Rory in my life, I'm not sure I can do that. How can I work in the bookshop, knowing he's right next door to me all day, every day?

I sigh and hit the 'call' button. Eilidh answers promptly. 'I'm two minutes away! Don't start the session without me! I've brought that book you gave me. The thriller? It was genius, Ava. You have to read it…'

I raise my eyebrows. 'You do know that author is Richard J.'s biggest rival? Apparently they hate each other.'

She laughs. 'They don't hate each other, that's just one of those things that the press made up. They're quite friendly. Speaking of which, Richard's actually here with me… He's coming with me tonight, if that's okay?'

'Of course that's okay, Eilidh. And I have some news myself.'

'You're staying in Ullapool?' she asks.

'The funding application for the book festival has been approved.'

'Oh, Ava, this is the best news!' she exclaims. 'Now you have to stay! It's all finally come together!'

I nod, my smile tight.

'Hello?' she calls down the phone. 'Why aren't you happier? And why aren't you here? I've just pulled up to the bookshop, and I hate to break it to you, but everyone is here apart from you.'

'I was out looking for… Never mind. Can you start the session without me? I'll be there soon. It's just… It's been a lot to take in. I don't know if I want to laugh or cry. Both, maybe.'

Eilidh lowers her voice. 'No problem. Look, I want you around, Ava. We all do. The bookshop has become part of the village now. But you need to do what's best for you. If you do decide to go back to London, you can always visit us in the summer, like you used to.'

I nod, even though she can't see me, and we hang up. The breakup bookshop is starting without me, but I can't face it just yet. I walk down to the seafront, pick up a long, flat stone, perfect for skimming, and attempt to slide it along the water's surface. Instead, it plonks straight into the sea. I can't help but giggle to myself.

Sometimes everything goes exactly as it should, and it still doesn't work out the way you think it will.

As the sun sets on the horizon, I wrap my cardigan around me. It's autumn now. The nights are fair drawing in, as Granny would have said. My time here has passed in a flash and a whole new season is approaching. I wonder what it will be like in winter. I've never spent time here in the colder seasons. I can picture the row of houses along the seafront dressed for Halloween, with pumpkins outside and children trick or treating around the doors – or 'guising' as they say here. Then the pumpkins will be replaced with Christmas trees as the festive season kicks off. Donna told me they host Christmas ceilidhs in the local hall. I can picture it all, here in the village I've always loved.

My thoughts turn back to the man I've got to know. Mackie, Rory, he's such an important part of my life here. Not just this time, but in previous years too. And I can't imagine letting him go. The seasons will change, but I'm certain that my feelings for him won't. I want to enjoy it all with him, from kicking the orange leaves during cosy autumn walks to opening presents together on Christmas Day.

There is no denying it. I'm not sure where I want to be, but I know I want Rory by my side. I sigh, wondering where the hell he's gone. I try calling him one last time, without an answer, before walking back up to The Next Chapter, where the breakup bookshop session is coming to a close. As I trudge up the street, I rehearse a cheery apology in my head. Although the group is there to offer companionship and support, I'm not ready for that right now. I have to make a decision. Go back to London alone, really on my own, and start a new journey? Or stay here and make it work?

Reaching the door of the bookshop, I peer through the glass window and frown.

Rory stands smack bang in the middle of the circle, where he's sworn he would never be. His eyes meet mine as I walk through the front door.

'Please don't say anything, Ava,' he says. 'Let me speak.'

'Rory, I—'

Chairs scrape along the ground as the rest of the support group mumble apologies. Eilidh grabs her jacket and nudges Richard to follow her, Donna and Pete whisper to each other while gathering their belongings. Fiona smiles at me, urging Margaret to pick up her stick and get moving.

'Give it a go, love,' Fiona whispers to Rory on the way past. 'No regrets.'

We lock eyes and I nod, offering Fiona a smile.

When we find ourselves alone in the bookshop, Rory takes my hands in his. I gaze into his eyes. He is here, with me. No Seb, no Elle, no Macy, just the two of us.

'I thought this support group thing was a load of shit,' Rory continues, after clearing his throat, and I can't help but smile. 'I genuinely couldn't understand why anyone would want to open up and talk about how they felt in front of a bunch of random people. I thought nothing could ever make me feel bad enough for that, until earlier today.'

His green eyes lock with mine. I open my mouth to speak, to try to reassure him, but he continues.

'I drove here as soon as the cake had been cut and the dancing started. I knew I needed to speak to you and make it up to you after our fight. But you weren't here. Seb told me that you were being offered some big job and were planning to move back down to London with him,' Rory says. 'I couldn't believe it. I've never felt so… so low. Despondent. I was completely gutted. It felt like I was losing you all over again.'

I blink. 'What do you mean, all over again?'

God, he is gorgeous. All I want to do is melt into a kiss with him, but I can't. We have to talk this through. We have to figure out what we want.

'Let me tell you my heartbreak, eh?' He smiles sadly to himself. 'There was a girl who used to come to the village every summer to visit her granny. I had a massive crush on her. She was my first love and she didn't even know it. I'd wait for her every June and then I'd be gutted every September when she left. One year, when I was sixteen, I decided I was going to tell her exactly how I felt, but she never came. Not the year after, or the year after that. But this year, she came back and I fell for her more than I ever thought possible. I'm not going to make the same mistake I did all those years and keep it bottled up, not telling her how I feel and risking her leaving and getting back with a guy who doesn't treat her the way she should be treated.'

My heart thumps in my chest and tears spring into my eyes at Rory's heartfelt speech.

I was Rory's first love. Not Elle. I was the one he fell for all those years ago, when he was known as Mackie. He'd waited for me to return and I finally had, years later. In that time, he'd transformed from a gawky teenager to someone who wouldn't be kicked off a catwalk. But I'd always been drawn to Mackie, and now to Rory, no matter his looks. As a teenager, I'd felt the same longing for him; I'd told Macy about the guy I'd shared all those deep and meaningful conversations with. This new Rory, with the gorgeous, kind eyes and broad shoulders, is the same person.

And now here he is, standing in front of me. And finally, I'm ready.

It feels like he is looking straight into my soul as he utters the words: 'Ava, please stay here, with me.'

Memories flash through my mind of heading away

from Ullapool at the end of every summer, tears streaming down my cheeks at the thought of leaving my granny and the friends I'd made. I hated going back to the city after months of feeling so free. I hated leaving the village and all its beauty. I dreamt of packing up and moving here. Now I'm here and living the life I dreamt of, I don't want to leave. Screw London. My heart is here. I can make this work. There is no other option, not if Rory really wants me. I can't risk losing him again.

I nod, looking straight into his eyes. 'Of course I will. I want this, all of this. And more than anything, I want you.'

Before I know it, Rory has scooped me off the ground and is kissing me. Truly, madly, deeply, we melt together. I never want to let him go. As I pull away, he offers me the widest smile and our foreheads touch.

'I came to the breakup bookshop tonight thinking Seb might still be here and I'd have to battle for your hand,' he confesses, before kissing me gently again.

I shake my head. 'I sent Seb packing. I couldn't go back there, not feeling the way I feel about you. I didn't get your messages until today. I thought you hadn't contacted me, but there must have been a malfunction with the bin technology.'

'Of course I contacted you. And you knew about Elle? She told me that she'd told the group she wanted to get back with her ex, but she wasn't sure if you knew I was her ex or not.'

'I knew. You didn't take her up on her offer then?'

Rory shakes his head. 'Elle's always been a friend. We tried being together, but it didn't work. She's feeling a bit stuck, like she's not where she wants to be in life, but we agreed that us getting back together isn't what either of us really wants or needs. That's not a reason to be with someone. And how could I be with her when it's always been you?'

It's always been me.

Impossibly, the grin on my face widens. 'Well, now you've got me. I'm officially part of the Rory fan club. The president, in fact.'

'About time,' he grins. 'We're finally on the same page.'

'What you said before,' I say, 'about waiting for me to arrive every summer and hating it when I left. Is it true?'

He nods. 'All true. I don't know why I was so embarrassed to say it before.'

'I'm sorry I didn't recognize you. We wasted so much time.'

'It's not your fault. I should have just bloody told you at the start. Turns out, being vulnerable isn't exactly my strong suit. I slated the support group because I couldn't imagine being part of something like this, but I see now how good it is for the whole village.'

'Does that mean you're going to come along and open up more often?'

'Let's not get too ahead of ourselves now,' he grins.

'Okay, let's make a promise,' I say. 'We talk to each other, even when it's hard. We're honest with each other, even if we feel embarrassed. And you wear a kilt for me every other weekend. Because damn, you looked good in that selfie.'

He throws his head back and laughs. 'There's one last thing I need to do to know you're staying for sure.'

'And what's that?'

'Let's get upstairs,' he whispers, pressing his forehead against mine, 'and remove those tiles.'

'Now you're talking.'

EPILOGUE

One year later

Rory swings me around the floor, a huge grin plastered on his face as he pulls me to a halt and then spins me in circles again.

'Will I ever learn the steps?' I groan when I finally slump back in my chair, regaining my breath.

'You know the steps,' he points out. 'You've just not quite taught your feet to keep up with them yet.'

'True. Anyway, I'm only here to see you in your kilt.'

He laughs and leans down to kiss me, ignoring the dancers all around us. I feel dizzy, and not just from the dancing, as his lips touch mine. He's wearing the full Scottish get-up, from top to toe. A MacGregor tartan kilt, white shirt, bow tie, the works. He's delighted with the hip flask in his sporran, with the whisky he's saved for a special occasion. It doesn't get much more special than today.

Pete grins at us as he passes by, Margaret on his arm. 'Got to watch your knee with that one around.' Through the breakup bookshop, Margaret and Pete have grown to be companions. They reminisce about the past and look out for each other.

Fiona dances past, with Lillian by her side. They laugh as they squabble over who should be leading the dance. Fiona claims to be a ceilidh expert, but Lillian is quietly confident in her execution. They live together now, in my granny's cottage. I'm a regular visitor to the house, which is filled with love and laughter, as they make up for the years they were separated. Lillian teaches in the local high school and there's more of a spring in Fiona's step every single morning when I pop in for my coffee.

I pull Rory's hand and guide him to the top table. I smooth my silk dress and take a seat beside Donna, while Rory sits on Finlay's left.

Donna's sporting a whole new look: blonde curls. She's firmly in what she calls her bridal era. Eventually, with a little persuasion from me, she opened up to Finlay. She told him her reasons for pushing him away. Finlay said he couldn't imagine his life without her, regardless of what their future held. He told her, in no uncertain terms, that whether they could have children or not, she was his family. He proposed as the clock struck midnight on Hogmanay, and she said yes.

Since then, she's tried out a range of hairstyles and finally settled on blonde curls for their big day. Finlay sits, proud as punch, in his full kilt, one hand around his dram of whisky, the other draped around his new wife.

So, I'm in my bridesmaid era, along with Elle. We make a great team and have spent months planning Donna's hen party over Teams calls or dinners when she's back in Ullapool. When Donna told Elle that Rory and I were a couple, Elle couldn't have been more supportive. She's brought her new boyfriend to the wedding as her plus one and, after a few glasses of champers, confided he may be 'the one'.

As I gaze around the room at all the familiar faces that have connected through The Next Chapter support group, I think back to where it all started. Bidding from Seb's flat on a property I'd never seen, after he trampled all over my heart. I heard through the grapevine that Seb and Macy split for good when they moved back to London. He's been promoted to director level, while Macy is seeing someone else. She's started posting on social media again, and she occasionally likes my posts. We don't speak, but that's okay. We're okay. My heart has healed.

'So, you two, are you all ready for the big adventure?' Donna asks as she adjusts her veil, which has moved to the side following a healthy dose of dancing.

Rory grins at me across the table.

I smile back at him. 'We're so ready.'

When Rory's parents, Patricia and Ron, returned to take over the day-to-day running of The Toolbox, I made a little proposal of my own. I asked Rory if he'd like to revisit the backpacking plans we'd discussed, Mackie and

I, when we were teenagers. Within a matter of weeks, we'd booked our trip. Europe, Asia, Australia and New Zealand are all part of the itinerary.

Patricia offered to look after the bookshop while we were away, but I had another interested party keen to take it on. Richard J. is moving to to be nearer Eilidh. A famous author running a local bookshop and living in my newly renovated flat seems too good to be true, but he's booked the removal van and is ready to go. Eilidh has even volunteered to take on the breakup bookshop sessions in my absence and will look after Rory's paintings. They've been selling like hot cakes in the bookshop and racking up healthy online sales. He's even been offered an artist's residency in Germany, which we've factored into our travel plans.

We'll be back in Ullapool just in time for the inaugural book festival, so I have a lot of planning to do while we're on our travels. Richard J. has agreed to headline the festival and has arranged for several of his author friends to get on board too. As soon as we return from our trip, we plan to offer creative writing classes and author events, as well as the regular support groups in the bookshop.

As the dance finishes, a familiar song begins to plays over the speakers.

'Caledonia'.

Donna and Finlay stand in the middle of the circle and we gather around them, holding hands. I glance around the familiar faces: Eilidh and Richard, with Harry and Caden,

Margaret, Pete, Fiona, Lillian and Jen. I squeeze Rory's hand tightly.

My eyes fill with tears as I listen to the lyrics, a love song to Scotland, a place we all call home. Ullapool has always been my spiritual home, thanks to my granny's legacy, but it has become my real home this past year, without question. Rory and I share an urge to travel and see more before we settle down here. We have the same hopes for the future: thriving businesses, our own house in Ullapool and, not too far in the future, we hope, a family of our own.

I can't believe I've been so lucky as to find him again. First love turns into forever love. The next chapter and my second chance.

Acknowledgements

Firstly, I want to say a huge thank you to Rachel Imrie from Atlantic Publishing for the vision and inspiration for *The Breakup Bookshop*. Rachel's passion for Ullapool and proud Scottish heritage was evident in every conversation we had. It's been fantastic working with Rachel on this novel, and it wouldn't have been possible without her. Thank you as well to my literary agent, Julie Fergusson from The North Literary Agency, for all her support, editing skills, ideas and advice.

When I finished university, I asked my boyfriend, Chris, if he would accompany me on a round-the-world trip. We set off with our backpacks on the adventure of a lifetime, from beautiful beaches in Australia and Thailand to small islands in Fiji, and stunning mountain ranges in New Zealand and Canada.

Almost twenty years later, with three children now in tow, I suggested a family trip to the Scottish Highlands.

Never one to miss an opportunity for adventure, Chris submitted a very last-minute annual leave request, and we set off the next day.

The research trip made me realise that Scotland is just as beautiful as anything I've seen further afield. Ullapool took my breath away. The seafront, surrounding greenery, the views of the mountains, the warmth of the locals and the bustling village with its cosy pubs and outdoor restaurants served as the perfect backdrop for a Highlands love story.

As a family, we went for long walks and hikes up the mountains, skimmed stones down at the seafront and took the Summer Isles trip that features in *The Breakup Bookshop*. So, thank you to Chris and our three mini travel enthusiasts, Orla, Leah and Calum.

While I was editing *The Breakup Bookshop*, I experienced my own heartbreak as my dad, Paddy, passed away. I miss him more than words can convey. This book is dedicated to my mum, Máire. I hope that she, and anyone suffering from grief or loss, can find comfort and strength in the people around them.

Atlantic Books

newsletter

Sign up to our monthly email for reading inspiration, author news and exclusive competitions.

Scan the QR code

Or visit our website: www.atlantic-books.co.uk